D1327995

THE VET'S APPRENTICE

David Basinski

IMPERTINENT PRESS

Copyright © 2023 The Vet's Apprentice by David Basinski

The Vet's Apprentice is a work of fiction. Names, characters, businesses, organizations, places, events, and incidents either are the product of the author's imagination or are used fictitiously. Any resemblance to actual persons, living or dead, events, or locales is entirely coincidental.

Published by: Impertinent Press (773) 345-3334 fax,
impertinentpress@gmail.com
Printed in the United States of America.

No part of this publication may be reproduced, distributed, or transmitted in any form or by any means, including photocopying, recording, or other electronic or mechanical methods, without the prior written permission of the publisher, except for the use of brief quotations in a review or as permitted by U.S. copyright law. For permission requests, contact the author at: thevetsapprentice@gmail.com

Cover artwork by Daniel Greenhalgh
Inside Illustrations by Fiverr Team & author
Edited by Cup & Quill
Interior design by Paul Salvette @BBeBooks

ISBN: 979-8-9861298-5-3 (hardcover)
ISBN: 979-8-9861298-6-0 (paperback)
ISBN: 979-8-9861298-0-8 (eBook)

First Edition: June 2023
Print Edition

Contents & Illustrations

Chapter 1

On each foot, five toes have we,

    four of five touch ground have dogs and cats

    three claws bear some birds and sloths,

    two hooves have cows and sheep

    but one is all the equids need.

HORSES COME AND horses go, so except for the unusually early hour, no one expected the unloading of this horse to be different from any other. The trainer, who always found an excuse to skip breakfast, chewed a stalk of hay while his empty stomach growled.

As the sun rose, the bleary-eyed handler stood by, winding and rewinding a lead rope. Paid by the hour, he could wait all day for all he cared.

The red-faced supervisor, whose wife always found a reason to fight before going to bed, had spent the night tossing and turning. He paced the stable doorway and, while bickering with himself, came up with chores for the groom to do. None of them commented on the time, nor mentioned the conspicuous absence of the new owner.

The groggy, curly-haired groom, leaning against a guardrail, outstretched his arms and yawned long and wide. The image of the girl he had kissed the night before broadened his smile. He rubbed the sleep out of his eyes and alerted the others to the oncoming rig.

The trailered hovercraft circled the lot before backing into the loading dock. The supervisor's cheeks flushed. "Heads up."

As the rig backed in, its steel walls rumbled, and its suspension swayed. Demons banging on the gates of hell could not have announced themselves better. The handler nervously clicked the lead rope snap while the trainer and groom undid the trailer latches. The ramp lowered. A dent-pounding *whack* caused the ramp to fly out of their hands. A cloud of dust blocked their view. Ear ringing banshee shrieks deafened. A dark, blurred mass lunged. Ironed flat ears, flared nostrils, and flailing hooves followed. Anything caught in its way was bitten, trampled, or stomped.

This horse acted like he wanted to bring back the bygone days of bronco busting. He kicked out a trailer door and flattened the trainer's boot. Guard rails toppled over. The stallion chomped the supervisor's shoulder and flung him across the landing. Rope burns scalded the handler's palms. Knocked over, the groom sat in the dirt, shaking cobwebs out of his head. The supervisor patted himself on the back as he hobbled off, partly to stanch the flow of blood but mostly to congratulate himself for getting away alive.

In the next four hours, the Wild West happened all over again, with chaos reigning up and down the stable aisle.

Observing from a hayloft, the calico barn cat swished her tail from side to side. She lay, content to watch. Only when a swarm of obscenities was sworn in a multitude of languages did she close her eyes as she scratched her whiskers.

Cat's Eye View

How no one got seriously hurt getting the frenzied horse into a stall was anyone's guess. The only witnesses left standing were the cat and stabled horses. They scored the first encounter, Horse–4: Humans–0.

The main event would take place that afternoon. Bookies would have their odds-on favorite. Two contestants: one big mean horse versus a slight but spunky teenage girl.

3

Chapter 2

The outside of a horse is good for the inside of a man.

—Winston Churchill

WHILE THE REST of her physics class exchanged notes and reviewed for Woodson's dreaded final exam, Luna Auer hefted the loaded electro-powered wheelbarrow down the stable aisle. The barn chronometer projected 13:13. By this time tomorrow, she would be done with AP physics and finished with her junior year. With no time to lose, Luna quickened her pace to get to the last stalls.

In her head, the morning's precalculus graphs and figures jumbled with tomorrow's formulas like the green nuggets of manure hopping around the wheelbarrow's tray. "The product of velocity and position uncertainties is greater or equal to Planck's constant over, over...." Luna said. Hearing Heisenberg's Uncertainty Principle for the second time, the horses quit listening and turned around in their stalls.

Undeterred by the horses' lack of interest, Luna pushed on, wincing whenever the wheel hit a rut on the floor. Every bump threatened to topple the whole thing.

13:14, 1,126 minutes to grab a bite, review my notes, and catch up on enough sleep to appear rested for tomorrow. I'll give Heisenberg one thing for sure. If this load drops, the poop will fall at 9.8 meters per *second squared, and I'll be in deep sh*t.*

At the last stall, she lowered the molded grips and rubbed her palms together, working the circulation back into her hands.

Over 4 π, where Planck's constant is…

The barn cat's meow announced her presence as she rubbed herself against the back of Luna's leg. Luna picked up and cradled the demanding feline. "Trulee, not now. I'm already on a tight schedule." She scratched the cat's chest, stroking her fingers up its neck. The trilling r's of the calico's purr confirmed her approval. Trulee's eyes floated dreamily as her lids closed, her chin inviting more.

"I can't spend as much time with you as with the horses," Luna explained. "Their stalls are bigger than your litter box."

Trulee worked her shoulders back and forth, burrowing into Luna's arms. Her eyes closed, ready for a nap.

"How would you like it if I came to your box with the prongs of a pitchfork?"

The cat stiffened.

"With you in it!"

Trulee's eyes shot open. She squirmed and pawed, demanding to be released. Before Luna could lower the fickle feline, Trulee flew from her arms and bound down the stable aisle. Raised at full mast, her tail bid farewell and good luck.

An inhaled bouquet of Cowboy Perfume—that aromatic mixture of molasses, hay, leather, and horse filled Luna's nose as she recited, "6.62607004 times ten to the…." *Why is the path to vet school littered with trivia? Facts I will never use.*

On the solar-paneled roof, the patter of drizzle erupted into a thunderous clap. Rain bounced off the carbon fiber roof, swirled through filtered gutters, and collected in ionized tanks.

Great, I'll get soaked by the time I get back.

Luna sifted through the litter. Centuries to innovate, stable architects had focused their designs on the horse's comfort. The fecal mass wavered on the pitchfork tines en route to the wheelbarrow. The grunt work still had to be done by hand. Normally, she would have lugged the wheelbarrow to the opposite side of the barn and unloaded it in the dumpster outside but not today. She evenly patted down the knobby green mass with a shovel, hoping to finish in the fewest number of trips. The barn record was seven loads for a stable of thirty horses. Luna was on her eighth, with twenty-eight stalls done and one more to go. The wall clock reading 13:19 flipped to 13:20.

The main door slammed open. Rowdy voices interrupted the munching of hay. Horses stuck their heads out of their stalls with their ears pricked forward.

"Guys, we were supposed to meet tomorrow," Luna said under her breath Her eyes rose to the ceiling. "Give me strength."

Clenching the wheelbarrow handles, she heaved and pressed the button. The wheel hit a rut and tilted to the brink of tipping over. The load shifted. Turds rolled.

Luna squeezed to the depth of her core, leveraged to counter the weight, and pulled up with one hand and down with the other. The tray righted, and her grip relaxed. *Newton's third law. Phew. Close one.*

Her friends from the school's Speeder Club had found their way inside. "Close the door," she said, loud enough to be heard yet soft enough not to sound bossy. Her friends waved and nodded. The door slid shut. *Why do things tend to go wrong whenever I'm being watched?*

Arnie, her ex-boyfriend and all-around class clown, led the

pack. "Hey, Luna, don't let us get in your way," he said, shaking the rain off like a wet dog.

The girls reacted in mocked horror while the guys burst out laughing and did the same. They tossed their gear aside and arranged hay bales in a circle before drying off.

Make yourselves at home, guys.

Based on how hard it was raining, Luna assumed her friends probably planned to stay awhile. Within seconds, loud, twentieth-century rock music reverberated off the stable walls. Horse people would have known better. There's propriety, an etiquette, if you will, to be followed in a barn. The horses didn't seem to mind. In fact, they nickered as their ears and tails twitched to the oldie but goodie.

Luna pitched the litter into the wheelbarrow, forming a higher yet teetering, green pyramid of horse apples.

Today, of all days, couldn't you guys be more like horses? They don't mind the rain.

She finished cleaning the stall and was about to slide the gate closed when the dapple, gray mare pooped. Again. And it kept on coming, plopping on the freshly cleaned bedding. "Really, Daisy? Saving up for a rainy day?" *Did a horse have to take a dump right after its stall had been cleaned? Was it an inside joke among equines?* Luna swore they did it on purpose. She scooped the last clumps and wiped the sweat off her brow. The gate closed with a satisfying click. *Not too bad. 13:43. Time to scoot.*

Despite Luna's effort to pat down the tray load, the manure mound had grown into a perilous tower. Luna balanced the shovel and pitchfork over the handles and, with a 'humph,' heaved forward. She pressed down on one handle and guided with the other. The wheelbarrow gradually turned. The load shifted. Her muscles protested. The wheel bounced over a floor seam. Her arms shook. The load threatened to topple over. She dug into her inner core, forcing an exhaled grunt. She pushed past the turn's crest. Only then did the wheelbarrow's legs come down.

Catching her breath, Luna spotted a new bronze nameplate on the opposite stall. *Not another one.* A rustle inside informed otherwise. Luna pushed the wheelbarrow out of the way. A chest-high dent in the stall gate obscured part of the name on the plate. Behind her, someone in the group cracked a joke, and the rest broke out laughing.

The nearby horses with box seats stuck their heads out of their stalls. They dialed their ears to full alert. They were not going to miss the rest of the show. Luna uttered the four syllables of his name, '*Bucephalus.*' "I'm over here, boy," she said, reaching for the latch. Maybe he had just arrived and hadn't soiled his stall yet. She crossed her fingers. *Please don't be anything like your namesake.* The stallion whinnied. The *thunk* of a hoof rattled the composite gate on its tracks. *That's gonna leave another mark.* What had the owner been thinking?

Bucephalus's new owner had purchased the horse sight unseen, guaranteed to be 'energetic' and in good physical condition. That's what he wanted. That's what he paid for. That's what he got. He figured the history behind the name had to be worth something. His country-club friends would have to be impressed with a horse like that. Just saying the four syllables exuded prestige. His daughter, Britânia, had requested a more spirited ride for her show-jumping competitions. She had falsely blamed her failures on the temperament of her mount, pleading, "But Daddy, all of my friends have trophies." How could he say no to his little girl?

Luna tried to understand why someone would pay good money for a major headache. *More coin than sense.* Like the blockhead who forgot to warn her about this arrival.

She undid the latch, slid the door a smidge, and peeked inside. The mammoth-sized equine took up the greater part of his stall. "You look like you're hiding Trojan soldiers inside," she said. "Hungry, boy?"

The horse was prepared to answer. He bobbed his head, held his ears back, and shook all over. His tail swished with his leg raised, locked, loaded, and aimed at the gate. A short fuse on a lit cannon.

"So you're gonna be like that?" As much as she wanted to slide along the sidewall, do a quick clean, and get out of there, she let the idea pass. Can't be nimble, much less quick, with a poop-filled pitchfork between us. But it had to be done. He also happened to pee like a racehorse. She slid the gate closed. The latch came down with a reassuring *click*.

It would be so much easier to pass on this one. Skip it. 13:59. Leave him there. Tomorrow, someone else could deal with it.

The horse tossed his head and whinnied. He gave the gate another resounding *thunk,* a 'go away' sendoff salute.

She had unknowingly left the worst for last. Luna impulsively wanted to kick the door. 14:01. And did. "Right back 'atcha," she said, though it did not make her feel better. Tired, impatient, and frustrated, she peeked over her shoulder. Her friends acted as if nothing had happened. They did not have to say it. She had lost the round. Horse–5:Humans–0.

"Think our wanna-be vet's got her hands full?" a voice said from the hay circle.

Arnie chuckled. "I think he just gave her the hoof."

The others snickered and giggled.

"Shh, keep it down," Arnie said.

Since we broke up, he hasn't gotten over it, Luna thought. The Beatle's song *Help* played. Swaying to the beat, the stable horses swished their tails. Like most kids her age, Luna knew the words and sang along. She looked over her shoulder. Daisy peered out of her stall with her large, soulful doe eyes. Their gazes met, and they bobbed their heads. "Might just work," Luna said, taking a lead off the wall. 14:03.

Luna led the mare into the aisle and placed her in a stall with another mare. She returned with a scoop of molasses-sweetened grain and filled Daisy's feed box. In a voice that resonated beyond the limitations of her petite frame, she said, "All right, you guys, take a break. Do me a favor and lend a hand. Bring over those bales."

There were the expected murmurs of dissent, but with Arnie's urging, everyone got up and brought their makeshift table and chairs.

Luna stacked the hay bales between Bucephalus's stall and Daisy's empty one. Leaving a gap in the improvised wall, she slid through and, without making a sound, carefully opened the stallion's gate latch. Her friends backpedaled. Before the gate was flung fully open, Luna dove through the break in her wall.

The stallion snorted like an annoyed dragon. He pawed the floor. His hoof sent litter flying.

Her friends vied for exits.

When the aroma of sweet feed hit the horse's nose, all irritation vanished. He trotted out, scraping his flank on the open gate, and crossed the aisle into the opposite stall. The sound of munching spurred Luna to push through and slam his gate shut. "Thanks, guys. Couldn't have done it without you." 14:13. "If you take back those bales, I'll finish up here." *If I rush, I might make it back in time to squeeze in the tail end of a study group.*

Her friends responded with grunts and sighs.

"What would've happened if he hadn't gone for it?" a voice asked between huffs from hauling hay.

Luna shrugged. "Since I couldn't appeal to his sense of civility, I had to tempt his stomach. Never doubted it for a second." She gave him a sideward glance and rolled her eyes.

They groaned in unison. "Yeah, right."

She considered herself lucky and was not about to press her luck. She unloaded the wheelbarrow, cleaned Bucephalus's stall, and returned Daisy to it with an added flake of hay. 14:29.

Her speeder group had rearranged the bales in a wider circle. Snacks and beverages appeared from nowhere. The background music mixed with their ecstatic voices and the occasional thunderclap. They carried on like they were at an indoor picnic without a care in the world. *They have a right to be jovial,* she thought. Their finals were over. *If I hadn't taken an extra major, I'd be celebrating, too. After work, anyway.*

Standing in the center of the circle, Arnie raised his beer can. "By this time next year, we'll be seniors and out of here." The others joined in the toast.

Luna gathered her gear. She, too, had a reason to celebrate. Her precalculus exam had gone well, with plenty of time to check her answers. Done here for the day, she would have to wait till tomorrow before taking a few laps at the track and letting her bob-cut hair down.

"Hey, Luna. Too stuck up to join us?" Arnie pointed his can at her. The others turned and looked at her expectantly.

She could explain her reason for leaving. They'd understand. But if nothing else, she was grateful. *I'd still be hauling bales without their help.* A thundering boom struck. *Planck's constant is 6.62607004 times ten to the minus thirty-fourth meters squared kilograms per sec. I got this. The storm will pass. Plenty of time.*

"No, Arnie. Thought I'd give you a head start before I embarrass your sorry butt tomorrow," Luna retorted, strutting up and squeezing in.

"We'll see," Arnie said before continuing his story. He bent at the waist with his fists extended at shoulder height. "So, where did I leave off? Oh, yeah. My turbojets are blowing ruts in the groomed track. Just as I lean into the curve, it's me and Jeff fighting for the rail. We both slide into Wipe Out Curve. My knee's dragging, kicking up clods, and my intake ports are sucking muck." Arnie pointed at Jeff. "Dude, you were right on the outside, you know, on the receiving end, taking soil samples."

Jeff put aside his cylindrical bong pipe. He blew a puff of smoke out the side of his mouth and frowned as he flicked the clods of mud.

Arnie held their gaze like a hypnotist. "So instead of easing up, as any sane person would, I bend the throttle."

Amy, the new, younger, blond girl, handed Luna a grenade-shaped beer can. "No thanks," Luna whispered. Her fingers rubbed against the outside of her knee, and, with the other hand, she pointed to the cooler. "Ginger ale, please."

Arnie clenched his teeth, bouncing on his knees. "Turbine's fighting me for every extra rev, vibrating below me, begging for mercy, threatening to blow. My speeder slides on the slippery surface."

Jeff nodded between puffs. "You were smoking, dude."

"So just when I think I'm about to skid out," Arnie said, "and by all the laws of Newtonian physics, it should." He gave his wrist an exaggerated twist. "I pop it, and it rights up. I'm back in it."

Arnie overheard me studying, Luna thought. Every particle in the universe attracts every other particle with force directly proportional to the gravitational constant times the product of their masses divided by their center's distance squared. *I'm ready.*

Arnie must have taken her smile as a sign. He slumped down next to her and squeezed in. "I'd have overtaken you at the last meet if—"

"You were in another time zone," Luna said, pushing him off.

Muffled smirks and snickers filled the circle.

Not missing a beat, Arnie put his arm around her and, with a thin smile, asked. "Come on, Luna, howz about a kiss? For old time's sake, or have you turned bashful without me?"

Luna batted her eyelashes and puckered her lips. She gazed seductively into Arnie's chestnut eyes. "Arnold, you're having one big love affair...."

Arnie relaxed, closed his eyes, and leaned in.

Luna shook off his arm. "... with yourself."

"Ouuuuuu," the girls said. The guys pounded their thighs and slapped each other on the back.

Arnie's cheeks flushed. He opened his mouth, but the words froze. For once, Arnie had nothing to say. In a huff, he trudged to the far side of the circle.

The thunderclaps sounded farther apart. The group chatted and laughed, as she hoped to do in twenty-four hours. 14:42. Arnie wasted no time regaining the attention of his captivated audience. *Almost time to leave.*

Luna turned to her opposite side and watched Jeff show Amy how to smoke a bong. He pressed the igniter button, placed his nose and mouth over the elongated cylinder, breathed in, and let the smoke out through his nostrils. Grinning, he handed over the pipe. "Now you try."

Amy hesitated. Then, before she reached for it, Luna

grabbed the bong and handed it back to Jeff. "No one sits next to me with bong breath, Jeff," Luna said. Amy sat by while Jeff shrugged and nodded. He puffed, careful of the direction he blew the smoke. "Time to vamoose; gotta go," she said more to herself than anyone else and picked up her helmet.

A sudden breeze announced the opening of the stable door. An underclassman entered. He looked around, careful as he stepped.

The floor's clean. What's your problem?

"Close the door! Whadyado, live in a barn?" her friends shouted, with a burst of laughter.

He approached the group and looked downward, unsure of himself.

"Give him a break; why don't ya?" Luna said. Everyone stopped what they were doing. All eyes were on the new kid.

He cleared his throat. "Luna, Principal Heiman has called you to his office. It's urgent."

In teenage harmony, Arnie led the group, singing teasingly, "Oh, oh, oh, oh, oh, oh Luna is in trouble."

Luna stood as if this were a routine matter. Hiding her concern, she grabbed her things and handed Arnie her soda. "It's the closest you'll get to these lips, lover boy." Arnie put down his beer and took the can.

"I had trouble finding you," the boy said. "You were supposed to be in Heiman's office ten minutes ago."

Luna wasted no time heading for the exit while she fumbled with the rest of her gear. She waited to get out of earshot before asking, "Do you know what this is about?"

"Dunno. I just do what I'm told," he said with a shrug.

She rushed to the door. Called into the office like this, there had to be something that could only be said in person, she thought, putting on her helmet. No explanation. Something terrible must have happened. "Be sure to close the door all the way," she said before starting her speeder and taking off.

*   *   *

WHILE THE RAIN bombarded Luna's helmet, an emotional explosion went off inside. Oblivious to the humming of her speeder's turbine revolutions, she weaved through traffic. A gamut of 'what ifs' filled overcrowded scenarios. *If it was urgent, it had to be something bad,* she thought. *Or maybe it's something good. But then, Heiman would have just 'commed' or found another way of letting me know. Why now? Has something happened to Mom? What if I've been awarded another scholarship? Maybe something happened in the lab? What else could she be responsible for?* Luna let off the throttle to scratch her knee. *Am I overreacting?*

"Watch it, dude," she yelled, honked, and swerved. "Stay on your line!" As if there was not enough to worry about, autonomous vehicles still couldn't recognize speeders in the rain. What if it's bad, really bad?

Luna arrived at the filled administration parking lot, scanning for an empty spot. *Afternoon finals must still be going on.* She squeezed between two student transports, oblivious to the following stares and sensors that would issue her a ticket. Without stopping to take off her helmet, she flew up the admin steps, taking them two at a time. Matted hair was the least of her worries.

Other than being another old-fashioned brick structure, Luna had never given the administration building much thought. For that matter, she had never been inside the principal's office, and the prospect of entering it now felt like going into Bucephalus's stall all over again. She took off her

16

helmet, and with one shake, her neutral, brown-colored hair naturally combed itself. Passing a mirror along the way, she wiped her face with a sleeve. A self-critique confirmed what she knew all along. Her speeder jacket and coveralls were all function, with no flair. Scraped knuckles were the only thing flashy about her.

You had to go through Ms. Watkins to see Principal Heiman. Luna took a deep breath before knocking on the oversize antique door. *Sweet feed won't do me any good in here.*

"Come in," came a woman's voice. Ms. Watkins wore a robin's egg blue dress with lace accents. A strand of antique pearls adorned her neck. The receptionist's reputation for having a short temper and outdated wardrobe was legendary throughout the school. Some hinted the elderly secretary should have retired long ago. Luna watched as Ms. Watkins manipulated multiple communication links with one hand while swiping video files with the other.

No way I could do that.

The matron's right hand paused as she granted a sideward peek while her left hand continued to swipe. "Yes?" she asked between frowned lips.

You'd think I barged in while she was taking a shower. "Luna Auer. I was told to come straight away. I just got off work." She brushed off her jacket. "Otherwise, I would have changed."

Ms. Watkins waved a finger over her comm links. They muted. "He will be right with you. Take a seat," she said and returned to multi-tasking.

Luna carefully unfastened her wet jacket, mindful to touch as few surfaces as possible. She put one boot over the other, trying to minimize the growing puddle on the floor. Ms. Watkins scowled as Luna set her helmet on the chair beside her. Luna raised her hand in a half-wave, and when that didn't get Ms. Watkins's attention, she stood and cleared her throat. "Sorry to interrupt, but I've come straight from work. I know I'm late, but I got here as soon as I could. Is it my mother? Is she all right?"

Ms. Watkins' scowl softened. She closed her eyes and shook her head.

That's reassuring.

The secretary began to reply when a student, with a flushed face pushed the inner door and slammed it behind. In a huff, he bumped into Luna. "Outta my way!" He caught himself and paused. "Oh! Luna, it's you."

Ms. Watkins cautioned, "Craig, mind your manners."

My physics lab partner. "What's up?" Luna whispered.

"You'll find out soon enough," Craig said. He shot for the exit. Before opening the door, he turned. He looked deadly serious as he spoke. "Watch out, Heiman's a—"

"Craig Hemsford," Ms. Watkins warned.

"Sorry. Never mind," he said, storming off and slamming the door.

From one of the desk's comm links, a gruff male voice said, "Ms. Watkins, the grass outside my window is thinning. Contact landscaping and send the next one in."

Ms. Watkins nodded and waved Luna in. "He will see you now."

Luna smoothed her overalls as she entered the modern office and was overwhelmed by the scent of men's cologne. The desk plaque dispelled any doubt that the man behind it was Principal Heiman. He sat back in his chair, his fingers laced behind his head, looking out the window. She recognized the face from three years of assemblies and the administration's school pictures. As he turned, his stiff yellow hair, puffy cheeks, and sagging jowls swiveled to face her. Up close, judging by his wrinkles and sprayed-on complexion, he could be anywhere from sixty to a poorly preserved six hundred. Did he think growing his hair long, combing it over, and dying it blond fooled anyone? Seriously? Luna might have sniggered, but this was not the time or place.

He swiped his middle finger through multiple files until he stopped at hers. "Auer? Luna Auer?"

"Yes, that's me," she replied. "What is this all about?" Without waiting to be asked to do so, she sat down in front of his desk. Her fingertips pressed against her knee.

"I'm sorry to inform you that circumstances have dictated that I cancel your Rockwood scholarships," Heiman said, scrolling through her academic records. "Because of unforeseeable circumstances, our corporate educational funds have been cut. We have been forced to eliminate scholarships to make up for the deficit. I'm sorry. Funding has to be appropriated where it will do the school the most good."

An electric shock could not have been more jolting. Fragged phrases tumbled from her mouth. "What about my university scholarship? I'm supposed to apply next year. I'll lose my application standing." She would have preferred to scream, 'You can't do this!' Instead, she said, "I'm enrolled in summer school." It came out sounding as pathetic as her desire to stay.

"Our bylaws state no student can attend classes, including summer school, until full tuition has been paid. Haven't your parents saved anything for your education?"

"But I'm surpassing the requirements. I have an after-school job." Her palms raised helplessly. "What more can I do?"

"I'm sorry. The situation is beyond my control." He

sounded apologetic, but it came out crappy all the same. "Perhaps your parents could arrange to finance the remainder of your education?" Squinting at the screen, he looked like a nearsighted pug. "I see that your father is gainfully employed. The Federation should have allowed him to save enough." The corner of his lip dipped, tossing out the accusation. "Has nothing been set aside?" His raised brows expected an answer.

"On such short notice?" Her knee throbbed. "You break your word, and now you're throwing me out? You can't do that."

"No, not throwing you out, Ms. Auer. Heaven forbid that. We're only asking you to pay your fair share." He pointed to the screen. "While you are an excellent student and your work ethic is commendable, it seems that ever since that unfortunate incident...."

If it was possible to saddle someone with guilt, Heiman had thrown in the bridle, blanket, and rope. Luna's nails clawed her knee.

"The university scholarship stipulates that you finish with a Rockwood diploma." He shrugged. "But all that doesn't matter now. Both of your scholarships fell through."

"I-I—"

"Your most recent academic performance has, how shall I put it, not been up to the same standard."

"But I'm way above the scholarship requirements."

"Look, let me be frank."

And I'll be Luna. You're something else; that's what you are.

"We've been forced to cut our budget. You're smart. You'll figure something out. Make financial arrangements. Take out a loan. Do whatever you have to." His cheeks blossomed. "Who knows? Maybe next year, university scholarships will be restored. Corporations are fickle that way.

You know how it is. You are aware how valuable a Rockwood diploma can be. Your future depends on it." He leaned forward. "Otherwise, I'll be forced to send your transcripts to an online institution. You wouldn't want me to do that."

Raising her lip in a snarl, she stressed the *s* and drew out the rest of the word. "*S*well."

"I'm sorry you feel that way."

Not sorry enough to do anything about it.

He tapped his fingers. His eyes wandered to the window.

"Well." He looked like a walrus struggling on a sofa as he rose off his seat. "You have a summer ahead of you," he said, extending his hand. "I suggest you make the best of it. Let us know what you decide. Say, by next month. There is a waiting list of student applicants."

Awash with disbelief, her bottom stuck to the seat. *This is unfair. What to do? Who to call? Mom's gonna throw a fit. Friends will freak. Forget about ever becoming a vet!* She buried her face in her hand. *Everything I've worked so long for, for what?*

He leaned over the desk and extended his meaty fingers.

She shook her head. Her grip strangled the armrests. *I ain't goin.' Sit him out. He has to come up with what was promised.* Her butt dug in, foxhole deep.

He waved the air to signal a handshake.

I get the message. You can keep your paw out there.

"Ms. Auer, must I call security?" He reached for the comm.

He'll do it. Justify himself with another excuse.

"You will lose everything. You have a fine academic record. Don't be foolish." He acted like a benevolent Caesar, granting a stay of execution. "Don't be like this." Even though he offered his hand again, his decision remained a final firm thumbs down.

She rose from the depths of the chair with her chin held high. *Don't give him satisfaction.* She abruptly did an about-face. *Shove it, Heiman.* As she pulled the office door open, her helmet fell from the chair with a *thunk*. *What else can go wrong?* The helmet rolled to her feet. "Super."

Ms. Watkins furiously flipped through files.

Bending over to pick up the helmet, Luna's head spun. *Forget about vet school? Why had I bothered?* A wreck, her finger traced the scratch over the helmet shield. *Ruined.*

"Ah, here it is. This might be of some interest," Ms. Watkins said, handing over an e-file.

Heiman's voice came from the intercom. "Ms. Watkins, insist they resod the lawn."

"I'm sorry." Luna shook off the dizziness. "Are you talking to me?"

"Don't let landscaping get away with seeding," the intercom asserted.

"Yes, Ms. Auer, this came last month. I posted it and filed it away because of a lack of interest. The Xerxes Corporation is offering a scholarship. A work-study program for someone your age."

"Ms. Watkins?" Heiman's voice asked.

"Work? Study?"

"A pioneer program. You'd be with a group of girls your age, doing statistical data entry and analysis for a Xerxes Corporation outpost. You would be visiting another planet, able to graduate with a diploma, and perhaps earn enough toward your first year's college tuition." Ms. Watkins handed up the electronic file. "For someone with your qualifications, they pay very well. Worth checking out. You'd better hurry, though. Today is the last day to apply." Her smile and approving nod urged Luna to think about it.

"Ms. Watkins, can you hear me? I know you can hear me," Heiman bellowed.

"Thank you," Luna said, reaching for the file, unsure what to make of it.

"Good luck with tomorrow's physics exam," Ms. Watkins said with a short wave. "Call me if you need any help with the application."

The bell rang. 15:00. In the hallway, she stopped at the stairs' edge. Students filed past. She raised her eyes from the file and gazed at the ceiling. *Where in the hell is Calcus?*

Chapter 3

"One's destination is never a place, but a new way of seeing things."

—Henry Miller

"I'm so terrified of being left behind that I don't care what lies ahead."

—Luna Auer

ON THE RIDE to the starport, Luna and Arnie recalled every 'remember when' good time spent between them: starting as freshmen speeder track rivals, to their first kiss, and dating during their junior year. What one missed, the other enthusiastically filled in. And then, as the inevitable approached, his self-driving rover changed lanes and, with it, the mood.

Over the dashboard and in the distance, the tips of fueling hyper-spacecraft appeared like spikes on an iron gate. The rover hummed as it merged onto the designated starport lane. At the far end of the port, enormous transports destined for the farthest reaches of the galaxy towered over the local planetary ships.

"I could come and visit," Arnie said, adjusting his side of the loveseat to face her.

"It's going to take most of the summer just to get there," Luna said. *I hope you're kidding.* "As it is, you've already put off your vacation."

He leaned closer and raised a brow as if expecting more.

How do I get it through your thick skull? "These days, hardly anyone travels beyond this planet, much less to the other side of the galaxy." She pinched his arm with her two knuckles like a snapping turtle to make her point.

"Ow," he said, rubbing the welt. "I'm not like other guys. I'd find a way."

"I know you would. But it's expensive to get there. I don't know how much free time I'll have or where you would stay." He turned away. *He's having a hard time dealing with this. Who isn't? There, I did it again. I hurt his feelings.* "Look, let me get settled first. When I do, we can come up with a way for you to visit."

With a brisk nod, Arnie's eyes brightened. He looked like his ole puppy dog-with-a-new-bone self.

Getting closer to the departure gate, they sat silently, buried in their thoughts, gazing through the rover dome. She snuck a peek at him.

While her friends had been sympathetic and a petition spread to reinstate her scholarship, it was Arnie who came up with a fundraising party. He must have commed the entire school and knocked on a hundred doors, spreading the word. No one, but someone who cares does that. His idea might even have worked, if most of the remaining students had not already left for the school year. Her smile grew as she recalled last week's benefit.

ARNIE HAD CORRALLED all the remaining students left over for summer school, and even teachers showed up. Despite her discomfort as the center of attention, it was a great going-away party. She played the perfect hostess, making sure everyone had a good time. Mingling with the crowd, Luna was repeatedly barraged with the same questions. "No, I'm not scared. Lost my scholarship, is all. I'm going to be traveling the galaxy while you guys are stuck down here." She discovered the easiest way to stop anyone from expressing how sorry they were or end their barrage of questions was to ask, "You wanna come with?"

Luna hugged Ms. Watkins when the secretary entered the gym. It had been no small feat to complete the required work-study documents before the deadline. Noticing her physics teacher, Mr. Woodson standing by himself, Luna took it upon herself to introduce the two. When she introduced the casually acquainted senior staff members, they connected easily. As Luna stepped aside, she overheard Mr. Woodson pass a compliment. Ms. Watkins blushed. Nothing was uncertain about how well they hit it off.

Amy, from Speeder Club, stood alone against the opposite wall with a cup in her hand. Luna came up from behind and gave her a nudge. "Tried the bong yet?"

Startled, Amy stiffened. "No, I haven't. It smells," she said, looking into the bottom of her cup. "Jeff keeps offering, but I turn him down… every time." She checked both ways and whispered in Luna's ear. "I applied for work at the barn. I hope you don't mind." She winced as if expecting a blow.

"Mind?" Luna's lopsided grin hinted at nothing of the sort. "Are you kidding? How's it going?"

"I like the horses and all. Just didn't know how much work was involved." Amy took a deep breath, appearing to summon up the courage to say more. "They took me because nobody else wanted the job." She leaned over in a conspired whisper. "I don't know how you did it." She took a long swallow. "And the new horse, he scares me half to death. I'm thinking of quitting."

"Boo?" Luna asked.

Amy looked confused. "That's what I call him anyway. He's a pussycat," Luna said, taking Amy by the arm. "Tell you what. Give Daisy an apple whenever you go to the barn, and I'll tell you Boo's secret."

"Boo? Bucephalus? Are we talking about the same horse? Ah, sure, I'll bring her an apple every day," Amy said excitedly. "I promise."

Luna cupped her hand over her mouth and whispered into Amy's ear. "He's got a sweet tooth. Carrots are his favorite. Just take it easy. Let him get to know you. He'll be eating out of your hand in no time."

"WHAT?" INSIDE THE rover, the moment faded with the breaking of the silence. "What is it?" Arnie asked, sounding concerned.

Luna shook off the image. "Nothing, just thinking about the party. It was fun, wasn't it?"

Arnie nodded. "Yeah, it was. Have you got everything?"

"Wow. I dunno." There wasn't much time to prepare for a year away from home. "The hard part was deciding what to take and what to leave behind." *If I forget something now, can I get it there?* "Twenty-five kegs doesn't allow much to pack."

"Twenty-five kilograms. That's it? Fifty-five pounds." His jaw dropped. "My speeder gear weighs more than that."

"Maybe that's why you're so slow."

"Aw, come on. I give you a run—"

"To take a nap," Luna kidded, snapping her knuckles.

"Okay, okay, you're the king of the track," Arnie said, submitting the title with a double-arm tap. "So, tell me. Where will you be staying?"

Queen of the track, Luna thought, thinking of a good way

to answer. "There's not that much to tell. The Xerxes website prepared a small packet that looked like an afterthought. YouTube University focuses on tourism, not some mining outpost in the middle of nowhere. And Google Galactic Maps showed only an aerial view of the facility."

He chewed his lip and began to speak, but there was no hiding his concern. Misgivings spread through the cabin like an uncovered sneeze.

He's worried about me. What can I say? I'm not exactly thrilled to be leaving. How often can I repeat, "It'll be all right?"

"Let's talk about something else."

Arnie swiped the radio and found a karaoke song they both liked. Luna joined the duo and swooned when he took the solo lead.

During the next song, Arnie continued singing while she tapped her leg against the hatch. *In my topsy-turvy world, maybe Calcus can turn things right side up.*

Arnie stopped singing, shifted in his seat, and during the next song, stared at the dash.

Luna silently ground her teeth. With everything going on, she dared not mention the fibs she had written on the work-study application.

Arnie turned down the volume and reached for the glove compartment.

Her mother's conspicuous absence also complicated Luna's decision to leave. Since hearing the news of her lost scholarship, her mother had not tried to hide her disapproval. *Mom has overreacted, as she tends to do.* In fact, three days had passed since they last spoke.

"BE SOMETHING ELSE," her mom had said.

Give up becoming a vet? No way. While her mother went on

and on, Luna felt at a loss for words. *I don't think of myself as irresponsible, or am I?*

"You're just like your father, using every excuse to leave."

Answering, 'I have to,' would only make her madder, Luna thought. During those exchanges, Luna tried to tune out, but the words kept coming back.

"It's a Godless planet. Serpents will consume your soul." To add insult to injury, her mother hounded, "Explain to me why you threw away your savings."

"Words hurt, Mom," she wanted to say.

LUNA CHECKED HER comm for messages, found none, and left her mother another text. *Seems that when Mom threatens not to speak to me, she means it.*

Spiraling rows of hyperspace craft stood on launch pads pointed at the heavens. At the last terminal, the biggest galactic transports readied for blast-off.

Arnie pulled a velvety black box from the compartment and nestled it in his hands. "You know, the way I feel about you. The way I've always felt. I…" He presented the jewelry box, poised to pry off the lid.

A ring! Oh, Arnie. Luna pressed her hand over his. "I like you too. But let's face it, we will be separated for a while."

Arnie gulped. "Are you sure? You don't have to." He squeezed the box till his knuckles blanched.

"You're welcome to come with."

"I already tried. The work-study program takes only girls. I even asked my parents." His grip on the box loosened.

"That's sweet," she said, scooting closer and taking his hand.

"I-I'm going to miss you. Who else is going to help me with my homework?" The tears welled in his eyes. "And give me competition at the track?" His head shook while his hands trembled.

"Come on now, quit that. You're going to get me doing it." She reached for his cheek and took his head in her hands. "Listen to me. This opportunity is a chance for us to meet at university next year. Do your part. Keep up those grades. That is if you really want that to happen."

"I spoke to my parents. They could help."

Luna put her finger to his lips. "Shush. I've got to do this." She leaned over and parted her lips to meet his. All too soon, the rover came to an abrupt stop. "You've been a great friend."

"You mean more to me than a friend." Arnie reached around her waist. "I love you."

She slid away and popped the door. "Before I forget. Remember the new girl, Amy? You saw her at the barn. She was at the party. Keep an eye out for her, will ya? She's a good kid." She put out her hand. "Please don't get out."

The hatch door released.

"It's going to be an adventure." Her finger snap exclaimed. "You'll see." She unloaded her bags and said, "Wish me luck."

Arnie glanced back at the rear compartment. "That's it? Got everything?"

"Got my ticket," she said, waving her comm.

And bringing more than I need and missing a lot of what I don't.

Arnie held out a roughly wrapped package, squeezing his eyelids with the force of a dam holding back a lake of tears. "Just in case I couldn't change your mind. It's from all of us. A going-away present." A string bow haphazardly held the wrapping paper together. Judging from the looks of the ribbon, Arnie had tied it himself. "Be sure to call."

The edge of the wrapping paper felt like… "A book? For real?" And stuffed the gift into her pack. "Thank you."

"We know how much you like to read. It was the best I could come up with." He wiped his eyes. "Call me as soon as you can. I'll get a hold of your mom. I promise."

"Thank you. Of course, I'll call. First chance I get." While she wanted him to remember her by a last-thrown kiss, her occupied arms allowed her to manage only a puny wave.

Headed for the terminal doors, the whirr of rovers came and went. Against the rustle of sports bags scraping against her sides, she strained to hear him pull away. *Go already.* A part of her yearned to fall back in his arms. Excited travelers, immune to another's burden, passed by without a care. Steps from the entrance, a porter's cart clipped her bag, sending her floundering to the side. Regaining her balance, she could not make out the signature whir of Arnie's rover. *Has he driven off?* Tempted though she may have been, she dared not look back. For as she passed the starport doors, the tears rolled steadily down her face.

*   *   *

EVEN IF ULTRALIGHT speeds were the way to go, as far as Luna was concerned, three weeks was too long to be out of touch. As the spacecraft descended into the layover planet's orbit, she bade farewell to the other passengers and crew. When the vessel landed, she sprinted for the terminal. At a con-comm booth, she tapped her foot as the screen connected and familiar faces filled the grid. "You put on a few pounds, girlfriend," were not the first words she expected to hear, even if Sandra, the girl from school, added ruefully, "On you, it looks good." Luna reached out to the screen with open arms.

"Where are you?" voices asked.

"Andromeda," Luna said, pulling out the book and waving it at the camera. "Thanks, guys."

"I've been there," a voice said.

"It's a layover planet," said another.

Arnie held up his hand, effectively placing everyone on hold. "From all of us…" He winked, "… We'd like to say how great it is to see you." He blushed, with a joyful smile.

As the last remaining cubes filled with faces, the center slot, the one reserved for her mother, remained prominently blank. An awkward silence followed.

Luna pressed her lids together, wishing above all else for the space to fill. Every time she opened her eyes, her heart plunged a little deeper.

"I stopped by your house. Your mom is all right," Arnie said. "She got delayed, is all."

A quick nod, dittoed. *Message received. Thanks, Arnie. She's still pissed.* Luna's pressed lips formed into a half-smile. "Yeah, that's it. Look, I don't have much time. My next flight is scheduled to take off soon." From the corner of her mouth, a mischievous up-slant formed. "What's up, guys?"

Twenty-seven screen portraits made a flash-mob impression of closing their eyes, frowning, and shaking their heads. "Same old, Luna."

"Take-off was a blast," Luna added without attempting to hide an unbridled giggle.

Groans replied. "No, really?"

"Well, I was supposed to board a freighter, but because my ticket arrived late, I missed my scheduled flight and got bumped to exclusive tourist class."

"Luckee!"

"Maybe if I come late for my next test, I'll ace it," Arnie said.

"How's that been working out for you?" Luna scowled. "Okay, so I got to the terminal, and a rep met me at the gate and relieved me of my bags. It's all taken care of until I get to Calcus. It felt kind of weird, to be relieved of the weight and miss it. Do you know what I mean?"

"No." Sandra raised an eyebrow while the others nodded.

"The trip got real when I exchanged my savings for Galactic notes."

"How much did you get?" Sandra asked.

"The cashier handed me a fistful of paper with colored symbols on it. Came to almost a thousand."

"I can spend that much shopping in one afternoon," Sandra said.

"Who cares?" the screen voices echoed. "Go on."

"Well, the rep introduced me to my fellow passengers. At first, I felt intimidated by the designer clothes, mounds of bling, and hills of luggage. I wanted to wait for another flight, feeling about as out of place as my knapsack and two canvas bags."

"You worry too much," Sandra said.

"Let her finish," Arnie said.

"We were escorted to the launch pad, where we met the crew and were shown how to put on our space suits. It was fun. We bonded, helping each other as we stepped into the unfamiliar bulky gear. While the others were careful not to wrinkle their clothes or muss their hair, when all zipped up, we looked the same, so in the end, it didn't matter what anyone wore. I grew so fond of my suit that I would have kept it for the track. Too bad I had to give it back."

"What was lift-off like?" multiple voices asked.

"Totally awesome. Pulling Gs is like speeding to a zillion in no seconds. After that, zero gravity is that suspended, hangtime feeling you get after coming off a speeder hill. Where you wish you could float there and never come down. Well, we played around, pushing off each other, until the pilot kicked in artificial gravity."

On-screen, the Speeder Club members closed their eyes and raised their elbows, like conductors waving their arms to a slow waltz. "Go on."

"The stewards assigned us sleeping pods, and we ate and slept the rest of the way. Chef-prepared meals..." she rubbed her belly. "And I got to try a Sumerian-crafted chocolate bonbon for dessert."

"And? How was it?"

"More than one, I'll bet," Sandra added.

Twenty-six pairs of raised eyebrows pointed warning shots at Sandra's square.

"Yummy. It's a lot better than regular chocolate: richer, a mellow sort of sweet. And yes, my favorites were the ones with nuts."

"Yeah, so go on," Arnie said.

"When the crew found out my destination, you'd think, by the way they treated me, I was some sort of modern-day Marco Polo. Crew members would drop by and ask if I needed an extra pillow, snacks, or my entertainment refreshed. Given all the attention, I kinda felt outta place. I mean, I even got offered space champagne."

"And... how was it?"

"Don't know. I stuck to my usual."

"Ginger ale," voices chimed.

"I've had champagne," Sandra said. "It's called pampering. Get used to it."

"Oh, I almost forgot. Going to the bathroom was quite an ordeal. The first time Tom Trevor, yeah, that guy, the rover designer, was on board. He must not have read the instructions. He—"

"Now boarding flight 27 for Calcus," the voice announced over the intercom.

The screen flickered. "Sorry, guys. Gotta go. Love you. We'll con-comm in a couple of weeks... as soon as I can... promise." She blew kisses and waved at the fading faces.

ON THE SHUTTLE ride to her next flight, Luna peeked through the passing portal windows to catch glimpses of Andromeda's rugged landscape. The solitary rust-colored rock and wind-blown dust did little to shake off the emptiness she felt inside. Stranded in a desert, she thought, clutching her knapsack. *I hope Calcus doesn't look like this.*

Transferred to a cargo ship for her final flight, it became clear that the crew did not have the time or inclination to be bothered by a teenage girl. Castoff coveralls replaced a proper flight suit, and a hissing, leaky valve above her cot made sleeping difficult. Her meals came in a tray of unidentifiable colored pellets surrounded by a fiber bar with the consistency of steel wool.

A crew member carrying a pitcher approached her. She made the mistake of holding out her glass. He passed by without so much as a nod. "Really? All I want is some water."

A thumb over his shoulder pointed to the galley.

AS SOON AS the ship touched port, Luna dashed for the exit. Homesick and anxious, she pushed through the cargo hatch without waiting for the passenger doors to open. However, without the shake of an onboard engine, she zig-zagged down the gangway like a drunken sailor back from the sea.

Unused to the planet's gravity, she grabbed a rail and

descended a long hallway as fast as her lurching legs could go. At the end of the hall, a solitary, unoccupied con-comm booth greeted her with a closed door. She placed her comm in the call port and counted off the seconds. The screen remained dark. An error message appeared. She repeated the process, and the same thing happened. She looked around. No one was anywhere in sight. She called out, "Hello. Is anybody here?"

Is this the right planet?

She removed her comm and tried again. The sounds of heavy machinery rumbled off the booth walls. An AI voice said, "I'm sorry, live con-comms cannot be completed at this time."

"What?" Luna said.

"Planetary interference is causing transmission delay. Please leave a message or try again later. Thank you for your patience and understanding."

Luna uttered a few inaudible phrases before she settled for leaving a text.

> Have arrived. Yippee! One more stop to base. Shouldn't be much longer. We'll comm as soon as I get there. Gotta go. Transport waiting. Miss you.

Loaded with the knapsack on her back, she looped a sports bag over her head while balancing another on her shoulder. Straps and handles dug in. Outside, the crew was loading ore and supplies. *Should I turn around and ask? Have the other girls already arrived? Am I even going the right way?*

Luna flung open the exit door and waddled past like a lost, overloaded pack mule. Unaccustomed to direct, natural light after so long, she took her first steps on Calcus with her eyes half closed. With each step forward, she adjusted. Gradually, one eye opened and then the other. Her stride lengthened. A smaller sun orbited its larger peer in a clear, peacock-blue sky. Had she brought sunglasses? Would she need sunscreen? She hadn't seen a list on the website. She shuffled through the loose gravel and plowed on. *This isn't going to be anything like summer camp.*

After having spent weeks in a cramped cabin by herself, she was surprised by a lone figure boarding the only vehicle parked in an open field. *That's gotta be my ride.* She quickened her pace and, to celebrate her arrival, tossed wiggles and hops to her walk. The two suns, shining against her back, cast a wide shadow that frolicked in step, leading the way.

XERXES TRANSPORT lettering plastered the side of a truck better suited for hauling rocks than passengers. Divided into three progressively longer sections, the pilot sat in the front cabin, port holes lined the middle, and thick, metallic ribs supported the rear. Next to the corporation's name, its logo—a drill and shovel, crossing over a miner's helmet—looked like a pirate's skull and crossbones.

Unused to seeing transports with wheels, much less monster ones like these, Luna approached, dragging her feet. The top of her head barely reached the wheel's rim. Standing within range of the tractor tread, the tire begged for a tap. "For luck," she told herself. She kicked the tire, lost her balance, and fell backward, flailing her hands and feet like a turtle trying to right itself. The brick-sized tire lug nuts stared down unapologetically. She wiggled and squirmed until a strap shifted off her shoulder. Fortunately, no faces peered through the pilot's side-view mirror or the passenger ports. No witnesses, no harm, no foul. Hefting one bag at a time, she climbed the Everest of steps. The truck's motor rumbled. Passengers' voices mixed with the chattering, braying, and mooing from the vehicle's rear. *What is this? Noah's got wheels?*

At the stair summit, the closest seats appeared to be taken. Her travel companions were dressed in overalls, and by the looks of their tattoos, long hair, and overgrown beards, she could have been in a biker club. The staircase door whooshed closed, and the pilot announced their departure. The transport lunged, and gears crunched. Animals voiced their complaints from the rear while Luna bounced off kneecaps, excusing herself. She tossed her bags aside and plopped into the far seat.

From overhead, the pilot introduced himself and suggested they make themselves comfortable for the trip to base. "Help yourself to the onboard snacks," he said, chuckling over the intercom.

Luna stowed her gear and settled in. On the fore cabin wall, the last Galactic Robotic Free-For-All championship streamed. Before leaving home, she vowed to use her travel time wisely. She turned on her tablet to the economics chapter on the applications of demand and supply. The game announcer shouted his take on the action, her cabin mates bantered, and the cacophony of animal sounds hampered her concentration. She put in earbuds, and for a while, it worked until the bumps in the pothole-plagued road forced her to reread incomplete sentence after incomplete sentence.

Her stylus flew off the screen. *For Pete's sake.*

"What did we do? Fall off a cliff?" a gruff voice yelled.

"He is aiming," a thickly accented voice replied.

"Basta pasta," Luna said to herself. "Enough already." She tossed aside the tablet.

"Hasn't missed a pothole yet," said the older man sitting across.

Forget this, Luna thought. *The quiz can wait.* She placed the tablet in her knapsack and watched the landscape through her portal window. *A lot nicer than Andromeda. Rolling green and no one around. Kind of pretty. This is what Earth must have looked like thousands of years ago. At least there will be places to walk around. Arnie would like it here if he could bring along his speeder.*

After the odd tree or shrub provided a few distractions from the monotonous scenery, she turned in her seat and faced the others. With nothing else to do, she passed the time, figuring out who they were and where they came from based on their name tags and accents. Tuning into their conversations, she learned they complained a lot and thought Sandra could fit right in.

Ziggy Konieczny, the oldest, bragged about the places he had been throughout the galaxy. Miguel Alvarado, of Chilean ancestry, touted his family's history of mining the Candelaria. Pieter Antebe had come from the diamond mines in Botswana. Vanya Feodorovich spoke about the hazards of hauling uranium and tellurium back in Mother Russia. Sitting in the middle, the apparent newbie, Bo Hastings, hailed from Appalachia. While the others exchanged stories, Bo's attention centered on the televised game.

Ziggy, the pockmarked man sitting across from her, looked to be having trouble with the new trend in smoking. He placed his face over the pipe's cylindrical opening but fumbled, trying to make it seal.

"Not like that, man. Over your nose and chin," Bo, the younger man, reached forward to assist. "Here, let me show you."

Ziggy blocked the offer to help with his elbow. He tried again, rolling the ends of his auburn mustache, holding them down with one hand while reaching for the pipe with the other. Repeated clicks of the igniter yielded the same result. He muttered under his breath, smoothed the ends of his mustache, and traded the bong for a can of beer.

On the forward screen, engineered hands ripped off another robot's head. Fluorescent green hydraulic fluid squirted from its staggering torso like Centurion geysers. The mayhem cut to a live news alert. Two business news correspondents spoke as stock symbols and prices scrolled below.

"Nooo," Bo bemoaned. "I was watching that."

"The big news on Wall Street today is the announcement by Xerxes's CEO, Amin Jun," the hazel-eyed, brunette commentator reported. The active corporation's stock price flashed. XERXES: 334.43k. "The street is keen to hear what this CEO has to say."

"Hold up, guys," Vanya said. "I have interest in this."

"Me, too," said Pieter. "I'm going to be paid in Xerxes stock."

"Hey!" Bo complained, but the two men raised their hands and shushed him.

"After Xerxes released their report three months ago, speculators have been having a field day," the goateed commentator said. 334.21

"That's right, Jim," she said with a look of concern. "The stock has lost 16 percent of its value since they reported a natural disaster on Calcus."

"What natural disaster?" Luna leaned forward for a better view of the screen.

"Shhhhh."

"It stopped their operations cold." Jim rolled up his sleeves. 334.09 "Here, we go. Let's cut live to the Xerxes Grand Auditorium."

A tall, silver-haired gentleman with a broad, white-toothed smile stood behind a podium. 334.13 "Good morning, ladies and gentlemen. After releasing our unfortunate episode on

Calcus, with diligent consideration—" 333.79—"we have decided to invest"—333.71—"in repairing the mining robots and electronics on-site." 333.42 "That will require trained personnel and the employing miners to keep our projections on track." 329.01

"That's us," Bo said.

Pieter and Vanya looked at each other with matching frowns.

"However, we have the right man on-site, supervising the technical staff restoring the on-site electronics and retrofitting robots and vehicles." 359.00 "Repairs are being made as we speak. Miners are stepping in for the robots until they can be made operational. I'm happy to report that analysis of Calcan ore samples promises to make this our most profitable venture yet." Amin Jun raised his triumphant clasped hands above his head. 389.98, 400.1, 404.33. He pointed to the front row of reporters. "I can take your questions now."

The news report switched to a Calcus promotional video. Snapshots of the Calcan operations and the surrounding region filled the screen. A woman, speaking with a British accent, narrated.

Vanya and Pieter toasted each other with broad smiles. "Early retirement, here we come," Pieter said.

"What happened to the game?" Bo asked.

"What natural disaster?" Luna said, waving her hand. *Hello? Anybody?*

"Your time on Calcus will be well spent," the female announcer's voice said. An aerial view of the mine and refinery portrayed an organized industrial complex. "We offer a variety of services and amusements. The humanoid inhabitants are friendly, and we provide excellent opportunities to explore their fine arts and crafts…"

Luna typed into her tablet: Calcus natural disaster. Between bumps, she read: *Feb. 16-magnetic polar reversal-electronics fried-mining robots stopped dead-abandon project-enormous unrealized investment.*

"The planet's ambient climate and Xerxes's diverse offerings feature...."

Ziggy gestured toward the screen with a thumb. "The way she's talking, you'd think we're here on vacation." He set aside a beer and removed a packaged cheeseburger from a cardboard box. The aroma of real meat filled the cabin. He squeezed a ketchup packet inside the sesame seed toasted bun and smacked his lips.

Bo reached over and shuffled through a basket of what looked like cellulose-wrapped scraps of tree bark. His face contorted like a child's when forced to eat spinach. He sniffed, bit off a piece, and washed it down with a glug of Orange Slide after a couple of chews. "They can't keep me here if this is all they're going to feed us."

"Eat that, and you won't be able to sh...." Ziggy's eyes swung in her direction. "...take a dump for a week."

Vanya shook his head as he tapped the brown, fibrous snack on his armrest. "Bowels of galaxy."

Luna put aside her tablet. "Yeah, the food's pretty—" she stopped speaking, realizing they were ignoring her. *What am I, invisible?*

Miguel pulled the tab on a beer and took long gulps. He drooled at the grease trickling down Ziggy's chin.

Bo looked at his snack with disgust and tossed it aside. "Eight months of eating this!"

"Fresh food is probably going to be expensive," Pieter said between bites.

Ziggy licked each finger with a satisfying smirk. He picked

his teeth, savoring every meaty morsel. "Engineered bars taste like swamp...." He glanced at Luna, "... muck," and reached for the pipe.

"That's it? They expect us to live on this?" Bo said.

"There are ways to eat better, but as always, cost is extra," Vanya replied.

"For what they are going to pay me..." Miguel puffed his chest and flicked his hand like he was shooing away a fly. "I don't care... is okay."

"For what it costs to bring us here, you can be sure they will work us until they get their money's worth," Pieter said.

Ziggy scrunched over in his seat. "Well, if you are what you eat, boys, then here is the last of...." he let out a tremendous, fluttered fart, "... burgers and beer."

Echoed hoots overtook Bo's groans as the young man waved his hands and leaned away.

Between laughs, "Don't light match," Vanya chimed in.

Luna wrinkled her nose and covered her eyes. *Gross. You gotta be kidding me. This, this is what I left home for?*

The rowdy atmosphere turned to concern when the vehicle's forward motion stuttered, and the overhead lighting and monitor flickered. Panoramic views of the Xerxes complex blurred to black and white. On-screen, a buxom woman in a bathing suit screamed in horror as she was carried off in the arms of a human-sized reptile.

"I know this one," Ziggy said. "It's a twentieth-century classic, *The Creature from the Black Lagoon.*"

The actress screamed in horror and pounded the creature's scaly chest.

"How did that come on?" Pieter asked.

The vehicle shook, and the men grunted, grabbing their drinks. The racket of screeching, mooing, and bleating from the adjacent wall drowned out the actress's cries. Everyone held on.

"Switching to combustion," the vehicle pilot announced.

The truck stabilized, and Ziggy muttered curses, bent over, and picked up his bong.

Bo also muttered choice words as he wiped his orange-splattered pants.

The black-and-white movie clip returned to the narrator's description of the compound. From overhead, the pilot cut in. "Sorry about that, folks. It seems there's been a MiPS. That's Magnetic Polar Shift for you newbies back there. Expect all electrically powered devices to malfunction."

These things are rarely supposed to happen, Luna thought. *This is the second one in five months.*

Everyone reached for their comm links, checked their screens, and shook them harder with every press of the power switch. Nothing. No one's was working. The vehicle stabilized. Power switches were tried again, and faces stared in disbelief.

"Mine's still not working," Bo said, tapping his comm against the tabletop.

"Auxiliary power provided by the Xerxes Resource Corporation. We appreciate your patience and understanding," the pilot said. "Your comms won't work until the poles reverse. Don't worry. MiPS rarely last long."

"How long is long?" Vanya asked, looking angry enough to spit.

Bo flicked the orange slime off his hand. "Great, that's just great," he said, looking around for something to wipe his hands on. "Nobody told me about no power."

Ziggy handed Bo his handkerchief with a shrug. "The natives don't bother with electricity."

"Primitives," Vanya said.

"Locals, natives, or whatever you call them. Have you taken a good look? Have you seen what 'they' look like?" Bo asked.

"Scalers. Their skin is disgusting." Vanya shuddered.

Miguel rolled his shirt sleeves below his elbows.

"Calcans. The people of this planet have red-pigmented scales. It's thought to be a genetic adaptation, the effects of two suns," Ziggy explained. "This place would be a must-see destination if tourists weren't concerned about sunburn."

"And could deal with having no power," Pieter added.

"We'll be underground most of the time," Vanya noted. "Nothing to see here, anyway."

"How come you know so much about this place?" Bo asked.

A bellow boomed from the rear compartment before Ziggy could answer.

Luna sprinted for the sliding door and squeezed through before the others could follow. In a rush to see what the commotion was about, once on the other side, she shuddered suddenly to a halt. Within the dusty, dark cabin amid the honks, bawls, and grunts, her eyes adjusted to the silhouettes of humps, snouts, and horns.

Feet away, in a makeshift pen, an open bear trap of a mouth greeted her with razor-sharp teeth. The animal, best described as the incarnation of a hippopotamus and Babe, the Blue Ox, slammed its sides against the stanchion bars. Panic-stricken eyes bulged from their sockets. Foam bubbled from its flared nostrils, and guttural groans spewed from its protruding lips. Bone on metal clanged. Its elbows extended from his barrel chest. Strands of saliva slid down the adjacent walls. It stomped its hooves and extended its beefy neck, fighting for breath.

She leaned back, bracing herself from being pushed forward by the oncoming throng. Two men dressed in loose-fitting clothes hustled from inside the compartment and leaned over the animal's pen. Their red faces, squinting eyes, and wine-colored scales revealed their Calcan identity. Clearly concerned, the younger of the two spoke into the other's ear. The older, burgundy-haired companion shrugged.

"Can't you do something? Anything?" Luna asked in a panic. "This animal will die if you don't do something."

Every time the creature thrashed, the onlookers winced or looked away. Desperate, she put out her hand, making the animal fling its head even more viciously. *The beast is its own worst enemy.*

"We should let the pilot know," Pieter said.

Barking diverted the younger native's attention, adding to the bedlam.

"He'll be dead by then," Ziggy said, putting his hand on her shoulder.

"Put animal down," Vanya said, shaking his head and turning toward the exit.

Luna refused to budge. "Come on, guys. Think of something." She reached toward the animal again.

"With what?" Bo asked, holding out his can.

The animal flung its head. "Look out, girl!" Ziggy yanked her back hard, but not before ragged teeth sliced through the edge of her hand, leaving a flap of skin dangling from the bleeding gash. Caught off guard, Luna pressed the cut against her side till the edges of her shirt seeped red.

Ziggy placed his hand on her shoulder. "Better go back. You need that tended to." He pointed the way with his bong. The other miners stepped aside. "There's nothing more we can do here." His grip on her shoulder tightened. "Keep pressure on that wound. You don't want it getting infected."

The Calcans turned, and the other miners checked over their shoulders. A weathered, windswept figure appeared from the rear of the animal compartment. As he came closer, he neither smiled nor frowned, looking like an off-season Santa whose trimmed beard had gone gray. He had the focus of a lion before a herd of gazelles. His gaze did not waver as he slid his oversized coat off his broad shoulders, methodically folding it before laying it over the stanchion bars. Oblivious to the ambient noise, he approached the beast with the solemn manner of a priest performing last rites. His wrinkled face remained calm as he nodded to the Calcan caretakers, rolled up his sleeves, and passed his mitt-sized hand over the beast's heaving chest. Seasoned scars, in jigsaw shapes and sizes, laced his thick arms. His being captivated the congregation.

He looks like a fantasy novel character, Luna thought. *Was he another Calcan?* In the limited light, she could not say for sure.

He scanned the cabin, stopped at Ziggy, and zoomed in on the pipe. Without saying a word, he put out his hand.

Probably Calcan. Doesn't speak our language.

Ziggy raised his pipe as if hypnotized. "You mean this?" He handed it over as though he were placing an offering in a collection plate.

The old man unscrewed the bottom combustion chamber, leaving a curved tube, and placed his fingers inside the mouth of the bong. Gray ash fell from the opposite end of the pipe as he twisted his fingers inside. His hand was too wide. He reached for Bo's beverage, and Bo held it out like an altar boy offering communion wine. The old man sniffed, shook the container, and poured the syrupy liquid inside. "This may change the taste of your smokes for a while," he said, swirling the tube.

Okay, so he talks and understands us.

So spellbound were Ziggy and Bo that they simply shrugged with their mouths agape.

The old man waved Luna closer and placed his fingers inside the cylinder, motioning for her to do the same. Unsure but curious, she held out her good hand while he poured the remaining beverage over her wrist to her forearm.

Yuck. The orange-colored slime felt gross. She turned her head and closed her eyes. "I don't know about this," she said, more to herself than to anyone else.

In the cramped space, the guys leaned in. "What's going on?" Vanya asked.

The old man stood behind her and held the tube, directing Luna's hand into the opening.

Pressed toward the tube, her fingers splayed.

"Make your fingers into a cone," he said, showing what he meant.

Is this nuts or what? Luna slid her hand seamlessly inside the cylinder to her elbow. The old man pressed her arm a step closer to the chomping maw.

The beast shuddered. Thrashings dwindled to tremors. Its eyelids drooped.

He plunged his first two fingers into the beast's nose as one would a bowling ball and lifted his hand above his head. Like raising a drawbridge, the enormous jaws opened. "No time to lose." Grids of coarse, misshapen, discolored teeth surrounded a slobbering tongue. He guided her elbow forward.

Luna's eyes widened as her encased hand came closer and closer to the cavern of cuspids.

"Don't!" Grasping hands extended to intervene.

Luna resisted, but her arm prodded closer and closer toward the chasmic gullet.

"No, not at an angle, straight on, below the dental pad." Her hand passed the first row of lower incisor teeth. The cylinder advanced. The animal's jaws closed. The tube rolled over and around the tongue, bouncing like a wave in a storm and taking her arm along for the ride. Crunches and grinds hinted at the havoc inside.

The miners gasped.

Luna pulled back, but the cylinder held, and the push on her elbow slid the tube deeper into the grinding abyss. On her toes and pressing her shoulder forward, so close that she could smell its breath, the tips of her fingers reached out, feeling deep enough to touch the animal's tail. A sudden tap prevented the tube from going further.

The old man beamed. "Foreign body."

"What? What did he say?" asked Bo, peering over Ziggy's shoulder.

He must have felt it through my arm. "That's it? That's the problem?" Luna asked over her shoulder.

He confirmed with a nod. He pushed her elbow, and her hand slid beyond the end of the tube and deeper into the throat.

"Extend your fingers and try to grab it."

Whenever the beast shook its head, her body followed like the tail in a game of 'crack the whip.' Between its breaths, she pushed. Inch-by-inch, her fingers clawed deeper into the gurgling pit. Her eyes widened. She touched a sharp tip and maneuvered the rest of her hand edged around a spiked sphere. An uncontainable smile widened.

"She's got it!" someone exclaimed.

Luna nodded vigorously. Yet, applause would have to wait because whatever it was still had to come out.

The old man gently pulled her elbow. Her hand and the

object returned to the safety of the tube. "Careful, try not to let go. Ready?" A tug on her elbow and the pipe and everything inside came out in one fell swoop.

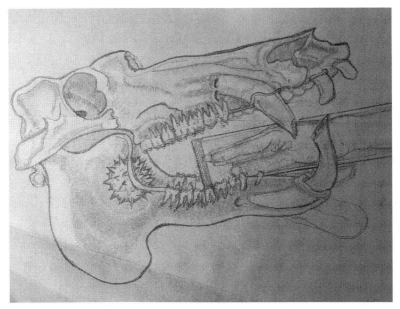

Foreign Body

The animal closed its eyes, lowered its head, and released a relieved belch. Like first-time maternity room fathers, the miners shook hands and congratulated themselves. As the tension dissipated, Luna felt at once exhilarated and exhaust-ed, as though she had, indeed, just 'had a cow.' The old man rolled down his sleeves and gathered his coat while the young Calcan embraced the beast.

Bo tapped Luna's shoulder. "What was it? What's in your hand?"

Luna pulled her hand from the pipe, revealing a baseball-sized spiked metallic sphere. High-five slaps were exchanged all around while she received congratulatory pats on the back.

Luna's gaze followed the old man's path to the rear exit,

but all she could make out was a disappearing white crescent on a wiry dog's behind and its wagging tail.

While the frazzled beast lapped water from a bucket, Luna exchanged nods with the young Calcan before turning to Ziggy with an impish smile. Handing back the orange-scented, saliva-dripping tube, she said, "Thanks, but I don't smoke."

The beast released an extended sigh.

Ziggy held out the pipe by his fingertips like a soiled diaper. "Thanks a lot."

"He didn't have any more luck smoking it than you did," she said, pointing over her shoulder. Tingling with exhilaration, Luna tilted her head back and winked. "I think he broke it in for you."

They exchanged smirks and nods before the rest of the guys guided her back to her seat.

Bo wiped his brow. "When I heard the grinding…," he said, staggering inside.

"Thought for sure you were going to lose your arm," Ziggy said, passing a finger along the bong's scratched grooves.

"El Milagro. Miracle, the thing is still alive," Miguel said. "Did you get a load of those teeth?"

"Thought the critter was a goner," Bo said, shaking his head and slumping into his seat.

"Toast," Pieter concurred.

Ziggy rubbed his belly. "No, boys. Not toast. Burgers." He laughed as he pulled the pin on another beer and handed it to Bo.

"Lazarus rises from the dead. Again," Pieter said, raising his can.

"Now we really toast," Vanya said, raising his shot glass, "Zazdrovye."

Luna wiped her arm and raised her can.

"Mind if I take a look?" Ziggy asked.

Metal spikes glistened in the cabin light. "It's pretty sharp. Wonder how it could've gotten hold of this, much less eaten it?" Luna asked.

"Eh! Those things will eat anything," Vanya said.

They passed the sphere around.

"Who was that old man?" Miguel said.

"I'll buy him a beer," Ziggy said.

Pieter held the device up to his portal window and pressed the spikes. "Looks like a spring-loaded burr. We see these on drill rigs. They are part of a driving bit."

Red droplets dripped from Luna's hand. "You're still bleeding," Ziggy said. "Let's get that tended to." Ziggy opened the onboard medicine cabinet while the others argued about wound cleansers and bandages.

"But that's going to sting," Bo said.

"Sting means is working. She can take it," Vanya said. "She's tough."

The others nodded.

Luna held out her hand. Once, when she was small, her mother had taken her for a manicure. Still, she had never felt more pampered than she did at this moment. Speeders and barns do not lend themselves to this.

Her companions cleaned the cut and applied a spray-on bandage. When they finished, Luna flexed her fingers. "All good."

"Wait for the bandage to thoroughly dry before you move your fingers," Ziggy said.

While her newfound friends recounted their impressions, she gulped from her can, closed her eyes, and held her breath until a long, satisfying, bubbly burp blasted from her mouth.

The others turned. Their faces froze. They were shocked

that a sound like that could emanate from someone her size.

Luna grabbed her cheeks with both hands—the picture of innocence. "Oh, my. Guess I'm made of grilled cheese and ginger ale."

Roars filled the cabin. Ziggy held his side, and Bo laughed so hard that beer spurted from his nose.

Suddenly, Luna felt like she was among friends again. How different could this place be?

Chapter 4

Elastic is sewn into the waistbands of the best of plans.

LUNA'S CHIN NESTLED in the palm of her hand as she lay cradled between the chair's armrests, her head resting on the cushioned edge. She might have stayed sleeping like that if spittle had not overflowed from the corner of her lip and trickled across her cheek. As she raised her hand to wipe it, her head slipped off the rest. In a groggy quest to adjust her position, she tossed and turned like a caterpillar shedding its skin.

Where am I? She needed more of a clue than a whirling hum. The last thing she remembered was nodding off in her seat. In the darkened cabin, her eyelids fluttered until she was sure everyone had left. Judging by the silence, they must have unloaded the animals while she slept. Rubbing the drowsiness from her face, Luna announced her return to consciousness with outstretched arms and a yawn resembling a lioness' roar. From a portal window, a faint glow greeted her.

"Ow!" she said, reaching behind and pulling a spike from her backside. Holding the sphere in her hand, a whiff of orange refreshed her memory. What kind of animal would put something like this in its mouth, much less try to eat it? Whatever the case, it would make an interesting Christmas ornament. It resembled a snowflake. She tossed it into her knapsack.

Looking around, she found Ziggy's bong propped between her two bags. An attached note read, "Dear Sleeping Beauty, We didn't want to wake you. Keep it for luck, Ziggy." She shoved the pipe inside her sack, but it was too long, and she could not close the zipper.

Gotta find some bigger luggage. Just got here and already have two souvenirs. Home sweet home. I'm here, everybody. Big deal. Who cares? Well, Mom does, but not the way I'd like her to.

One by one, Luna gathered her bags and took them down the transport steps. If she were home, she'd be a starting senior on the welcoming committee, greeting the incoming freshmen class, waving the school flag, and parading around campus with the Rockwood Rhino mascot. *But that was there, and I'm here,* she glumly reminded herself, loading up.

She trudged toward the dim compound entrance, engulfed in the shadows of silos, smokestacks, and twirling turbines. While banners and bright smiling faces were not there to greet her, two sickle-shaped lunar crescents shined in a cobalt-colored sky, illuminating the way. *That's okay. I wouldn't stay up this late for me, either.*

Steps away from the truck, she heard crunching footsteps behind her and tightened her grip on the canvas handles. She dared not turn around for fear of slowing down. It sounded like whoever was behind her was closing fast. A sideways glance confirmed it was a man, but that's all she could tell. The bags bounced off her sides. If threatened, her lungs were loaded, and she was ready to scream, and her legs were pumped to bolt. *Drop 'em and run for it,* she told herself.

The man came alongside with a curious smile. He was tall, thin and wore his hair in a bun. Calcan scales sprouted from beneath the collar of his silk shirt. Luna lengthened her steps.

"Can I help you with those, young lady?" he asked in a high-pitched voice.

"No, thank you, I've got this." Sweaty armpits and moist palms added to her discomfort. At this time of night, she wanted nothing to do with a stranger's help.

"How impolite of me not to introduce myself. My name is Rizzo." He walked alongside, turned to face her, and extended his hand. "What is yours?"

Don't stop. "Sorry, my hands are full," Luna said, maintaining her stride. She raised her shoulders and flexed her arms to keep her bags' straps from falling off.

Rizzo placed his hand on hers and gave it a one-sided shake. "Now that we know each other…" he picked up the pace with a mischievous grin. "Perhaps I can interest you in some Blue Glass?"

"Blue what?" A strap teetered on the edge of her shoulder. *Keep your eye on the gate*, she told herself. *And don't stop.*

The determined man backpedaled, keeping in step, fixing his eyes on hers while maintaining a distance slightly in front. "Yes?" He sidestepped in front of her and slowed the pace.

Luna did not follow his lead by slowing down. To avoid bumping into him, she double-stepped around his small frame. "No, no thank you, I'm good." Both shoulder straps fell. With the full weight held in her hands, the left handle buried into the cut. She grimaced.

Undeterred, he came alongside. "I understand. Is late. Lady is tired. If anything I can do for you."

Her arms shook. Pressure on the knapsack. *Don't stop. What's he doing? Don't look back.* Her biceps quivered down through her teetering hands. *Don't trip. Almost there.*

The Calcan stepped aside. "People like Rizzo. Rizzo good

for people," he said and magnanimously waved her on like a gallant knight for a lady in waiting.

The Calcan welcoming committee could use some work.

"You come back," she heard him say. "You people always come back to Rizzo."

Once inside the entrance, she dropped her bags and rubbed the circulation back into her hands. Two uniformed guards sat at each side of the gate, leaning against a wall, with their eyes closed.

"Excuse me, guys," Luna whispered. "I hope I'm not disturbing you."

The guards might as well have been under anesthesia. The heavyset guard breathed from his open mouth while the tall one twitched like a dog dreaming about chasing rabbits.

"You are entering a Xerxes-owned and operated facility," a female voice said, "State your business."

Luna stretched her neck and rotated her shoulders. "Auer, Luna, reporting."

A green light blinked. *That's it? Thanks a lot. You shouldn't have gone to all that trouble.* Luna grabbed her bags. *Don't bother getting up, guys.* She obeyed the voice's instructions, following the flashing floor arrows through a maze of corridors. Battleship gray-colored pipes, cables, and wires hung overhead like a vine canopy. One of her bags bounced off her leg and slammed against a duct. The noise echoed through the muted hall. The arrows stopped, and a pod door opened. *Hooray, Home at last.* The lights turned on.

In the unfamiliar surroundings, she grinned sheepishly and craned her neck. "Hello, is anybody here?" she asked before stepping inside.

She dropped her bags unceremoniously to the floor while she waited for an answer. The portal closed behind. *Looks like*

I'll be having the place to myself. Not bad. A nice change from sharing a bunk bed. She unfastened the knapsack and, one by one, laid the sphere, bong, comm, tablet, and book on the bedside table. Everything was there.

In the bathroom, she flexed her hand. The cut was not as bad as it looked. A little red but healing nicely. Vanya was right; it didn't hurt. In front of the mirror, she wiped her tongue across her teeth and opened her mouth wide enough to look down her throat. *No foreign objects.* She placed her electronic toothbrush on her forefinger and applied Xerxes Dental Toothpaste from the wall dispenser. While she brushed her teeth, she sang the Xerxes jingle, "We clean, 'n' calcify, dental caries need not apply, tooth decay will stay away…." Her eyelids drooped, as bubbles foamed from her mouth. She looked as rabid as she was tired.

She plopped onto the mattress and mumbled, "Off." The pod lights and monitor powered down.

The Xerxes logo glowed from the wall night-light.

*   *   *

ALL FIFTEEN MEMBERS of the Xerxes board of directors sat physically or virtually in attendance at the conference table. Heads shook, elbows clasped, and voices conspired. Every man and woman present were, in one way or another, related. At the head of the table, the CEO, Amin Jun, did not have to clear his throat to get everyone's attention. Although he could no longer frown or wrinkle his brow since his last cosmetic surgery, there was no mistaking the sound of concern in his voice. "There's been another one."

"Oh no! Not again," a member cried, shaking his head. The meeting erupted into a free-for-all of flailing hands and voices talking all at once.

The CEO placed his folded hands on the glass-covered table. Effective as a remote control, everyone paused on mute. "We don't know how bad it is. Since late last night, we have been unable to reach Calcus."

Samantha, director of research and acquisitions, rose and addressed the board. "Let's cut our losses and get out now."

Voices rumbled. Not everyone agreed. The dissenters countered.

"We've already made an enormous investment."

"Short sellers will have a field day. I'll go bankrupt."

"Squeezed."

"We all are," the others added.

The CEO slammed his fist on the table. "First things first. Nothing we say here gets out. Am I clear?" He stared at the man sitting to his left. "And that means no short selling on your own behalf, Jonathan."

The relations director crumpled. He gritted his teeth and nodded.

"It may not be as bad as all that," Amin Jun said. "Our geologists report that this usually is a temporary glitch and will not affect the updated electronics."

"The same ones who said that these shifts weren't supposed to happen in the first place," Jonathan said.

"At the time, they did not have sufficient data to make that claim," Sheila, the science director, said defensively. "I—"

Amin Jun raised a finger. "Our man in place has adapted the repairs and upgrades ahead of schedule. He has never let us down. The improved electronics are supposed to be impervious to magnetic quirks."

"Except for communications," Jonathan added.

"Except for communications," Amin Jun said, conceding

the point. He winced as he massaged his temples.

"Communications are not impervious to magnetic aberrations," Sheila said.

"Remember, Valdeez pulled us out of the Sigmoid fiasco," Samantha said. "No one else would come near that one."

"His methods are unorthodox."

"He's getting production going again," Sheila said.

"At 6 percent of where we ought to be," Samantha said, pointing to the figures on her tablet.

"Sammi, you're such a pessimist," Sheila said, twisting her wedding band.

"Valdeez wants to get the locals involved."

"What is that going to cost us?"

"He offset the wage expenses by discontinuing our scholarship programs," Amin Jun said. "Take the money from one pocket and put it to better use in another was the way he put it. And that is helping our bottom line."

"Not a popular decision among some of our consumers, I might add," Samantha said.

"Who cares? Valdeez gets the job done. That's all we should be caring about," Jonathan said with a shrug.

"He's a loose cannon."

"Wasn't there a problem during his last assignment?"

"A Federation agent came up missing," Sheila said.

"This Valdeez could prove to be an embarrassment," Samantha said.

"Can anything be traced back to us?" Jonathan asked, biting his thumbnail.

"Nothing more than a malicious rumor," the CEO assured.

"Forget that. He has hinted at a seat on the board," Samantha said. "Will we consider it if he succeeds?"

Jonathan disengaged his thumb. "Can we afford not to?"

"Valdeez is not one of us. What do we really know about this man?"

"How can we trust him?" multiple voices asked. Their eyes switched to Amin.

Fingernails tapped on glass. All attention spun to the far end of the table. The security director rarely spoke, much less made his presence known. A man of slight build and unremarkable features, he remained the black sheep of the family. His eyes raised to meet theirs.

"My man is on him."

Chapter 5

Friends are the siblings God never gave us.

—Mengzi

THE ROOM'S AI monitored Luna's rapid eye movements, breathing rate, and pulse while she slept. Xerxes algorithms determined the minimum amount of sleep required for every occupant's optimum performance based on an occupant's age and expected productivity. At the end of her fourth REM cycle, the waking process began. On the wall behind her bed, an image of the Terran sun rose from the floor. A flute played softly as birds chirped, and string instruments subtly joined in. Luna's occasional snorts added a wind element to the musical ensemble. The volume gradually increased. As the room brightened, Luna turned on her side and watched a new day begin.

A life-sized female image dressed in casual attire appeared at the foot of her bed. "Good morning, Luna," the voice said. "My name is Xena. Welcome. I will be your guide and mentor during your stay. I trust you slept well."

Luna swiped her hands over her face and worked her fingers through her hair. The music and voice were subtle touches. Sweet, even. Definitely an improvement over her roommate's alarm. That is, if anything could be considered sweet first thing in the morning. *Where am I again?*

"Yes, it was fine. I'm up," she answered, rubbing the last sleep out of her eyes. "I'd like to comm home, please." Her shirttail stuck out of her pants. She picked up a rumpled blanket off the floor and snuggled it to her chin.

"I'm sorry, Luna. There's been a Magnetic Polar Shift."

"Yeah, I know. When can I call home?"

"Based on historical data, this inconvenience should be temporary. Can I help you with something else?"

"Let me know the moment I can, please." Luna's gaze drifted to the screen. Xena appeared to be a beautiful woman with a light olive complexion, almond-shaped eyes, and long, dark, straight hair. *If they keep making AIs this gorgeous, what hope is there for the rest of us girls?*

Except for Xena and the workstation, everything else in the room was a drab shade of bleak. She noticed a lack of windows. *I won't be spending my time shopping for curtains.* She chuckled. While school dorms maximized space with functional furniture and floors designed for Robo-cleaning, there was always a place for students to help make themselves feel at home. *This isn't school,* she reminded herself. *A roommate would have been nice, but I can get used to this.*

She swept aside a cargo bag and dug out a picture frame from the other. She moved the book over to make room for the frame. *Where's the sphere, thingy? I could have sworn I left it next to the bong.* She looked under the table. The spikes would have prevented it from rolling off the table. She reached under the bed, rummaged through her bags, and turned the knapsack inside out.

"Xena, do you have info on a spiked metal sphere on my side stand?"

"Checking… for the item as described. I have no matching entry in my database. Do you have an alternate description?"

"No, that's okay." *If things keep disappearing like this, maybe I won't need more luggage after all.*

Her comm screen remained blank, even after several attempts to restart it. "Xena, when you said 'temporary,' how long is that?" she asked, shaking the comm.

"It's impossible to calculate. Sometimes a MiPS lasts for mitts or theoretically longer. I will continue to monitor and let you know when the situation changes. In the meantime, please take forty mitts to acquaint yourself with your immediate surroundings. Feel free to ask questions. Orientation begins at nine rays."

"Wait a minute. What's a mitt? What's a ray?"

"Not to be confused with a MiPS. A mitt is a unit of time based on a fraction of this planet's equatorial rotation in relation to its two suns. Equivalent to 1.6785 Terran minutes. Sixty mitts equal one ray."

Luna unpacked her bags and placed her limited wardrobe in spring-loaded closet racks alongside hanging Xerxes jumpsuits. Smaller items went into designated drawers. Shoes were placed on a tray on the floor for automatic cleaning. Could the sphere have slipped inside the bong? Instead of a rattle, a shake of the pipe produced an unexpected shuffle. There's something in there, but it's not metal. She unscrewed the bottom combustion chamber and, from it, removed a plastic baggie. Holding it up to the light, blue crystals sparkled like tiny sapphires. The Calcan, at the gate, must have put it there. *What was his name... Rizzo?* He had mentioned something about Blue Glass.

"Xena, what's Blue Glass?"

"Blue Grass is a kind of country music, primarily of the twentieth century, influenced by jazz and blues."

"No, not bluegrass, Blue G-L-A-S-S, as in crystals."

"Amphetamine. An addictive stimulant that appears as glass fragments. Chemical formula: C9, H13, N. The chemicals involved include red phosphorus, hydriodic acid, and...."

Before Xena could finish the list of components, Luna had emptied the bag into the toilet and flushed it with a 'swoosh.' She had heard of Rockwood students using drugs. Even Arnie had confessed to having taken something before his biology final. But she never considered drugs would be available so easily, so far from home. Yup. The welcoming committee could use some work.

While she showered and dressed, her worn clothes were washed and pressed on cleaning racks.

"It is now nine rays. Beginning orientation module," Xena said.

Luna zipped her uniform up to her neck. "Go ahead."

"Your pod is divided into four zones. Everything is self-explanatory."

Luna found the automated laundry attached to the modern bathroom more convenient than going down a hall at school. *Check.* The workstation hutch had high-tech features she was unacquainted with, but otherwise, nothing new. *Gotcha.*

"The food dispensary provides your daily nutritional requirements. Select the meal, bar consistency, and flavor settings."

Her stomach growled at the corner vending machine. She scanned the menu and said, "Breakfast, oatmeal, crispy, kiwi 'n' strawberry."

The dispenser whirled and churned.

"And hot chocolate, extra creamy." A bar and cup plopped in their respective solid and liquid trays. Between bites, Luna sipped her drink. School food had always been something to complain about or a bad joke. Her roommates used it as an excuse to ask for care packages from home. Of all the meals served, Mac 'n' Cheese Fridays was her favorite meal of the week. She closed her eyes and could almost taste the velvety goodness.

"Once you have finished breakfast, we will begin," Xena said.

Luna tapped the bar on the workstation desk and nodded. *Not bad. At least it tastes better than it looks.*

"Once your work quota has been completed, you are free to pursue academic or personal interests. Do you understand?"

"I do."

"You have committed ten employment tykes and have selected chemistry, economics, galactic history, calculus, and environmental science. Your classes are stored in my database and at your disposal during that time. Please authorize."

Luna turned about the stark room. *A year in here?* The same sports bags she had brought to school three years ago lay on the floor, a few things on the side table, and an unmade bed were all that attested to being here. She had arrived at Rockwood much the same way, without friends, and worried about how the other students would take to an outsider. In the end, she thrived and, as a bonus, got to work with horses and develop riding skills. While her mom may have been wary of sending her off, she had to feel proud that her daughter attended a prestigious school on an academic scholarship. *This isn't quite the same, but I'm here, and everything will turn out right. Besides, it's too late to go back now.*

Luna closed her eyes and took a deep breath. "Auer, Luna Auer, I authorize."

Luna laced her fingers and stretched out her arms. Psyched for the first day, she said, "Let's do this."

Xena's casual attire morphed into a company suit with the Xerxes logo on the lapel. "Initiating data protocol and analysis tutorial." On the monitor, a series of digital tables appeared. "The program divides them into individual files according to category: input, output, purity, contamination, toxicity, depreciation, utilization, and waste," she said. A file was supposed to deploy one onto another and then align the two with the other parameters for a three-dimensional report.

Luna followed the file melding protocol as best she could, but data points flew off like they had minds of their own. Red arrows and orange exclamations flagged her errors. She pushed a hand forward to get on the axis of one heading, and a previous set of values dissolved. The screen filled with flashing warning signs.

Luna lowered her uniform's zipper. *Is it getting hot in here?* She threw up her hands at the screen. *Good thing AIs don't lose their patience. Maybe they're still hiring at the mine.*

Replacing the images of tables, charts, and graphs, Xena reappeared. "You have been at this for three rays and are eligible for a twenty-mitt break."

Luna covered her mouth as she yawned and nodded. "Yes, thank you, Xena. Please try calling again. I know it's early their time, but I have to comm home."

The screen turned blank. "I'm sorry. Communications beyond this compound cannot be completed at this time. You may begin your break." A treadmill slid out from under the food dispenser.

Is this where adventure goes to die?

Luna swapped her uniform for running gear. *I'm not spending my free time here.* "Think I'll go out for a run, Xena. Configure compound, please." A map with flashing arrows appeared directing her through a labyrinth of hallways. Luna made a note of the layout as she laced her running shoes. The door opened, and gray floor arrows pointed the way.

Along each side of the corridor, rows of identical doorways lined the wall. *Time to meet the neighbors.* Every door portal looked the same. At school, stuffed animals, posters, and 3D–printed creations always hung on dormitory doors. The personalities of those inside were known without having to knock.

A technician, judging by his lab coat, came her way.

"Hello, I'm new here," Luna wanted to say. He approached like a plow horse wearing blinders and passed her by. There was a wedding band on his finger. *Maybe his wife is the jealous type?* Luna had better luck with the next passerby. The woman judged Luna worthy of a brief nod. Even Rockwood's most stuck-up students bestowed an occasional heads-up.

Before entering the park entrance, she peeked inside a room designated GAMES. The usual hovercraft, flight, and robot simulators were there, but, to her disappointment, a motorcycle was unavailable to play 'Biker Warrior.' *Another thing I'm going to lose in common with my friends.* She reminded herself that she had not come this far to play games.

The floor arrow flickered at the park's arched entrance. Inside, the domed roof's artificial light projected a clear, blue sky, and the walls displayed autumn foliage. She stretched, holding the entrance rules sign with one hand while grabbing her foot from behind with the other. Ahead, preschool-aged children played in their allotted area. The boys ran around the swing set while the girls claimed the sandbox. The adults watched mindlessly from the refuge of park benches. *No matter where they are, people behave the same.*

Luna would have preferred to run on turf, but as this was

her first day, she stuck to the designated asphalt track. Warming up at a jog, she noticed a boy trip at the side of the pavement. By the time she arrived, he was sitting off to the side, crying and holding his knee.

"Are you okay?" From what Luna could see, the boy needed more consolation than medical attention. Her lower lip pouted. Her eyes searched for recognition. "That was some big tumble you took."

Beneath a mushroom-shaped hoverboard haircut, the chubby, freckled, frowning face of a five-year-old revealed itself. His hazel-colored eyes met hers for an instant before returning to his knee. "Yes, I know. I fell down. It really hurts," he said, hugging his knee.

Luna knelt alongside and outstretched her hand. "Hi, I'm Luna. Can I help you up?"

He shook his head without responding to her hand as he rocked back and forth.

No one was around. "Are you here with someone?"

The boy's chin dipped to a nod.

"Sometimes when you rub where it hurts, the pain goes away faster. Do you want me to try?"

The boy tilted his head as if he didn't understand. He pointed his finger at her knee. "Did you hurt yours, too? Does rubbing it make it feel better?"

Her cheeks flushed. "Guess I did," she said, lowering her shorts' pant leg, and sat sideways, with her knees pointed away. "Does that feel any better?" she asked, massaging his knee.

His frown undid itself as he nodded like a bouncing dashboard bobblehead. He gave the thumbs up and took her hand. They raced back to the benches, skipping all the way.

"I'm gonna beat 'cha," she said.

"No, you're not," he said breathlessly. "I'm the fastest."

A woman, wearing an identical mushroom-cut hairstyle sat by herself, her nose plastered to her comm screen. As Luna and the boy approached, the woman raised her head enough to reveal narrowed eyes and pinched features. She pressed a finger to her ear. "Look, I'll have to get back to you. Something has come up."

The woman's frown deepened as she crossed her arms. "Did you fall again, Hunter? How many times have I told you to be more careful? Look at what you've done to your pants."

The boy released his grip on Luna's hand. His arms hung at his sides, and his chin dropped to his chest.

"I saw it happen," Luna said. "He tripped on the path edging. It could have happened to anyone."

"Yes, yes, thank you. He'll be all right."

"Excuse me. Is your comm working? Have the poles shifted?"

"No, not yet," Hunter's mother said. "This works only within the complex." The woman turned to face her son. "You're okay now, Hunter, aren't you?" Without giving the boy a chance to answer, she searched inside her purse while maintaining a firm grip on her comm. "Would you like a piece of candy?"

Hunter's attention was diverted by the crinkling paper.

"It was nice meeting you, Hunter," Luna said, waving goodbye.

Hunter turned for a second. His eyes shot back and forth. Ultimately, they clung to his mother and the silver wrapper. Only his mother's enthusiastic return to her comm surpassed the boy's attack on the candy.

Luna shrugged off the encounter. Break time had to be ending soon. She jogged to the park entrance and spoke to the electronic directory. "Luna Auer, pod guide." Gray floor arrows flashed.

A well-dressed girl about Luna's age, with long, straight black hair, stood in the gray arrow's path. She had round, expressive eyes, a finely shaped nose, and a beaming home-coming queen smile. The girl opened her arms like her team had just scored a touchdown. "T-there you are. I've been looking all over for you," she stuttered.

Luna looked over her shoulder and then pointed to herself. "Are you talking to me?"

"Of course I am." The girl's pinched face, closed eyes, and pouted lips revealed her struggle to get out the two syllables. "Wel-come."

"Oh, uh, hi." *Who better to send than a cheerleader to make some-one feel welcome?* She put out her hand and found herself hugged in two coils of a python's grip.

"Hi, I'm Jazz, Jasmine actually."

Awkward. The touchy-feely show of emotion, especially from a stranger, was beyond Luna's comfort zone. Out of politeness, Luna reciprocated the hug with a pat on the back. "Just got in."

The girl smelled of sandalwood—elegant, smooth, and expensive, just like her silk blouse.

"I know. Work-study, right?"

Not to state the obvious, Luna quashed her reply with an impish smile. "Not exactly. I came to party."

Jazz flinched. "Uh, p-party?" She froze, her face utterly blank.

Did I push too far, too fast? Luna broke into a wide smile. "Just kidding. Where are the other girls?" Seeing the same bewildered look on the girl's face, Luna continued. "Haven't the other girls arrived?"

Jazz blinked. "You were joking." Her confusion turned serious. "Janice stepped off the transport, looked around, and got right back on. The other girls stayed the night before they took off. You must have just missed them." Jazz stood back and looked Luna in the eye. "You're not thinking of leaving too?" The corner of her lip quivered.

Luna stroked her chin. "Well, I won't be able to make up my mind…" she bounced her eyebrows "… until after the party."

"What par…?" Jazz's stutter ended in a frown. Her hesitancy spread into a beaming smile and then a giggle. "Why, of course. A formal affair, black tie. I assume you brought your gown and heels?"

Luna chuckled. "Yeah, sure, Cinderella. Right along with my tiara. Left them in my pumpkin carriage waiting outside."

Their matched grins burst into laughter before Luna turned serious. "No. To answer your question, I haven't seen anything to get me to leave. Anyone else besides us?"

"No. Not really," Jazz said, shrugging. "Sorry. We're pretty isolated out here. Techs mostly, young couples with little kids."

"Guess that frees up my weekends."

"We'll figure it out. Getting settled in all right?" Jazz's voice rose, sounding helpful.

Luna half shrugged. "I'm here to finish school and earn enough to pay for college. My scholarship fell through."

"Tough break. Is there anything I can do?"

"Well, since you asked, I really need to call home."

"Sorry, nobody can. Part of the planet's mystique? Sorry. That's not funny. I can imagine how homesick you are." She paused. "MiPS usually revert quickly, at least during the time I've been here. This one's taking longer than expected.

Everyone gets paranoid when they last more than a few mitt*s*. Uh. Minutes, back home time."

"Yeah, right. The time around here takes getting used to."

"Time is all messed up when chronometry is based on two suns. Anything else?"

"I'm having problems melding data into the core feed."

Jazz pointed to herself. "Just the person you're looking for. No biggie. Think of me as your computer guru. I'll have you running that program in no time."

Luna knew a couple of girls like Jazz. They dressed in the latest fashions and were outgoing, gorgeous, and smart. Not to mention having the kind of figure boys flocked to like pigeons to popcorn. She could be the school president or captain of any club she wanted. Well, maybe not debate, she thought. "I'm coming off a break and have to get back. Xena isn't cutting me any slack."

"One computer nerd reporting for duty," Jazz said, raising her hand in a salute. "How does right now work for you?"

"Uh. sure."

Jazz looked at the floor arrows between her feet. "Yours are the gray ones?"

"That's what I was assigned last night."

"Well, we can fix that." Jazz stopped in the corridor and turned away. "Does the stutter bother you? You don't have to be nice. I know it does some people," she said, covering her mouth.

Luna gave a 'come-along' wave as she passed her. "I snore. My roommates used to say, 'like a dinosaur.' It's the same thing, only asleep."

Jazz snorted. "I never thought of it that way. So, what's your favorite color?"

"Turquoise."

"Then that's the color your arrows will be," Jazz said, extending a hand, accepting Luna's lead.

"You can do that?"

The two girls spoke freely as they walked. In no time, they were giggling and fooling around like lost sisters catching up. Jazz had millions of questions about her hobbies and friends. Did she have a boyfriend? What did they think of her coming here? Was the new music just imitating the classic era? Did she think Struttle had really broken up with Corina?

As THE POD door opened, Luna said, "Got in late last night." She straightened out the blanket on her bed, picked up her bags, and invited Jazz inside. Xena's screen image appeared, paused from the last session. "The filing system doesn't like me."

"Oh, don't worry about it. No biggie, we'll have you going in no time," Jazz said, scanning the room until she stopped at the side table. "You smoke?"

"No, the bong? Got it on the way here. It's a long story."

Jazz's eyebrows rose. "A book?" Her fingers swiped over the binding. "Don't see many of these lying around."

"Going away present. What can I say? I've got weird friends."

Jazz spoke to the monitor. "Activate. Jx7T1-COMMAND: file. Copy <V.C.N >." She turned to Luna. "Say your full name for ID."

Luna shrugged. "Luna Auer."

"Shift Sagitta chrome sequence G flat to T-100. Xx7TO, hold tutorial phase." Jazz did not stutter when she spoke computerese.

"What was that all about?" Luna asked.

"I changed your arrow color and gave it a neon kick. Hope

you don't mind."

"Do I mind? Are you kidding? Can't wait to go somewhere. What did you do to Xena?"

"Chronostatic hold." Jazz picked up the picture frame of young Luna with her parents. "You and your family look very happy."

"Seven years ago. Those were the good times."

"They let you go?"

"It's kind of just Mom and me. She wasn't exactly thrilled by my coming here," Luna shrugged. "You know how mothers can be."

"My mum died eight years ago." Jazz lowered her head.

Luna gulped. "I'm sorry."

Jazz's shoulders slumped. "That's okay," she said with a sigh.

"I've gone too far," Luna said to herself. Now it was her turn to fumble for words. Talking about personal stuff never ended well and was best avoided.

"When we were a family, things were great. But then Mum came down sick and died soon after." She took a second to compose herself. "Papa always worked hard, but Mum kept his priorities straight. Now that she is gone, I'm no longer a part of his life. I might as well not exist." Jazz embraced the picture frame. "Hey, enough about me. What about you? What's your family like?"

Luna stiffened, preferring to be talking about anything else. Quid pro quo. *What to say? Tit for tat. Where to begin?* "Ever since I can remember, it's been Mom and me. My father always seemed to be away, going from one Federation deployment to the next. The only time the three of us were together was between his assignments. Mom moved us around to make that happen as often as possible. I think she gave up when I entered high school. In fact, my last three years at Rockwood were the longest I've ever spent in one place."

"I've heard it's one of the best schools," Jazz said, scrutinizing the family portrait.

"That was taken for my tenth birthday."

"I can understand why your mum had such a hard time letting you go." Jazz's finger traced over the edge of the frame. "Everyone looks so happy." She pointed to the young girl in the picture. "Look at you with those bangs."

Luna propped a pillow against the wall and leaned back. "My father spent so much time away that I thought of our family as just Mom and me. And then, unexpectedly, my father made it home for my birthday that year. You would not believe how happy my mom was when she received the news. I was excited for her. I guess I was happy for me, too. Finally, my dad was coming home. We would be together again—a family, just like the other kids had." Luna pressed her fingers against her lips as she recalled the glowing page in her album of memories. She shook off the image. "Hey, I'm sorry. I get caught up. Let's talk about—"

"No, no, please, please go on," Jazz said, taking a seat at the foot of the bed.

"Mom cleaned the house, had her hair done, and got all dressed up. Even made me change my clothes." Luna smiled as if this were a private joke. "You can't imagine what it takes to get me to put on a dress."

Jazz scooted closer, listening intently.

"When he came through the door, Mom threw her arms around him just like I'd seen her do in the early pictures before I came along." Luna raised a tuft of hair over her ear. "He kind of looked like me. When I wrapped my arms around their legs, he reached down and put his hand on my head."

"Go on."

"I was so happy. Mom rattled questions at him, but before he could answer one, she threw out another. That's what I imagined a family looked like. Dad opened his bag and brought out a large, wrapped box, and gave it to her. She was ecstatic when she opened it. It was a new dress, the kind she liked with frills on the sleeves. I thought it was too short. Well, we went upstairs, and while he unpacked, I stood aside while they talked. When he finished putting away his things and they left the room, I stayed behind, hoping there might be a surprise left inside." Luna's gaze extended to the door. "The bag was empty." She scooched over and sat on the edge of the bed. "Disappointed at first, I got over it, since seeing mom happy was the best present he could ever have given." Luna shook her head and started to rise off the bed. "Are you sure you want to hear this?"

Jazz urged her back. "But I do. Please go on; what hap-pened?"

"That night, I lay awake, thinking about the great time we'd had. I couldn't believe how much Mom had changed into her old self. But then, when they thought I was asleep, I overheard them arguing. I hoped they were not fighting because of me. Not knowing what to make of it, I stayed awake until their door slammed, and their voices quieted down."

Thumbing through her memory of that day, Luna paused and closed her eyes. "I got up early the next morning, careful not to wake them, and tip-toed down the stairs. Mom had promised to make me a birthday cake. I was all excited. She had been a pastry chef before they got married. This time, we were supposed to make it together. It was going to be my favorite, German chocolate cake with real chocolate and coconut and walnut frosting."

Jazz parted her lips. "I'd go for a piece of that."

"I got up early the next morning and put on the apron my mother had bought me for my birthday. Ever since I was little, I watched her bake. Having the recipe by heart, I laid out the ingredients, utensils, and mixing bowls. When everything was arranged just right, I imagined how surprised she would be. While waiting, I'd pretend to scoop a cup of flour, break the eggs, and butter the frosting so I would be ready to do it for real when she came down. Time passed. I moved a bowl here and rearranged a spoon there. All perfect. I listened for her bedroom door. It was getting late. I thought about waking her. When morning turned to noon, I fretted the cake would not be ready in time."

"I know what you mean," Jazz said, shaking her head. "When you're a little kid, a few minutes feels like forever."

"Mom came down an hour later. I sat up and folded my hands, anticipating her reaction, eager to start, and she just passed me by. Her eyes were red and puffy, and her shoulders drooped the way they do when a person hasn't slept. I called out, but she didn't respond. I took her by the hand and pointed to the table. 'I don't feel like it,' she said. She was not in the mood, and that was all there was to it. As you can imagine, I was devastated. When I pressed, reminding her she had promised and that it was my birthday, she said that she had never promised, but only said 'we might make a cake,' and turned around, leaving me alone in the kitchen."

Luna buried her teeth in her lip. "I sat there, crying, over-hearing them argue. Crushed, I wished he had never come. My father was why Mom was crying, and I wouldn't have a cake."

Luna sat up and placed her feet firmly on the floor. "When

I was the angriest and feeling the most sorry for myself, he came into the kitchen and sat beside me. He looked at me with those big brown eyes of his. For some reason, I felt I had to give him my side of the story. Someone had to believe me."

I haven't told this to anyone else.

"He said, in words that I will never forget, 'I'd make a cake with you.'" My eyes met his. Then he added, 'But I don't know how.'" Luna wiped the side of her face. "I don't know how he did it, but somehow, those few words made me feel better." A grin sprang from her lips. "I've had my share of German chocolate cake. It's not that I don't like it anymore, but now I prefer pie."

The girls sat in silence, side by side, until Jazz put her arm around Luna's shoulder. "If you like, I can come back another time."

Luna wiped her eyes. "No, let's do this, or it'll never get done. Let me show you where I get stuck." She activated the workstation, and the paused figures and tables spread across the screen. Her wrists dragged, and finger flicks jerked. The tutorial surface was filled with red flags.

Looking over Luna's shoulder, Jazz said, "You're making it harder than it is," and placed her hands over Luna's.

Luna followed along and soon was nodding and smiling. Her hands and fingers waved, twisted, pushed, and pulled. Within minutes, she became a conductor, leading an orchestra of figures, tables, and columns.

"That's it, now you've got it."

Luna flew through drill after drill. What started as clumsy movements became fast and fluid. "Thanks. You've made this so much easier. Where the tutorial told, you showed."

"You'd have gotten it on your own," Jazz scoffed. "Eventually."

"All right." Luna said, yielding the point, "I deserve that. Thank you."

Suddenly, lights flashed, and the on-screen tables faded. The girls looked at each other.

"Weird things happen during magnetic shifts," Jazz said.

"I know. Great. I'll be able to comm home."

The monitor image faded and then turned black and white.

"The same thing happened on the way here. Does the same old movie clip always appear?"

"Excuse me?"

The fuzzy screen changed to an image of the Xerxes logo and then to text. "**TOP SECRET**: Authorized Personnel Only. The Acquisition of Calcus Native Labor." The girls' eyes widened, staring incredulously as they read. "BREEDING ANIMALS MUST BE SYSTEMATICALLY ELIMINATED." Luna's jaw dropped, and Jazz covered her mouth with her fingers.

"We sh-shouldn't be seeing this."

"If generous compensation cannot lure natives to the workforce, then we must quash their means of livelihood. Selected ranchers' breeding animals should be dealt with individually; failing that, entire herds must be eliminated. Actions must be taken to minimize witnesses or potential causes for embarrassment. If our expansion of—"

The lights flashed on and off and back on again. The girls looked at each other. Luna reached for her comm while Jazz's comm flashed and then turned blank. The screen text reverted to columns of numerical data.

"Did you get that? Xerxes is going to kill livestock to get workers." The screen on Luna's comm remained blank. "Getting anything on yours?"

Jazz shook her head. "MiPS blip. Nothing. How about you?"

"Nope. Nada. The authorities need to know about this."
Luna handed over the pipe to Jazz. "Well, this is happening,
and I'm in the middle of it."

Jazz awkwardly balanced the bong in her hands.

Luna told Jazz why she had put her arm through the tube.
"This is for real. Last night, I left the burr on this table, and
now it's gone."

"You must be mistaken. Are you sure?"

"Don't you get it? I thwarted their attempt on that animal's life." Luna jammed her fingers in her armpits and
rocked herself side to side. "Now that they know I'm involved," she said, closing her eyes and feeling a chill, "they'll
get rid of me too. I should never have left home."

"Hold on, not so fast. You know that unaccountable electronic signals happen during polar shifts."

"That wasn't some creature feature movie clip we just saw.
This is for real. Nothing changes the fact that Xerxes has to be
stopped."

"It could be a mistake. Comm signals screw up all the
time. And even if it was true, it would be your word against
theirs. What we need is proof."

"The sphere is gone. Isn't that proof enough?" Hearing
her words aloud, she realized how flimsy the evidence
sounded. Pathetic. "Can't call home. What am I supposed to
do? Who can I tell? Well, I can't stay here and pretend this
never happened." At a loss for answers, she vented with a heel
kick to the closet door. "I know what I saw."

Jazz did not seem entirely convinced.

"You believe me, don't you?"

"Of course I do, but we must be smart about this. Has
anyone else seen it? What if the screenshot is phony? Let's find
out for sure." Jazz jutted her chin with conviction. Her

stuttering was less pronounced. "Promise me you'll keep this to yourself. At least give me a chance to check it out." She poked Luna in the shoulder. "The party can't start without you."

"Guess I owe you that much."

"You've just arrived. I can't afford to lose a best friend."

"That's right, you can't." Luna gave it some thought before she begrudgingly agreed to Jazz's request. "All right, I promise. For now."

"Thanks. I'll let you know what I find out as soon as I know something." As Jazz rushed for the door, candy-apple red floor arrows flashed.

Chapter 6

Courage is grace under Pressure.

—Ernest Hemmingway

LUNA SPENT THE rest of the day sharpening her data filing skills and used her breaks to futilely comm home. During those times, she thought about what she would say and how she would say it.

"Hello, everybody. The weather is great. At least the day I've seen of it," and maybe, in the most sarcastic way, "Food is lousy. There is a plot going on to kill animals that I'm involved in. Oh, and what's new with you?"

When she finished the tutorial, Luna peeked out the door, checking the corridor—nothing. No flashing arrows and no one was in the hallway. She stepped back, and the door closed behind her.

"Xena, let's continue with chemistry."

Xena's figure ghosted into a middle-aged man, wearing a white lab coat with the name, Walter White embroidered on the pocket. He pointed to the right side of the Periodic Table, the second row, below nitrogen. "The fifteenth element is phosphorus, symbolized by the letter 'P.' By itself, the element is highly reactive."

He scooped red powder from a jar with a pinch-sized spoon and held it over a Bunsen burner. "In the air, see how phosphorus radiates light in the dark." The screen darkened, and a pink flame flared. "Phosphorus has been used to manufacture match heads, fertilizer, gasoline additives, insecticides, and...."

"Xena, pause lecture, please." Luna's knee bounced furiously against the side of the desk. *What am I going to do? If Mom finds out what they might do to potential witnesses, she'll freak.* She tried to distract herself by working up a sweat on the treadmill, but her thoughts overpowered everything else. Running to the point of exhaustion, she propped up her pillows and plopped into bed. *'Eliminate entire herds.' No one will believe it.* As she caught her breath, her eyes darted about the room until they settled on the side stand. *Why would Arnie choose a book about a crazy old man who jousts with windmills?*

She reached for the book, opening *Don Quixote* to a dog-eared page showing an illustration of a gaunt man on a decrepit horse, holding a lance, pointing at distant windmills, and beside him, his overweight companion, Sancho, riding a donkey. The caption read, "Do you see over yonder, friend Sancho? Fortune has provided me with thirty or forty giants to encounter."

Bucephalus might have stomped me. Heiman blocked me. A beast bit me, and now Xerxes. I've had my fill of 'fortune.'

Luna put down the book and pulled up the covers. "Xena, you can go to sleep, too."

*   *   *

BO WISHED ZIGGY was here. As the youngest member of the team, he had expected to be given a hard time. Hazing the new guy is a rite of passage, but the taunting never stopped. Bo had stood up for himself against the other men, but they outnumbered him. The guys were merciless. They called him 'kid' and made fart noises behind his back. Someone put a donkey sticker on his helmet. They teased him about everything. He especially disliked comments about his girlfriend and had rolled up his sleeves, ready to fight, a couple of times. It would have gotten out of hand if Ziggy had not stepped in. Ziggy kept an eye out for him. *Devil, take the others.* In no time, he would be making enough to be rid of these guys and do whatever he pleased. Still, he wondered where Ziggy had disappeared to.

Nothing prepared Bo for the heat. It had been nice to get out of the suns and into the shaft, but the further down the elevator went, the hotter it became. The humidity spiked. In here, they put you in a sauna to cool off.

They stuck him with carrying the jackhammer because he had 'young bones.' They made snide comments as he fumbled for his helmet's light switch. "If you can't find a switch, what else can't you find?" He got no slack when he put on his gloves, and the drill slipped out of his hands. "Is that all you fumble?" How was he supposed to hold a drill and keep the sweat out of his eyes at the same time?

In the cramped cage, perspiration saturated his clothes, and there was still a ways down the shaft to go. Bo closed his eyes and struggled to fill his lungs. The bang of the elevator cage hitting the bottom could not come soon enough.

The moment the gate flung open, the men ran toward the shaft air conditioning. *So, I'm not the only one who feels it.* The older guys pumped their unbuttoned shirts in the duct's cool breeze as the mine supervisor reviewed the safety regulations. It was the same mumbo jumbo Bo had heard before.

"Don't get separated, don't get lost, and don't get dehydrated," the supe warned. Of course, as soon as the supervisor's back turned, Bo's team took off without him.

By the time Bo collected his gear, lantern flashes at the tunnel's far end were all he could see. He picked up the pace. Sweating did not help. His helmet kept slipping over his eyes. He got further behind. When he switched to holding the jackhammer in one hand, it threw him off balance. His tool belt fell below his waist when he held it with both. The other guys made it look so easy. Sweat stung his eyes. At this point, he was ready to quit and be rid of this place and the whole lot of them. Leave in his long johns if he had to.

Within the tunnel's depths, he took longer steps as the walls closed in, and laughter echoed. He closed his eyes to ease the sting while juggling his helmet, belt, and drill. When they opened, his headlamp's beam offered a choice of tunnel walls. Whispered echoes taunted. He chose the closest and hastened into the abyss. The voices sounded closer. Perhaps they had turned off their lamps. Just the kind of joke they would pull. When he was sure he was upon them, he tripped over the drill and fell over. Blood trickled down his leg. He would have called out but preferred not to give them the satisfaction.

"I'm so going to get y'all," he mumbled hoarsely.

Too exhausted to continue, he gathered his helmet and sat against a jagged wall. Let them come to him. Parched, he patted his hip. His water bottle was missing. "Guys." The bottle must have slipped off when he tripped. They would show him no mercy. He used his helmet like a flashlight, widening his search of the dust-covered floor. Reaching along the wall, he grasped the canteen's cool, smooth metal surface. Gulp after gulp, he quenched his thirst and raised the bottle over his head. Empty. Was that a glow he caught in the corner of his eye? He leaned down till his head almost touched the floor. A crescent-shaped luminous patch shined off a narrow chamber. Bo brushed himself off, put on his helmet, and pulled the drill closer. He considered shouting, then thought better of it. Perhaps he could take a sample, stake a claim, and return later. He'd show them.

Flat on his belly, he crawled into the cramped passage. Using his elbow as a guide, he wormed his way through the hole, dragging the drill behind. He crept closer and closer, pausing only to clear his eyes and spit dust. Ahead, an overhanging rock threatened to block his way, but he squirmed and twisted around it. Once past it, he entered a cave large enough to stand up.

He passed his hand over the irregular, radiating rock surface, feeling for a spot to set the drill. *Maybe it was one of those precious 'ums': Radium, Curium, Einsteinium.* If it was valuable, he'd show those guys. Maybe give Ziggy a share. The others would treat him differently then. Maybe he'd get out of his contract. Could this be a vein leading to the mother lode?

Bo raised the jackhammer. The pounding shook down to his toes. Sweat flew from his forehead. The drill bit chewed deeper and deeper into the uneven rock. Between pulses, Bo thought he heard clicks. They were getting louder. He repositioned the drill. The clicks faded and then altogether stopped. He pressed the drill, and the clicks intensified.

"Bo" echoed from the main tunnel but went unheard next to the pounding drill.

He widened the hole enough to squeeze his arm. The clicks amplified. The glow glimmered in the limited space. He heard them calling his name but ignored it, reaching deeper into the hole, to his shoulder. Won't they be surprised? He tapped the farthest reach of the opening and felt his fingertips tingle. Pain seared to the bone. Bo screamed.

From the main shaft, "Bo, come on, man. This isn't funny,

dude. Where are you?"

Bo sensed a burning sensation in his fingertips and withdrew his arm. Had he touched acid? There was no more water. When he forced the glove off, his fingers dissolved into stumps. Like a deflating balloon, his hand lost shape. Blood spurted from his wrist. Pain shot up his arm. His brain cried out. Before he could scream, his windpipe dissolved.

His helmet fell, jouncing off the wall and landing with its beam shining on a jagged corner.

"Bo, Bo. Where are you, bro?"

Chapter 7

Without Danger, there is no Adventure.

BEFORE THE FAUX sun rose, the flute played, and the birds had a chance to chirp. Luna shot out of bed and darted across the room to the water dispensary. With every slurp, shreds of bad dreams rinsed down the drain. Quenched, she tapped her comm—no signal. On the far wall, the first rays of sunshine peeked over the floor.

"Wakee, wakee, Xena," Luna said gleefully, deriving unfounded satisfaction in activating an AI. Not only did Luna resent Xena as the personification of Xerxes, but it irked her that no matter how good the artificial looked or how sweet she sounded, it did whatever it was programmed to do, unable to think for itself. *Too bad they don't make them with groggy faces.*

Xena appeared in casual attire. "You have not completed your REM cycle," she said in a deep voice that sounded concerned.

"If I could call home, it would put my mind at ease," Luna said, wondering if Xerxes also had control over outgoing comms. *Mom must be frantic by now. Did Mom care? Of course she did. Moms don't hold grudges—for too long.* Luna's smile danced at the thought of her mother throwing a fit with Xerxes's human resources.

"What do you mean I can't get a hold of my daughter!"

Luna imagined her saying.

Go get 'em, Mom.

"There has been no change in polar rotation," Xena said. "I'm sorry."

Work-study? I might as well be serving a prison sentence. Even jail cells have windows. All that's missing are bars on the doors.

While making her bed and putting on a clean jumpsuit, Luna owned that she had allowed herself to be put in this position. Despite being unable to act until some unseen Calcan force of nature reversed, she stared at the blank screen while crunching the last bites of breakfast. *Finishing early will leave me with one less thing to worry about.* Breakfast's cookies 'n' cream flavor topping did nothing to improve the bitter taste left in her mouth.

"Start data analysis," Luna said, wiping the crumbs off her lip.

Xena's algorithm must have noticed the tone of Luna's voice. "You look very smart in your uniform," Xena said cheerfully.

In no mood for Xena's attempts at chitchat, she managed the reports with ease thanks to Jazz's tutorial and some things she'd figured out on her own. With nimble, coordinated slides and twists of her hands, data packets melded seamlessly. Parcels of details, figures, and statistics slipped into the processor core. *This isn't so hard. I was making too much of it. If I end up doing this every day, they will put the loony into Luna. Maybe the guys can use some extra help at the mine.*

By mid-morning, Luna finished entering the latest provided figures from the previous saul.

"You have completed today's calibration analysis report," Xena said. "In record time, I might add. Since you have executed your work requirement for today, will you spend the rest of this period exercising, playing games, or continuing with classes?"

"Compound map," Luna said, looking in her closet. "Not this morning. I'm going out for some fresh air."

No way am I going to wear a Xerxes uniform any longer than I have to, she thought, unzipping the jumpsuit. She would have asked what Calcan girls wore, but the less Xena knew about what Luna intended to do, the better.

The digital map appeared with directions to the commissary, game room, and park highlighted.

"The affected knee should be uncovered as much as possible," Luna's preflight medical scan had reported. "Exposure to the sun may prove beneficial."

I wonder if my red knee can help me pass as a Calcan. Luna grinned at the thought. *Shorts it is.* "Directions, gate entrance."

Xena's eyebrows narrowed. "Given the terms of your contract, you have placed yourself in our care. We are responsible for your safety. You are not allowed to wander beyond the perimeter unsupervised. Absence after twenty-one rays will violate your contract and…."

Curfew. Luna grabbed her knapsack.

"… will result in appropriate disciplinary action and the removal of privileges."

What is she going to do? Take away my comm? Luna's pod door opened with a whoosh. Neon turquoise floor arrows flashed.

Any misgivings about being stopped vanished when she arrived at the gate and was met by the backs of two uniformed guards talking to a Calcan. The native turned out to be Rizzo, who looked quite handsome in the light of day with his tied-back maroon hair, ruddy complexion, and high cheekbones. From a gold chain around his neck, symmetrical scales appeared to climb like red ivy tattoos. He stopped mid-sentence and greeted her gaze with a nod and a welcoming smile. The security pair turned long enough to blink before returning to business.

Luna checked her blank comm screen for a signal before a series of toots, honks, and beeps barraged her. Upon arrival, what had been a dark, empty lot was now a beehive of activity. Steps away, motorized vehicles whizzed by. Her nose wrinkled at the unfamiliar smell of exhaust. In the crowded lot, everyone scurried to be somewhere. She could hardly wait to join in.

Unused to crossing a street without a signal or curb, she cautiously approached the makeshift road. Inches away, a dump truck zoomed by, leaving the air saturated with soot. She sputtered a glob of dust. Before the air cleared, numerous wheeled vehicles had passed her by. Determined to get to the other side, she dodged the gap between bumping into and being run over. She went for it and would have made it cleanly had she not paused to gape at an honest-to-goodness, two-wheeled, chain-driven motorcycle ridden by a Calcan.

'Beeeep' blasted behind. She tucked in her bottom and just missed being goosed by a truck fender.

Looking over her shoulder, she yelled, "You missed." But the words were lost in the ruckus.

Safe on the other side, she dusted herself off and made her way to a makeshift market bustling with Calcans trading their wares.

So, this is why the halls are deserted.

Whoever wasn't working inside was outside, using hand gestures and pointing fingers to buy knickknacks and food. She scanned the crowd for a familiar face, but neither the miners nor Jazz was anywhere in sight.

She strolled through the aisles, wandering through the

crowd, occasionally glancing at a vendor's wares. Nothing caught her eye. Besides, she came to make money, not spend it. She thought she had seen all there was to be seen and was ready to go back when a three-wheeled auto-rickshaw whisked by and turned off the road. A hand-painted sign on the back spelled TAXI in crooked letters.

A pat on her thigh pocket confirmed she had brought along her stash of Galactic notes. She followed the taxi to a stand of vehicles that looked like rolling cake wedges. They had open sides and tin roofs and came in flashy colors and designs. In front, the driver steered using handlebars, and passengers squeezed onto a narrow, padded bench behind. A vehicle's rubber horn stuck out from a nearby deserted cab. Its orange bulb protruded, begging to be pressed. Holding her hands behind her back, she looked away as she accidentally, on purpose, leaned against the horn. *Ahwoogah.* Her cheeks reddened. Ruddy, scaled faces stared as Luna innocently looked around.

She would have preferred to rent a speeder, or better yet, a motorcycle, like the ones featured in the game Biker Warrior, but would settle for a ride in one of the wheeled cake slices. She strolled toward a group of Calcan drivers congregated in a circle. "Taxi?"

Her request fell on deaf ears. Undeterred, she tapped the closest Calcan on the shoulder. Scales covered the back of his neck and ran down the side of his arm. "Excuse me, how much for a ride?"

Without turning, he held up ten fingers.

At least he understands me. "Are you kidding?"

"Nine," he countered instantly.

She thought about counteroffering two when out of the corner of her eye, she noticed Ziggy sitting in the rear of one, waving his hand. He urged her closer.

"Come on, plenty of room," he shouted, pointing to the space next to him.

"Thank you, maybe next time," she said to the Calcan's backside, happily greeting Ziggy's familiar face.

"Well, now, if it isn't the little miracle worker, Ms. Rip Van Winkle, wide awake," Ziggy said with a bright smile. "Had enough of this place? Looking for a ride in a tuk-tuk?"

"Hi, Ziggy. Sure. Tuk-tuk, huh? Where are you headed?"

"The only place to go, town, village, whatever you want to call it. Any place that serves cold beer." He scooched over. "Did you find my pipe?"

"Certainly. Even in the dark, it's kinda hard to miss." She grabbed hold of a rail. "It's my only orange-scented memento," she said, stooping and swinging inside.

Chuckling, Ziggy tapped the driver on the shoulder.

As the tuk-tuk surged, her pant leg rose, and before she could settle and lower her shorts, she was slammed into the back of the seat. "Whoa," she said, covering her knee.

"Not an air-cushioned hovercraft, that's for sure," Ziggy said, barely audible.

For all the rattling going on, she might as well have been sitting on a blender, listening to a mufflerless, gas-powered lawn mower. "How are the guys?"

Over the racket, he covered his ears. "Enjoy the ride," he mouthed.

The driver abruptly made a U-turn. Her body twisted with the force of a ballerina's belly button during a pirouette. One of the rear tires rose until the driver's weight shifted, and the third wheel came down in a spinning plop. With no doors or seat belts to keep them inside, there was nothing to do but hold on.

The tuk-tuk merged into the road, weaving among potholes. Luna imagined herself behind the handlebars. How much different could it be from riding a speeder? She flicked a fingernail above her head. *Tink. Tin roof?*

She had read about combustion engines and could not wait to look under the hood. *There has to be an engine in this somewhere.* She bent over to listen. Judging by the sound, the driver was sitting on it.

Ziggy's forefinger flew under her nose, directing her gaze to the animals grazing in open pastures. Another revelation, since the only free-roaming animals Luna had seen were during a trip to the Xerxes Grand Canyon Corporate Park. Yards away was a herd of the same animal encountered in the transport. In daylight, she could see they came in shades of gray and blue. For as big as they were, she admired their agility as they rambled across grassy fields. Their thick legs moved in a gait that was difficult to describe. Too slow for a gallop, too smooth for a trot, and too fast for a walk. Luna settled on "sauntered" as a reasonable description of their movement.

A nudge drew her attention to Ziggy's side of the cab, and his thumb pointed up. She leaned over and craned her neck. In the sky, in synch with one another, hundreds of plum-colored birds flew in ever-changing directions. Her jaw dropped. *Chaos Theory in nature.* This is what Heisenberg might have been looking at when he came up with his principle.

"Wow!" Her response was not exaggerated from someone whose planet had decimated most of their wild bird populations.

Ziggy changed places with her, and the tuk-tuk wobbled as if they were in a canoe. She gaped, using her finger to trace the birds' whirling, irregularly regular flight patterns. When they flew out of sight, she mouthed "Thank you" to Ziggy.

The road improved, tuk-tuks zipped by, and farmhouses appeared closer and closer together. Made of lumber, adobe, and brick, their buildings looked nothing like the townhouses and prefabricated block structures back home. Like their tuk-tuks, Calcans painted their houses in a variety of colors. Ruby-colored ceramic tiles arranged in fish scale and herringbone designs covered their roofs, picture windows filled their walls, and ornate gardens accented their yards.

The driver slowed to honk his horn or wave at people walking along the sidewalk. Storefronts appeared with shoppers. The Calcans wore smiling faces right along with their complexions and scales. Sensing this was as good a place as any, Luna nudged Ziggy and tapped the driver on the shoulder. "How much do I owe you?"

The driver shrugged.

Ziggy raised his hands. "My treat," he said, shaking off the offer. "Sure you don't want to come with?"

"Thanks, but no thanks. Maybe, next time."

"Okay," Ziggy said. "I'll keep an eye out for you on my way back. If you like, I can meet you here in an hour or so."

"I'll manage. There are plenty of tuk-tuks around. Worst-case scenario, I'll make my way back." Luna waved off the tuk-tuk and continued walking in the same direction. *There's no sense going back the same way I came.* A breeze filled with fruity, chili, and spicy smells enticed her forward. Who needs arrows with yummy smells pointing the way? She got her stride going and, having no place to be, enjoyed the walk for the sake of walking.

A Calcan man came toward her and tipped his wide-brimmed hat. A mother nodded in synch with hers while her two children gawked. Luna hoped she would come across the mysterious man from the transport. If she kept walking, he might even pass her. Maybe ask someone? But how to approach a Calcan? "Excuse me," she could say, putting her hand above her head. "Well, he's about this tall." Not getting a response, she imagined she might scrunch her face and press her chin. "And he's old. Older than me. And he's got a beard." Perhaps point at her arm, "Like my skin. Not like yours." Or maybe forget *charades* and keep walking.

She quickened her pace at the sounds of music and laughter. Crossing the street, side-by-side stands encroached on the sidewalk and ended at what appeared to be a large entrance. Aromas wafting from inside invited. Although the flux of Calcans coming and going made it even more tempting, the passageway resembled no mall she had ever been in, and she decided to continue.

On the other side of the entrance, she came upon a stand featuring pipes and hookahs that reminded her of bong-smoking Jeff. The vendor must have noticed and held out a version of what she was used to seeing back home. "No thanks, I've already got one." She shook off the offer with a wave. The universal 'not interested' message was received, for he shrugged and waved back.

Intending to circle around the block, Luna walked over one street. She noticed two boys, Hunter's age, squatting over what appeared to be a spotted kitten. She peeked over the boys' shoulders. The closer boy wiggled his finger, fencing with a hand-sized kitten with the most ornate ears she had ever seen. *Trulee would love it here.* The kitten lay on its side, with its extended paw, playing like any young cat back home. They played finger tag while the boy's younger friend watched. The ball of fur reached out and scratched the boy's finger. Touché, she thought, bracing for what revenge the boy might take.

Nicoleta Dabija

Calcan Kitten

Instead, he shook his finger and inspected the cut. The kitten froze, then tilted its head as if to wonder why the game had stopped. Instead of retaliating, the boy sucked his finger, scanned the ground for a long piece of straw, and used it as an extended sword to continue to play. The kitten readily took up the challenge.

What's with these animals' affinity for fingers? Standing up, she caught sight of a wiry-coated dog trotting around a distant corner and followed. Remembering the same crescent pattern on a dog's behind from the transport, the chase was on. If the dog belonged to the old man, she hoped he'd lead her to him. By the time she reached the corner, the dog had disappeared.

A door-to-door search came up with blank Calcan faces. "Sorry," Luna said, in too much of a hurry to mime a request for the whereabouts of a particular dog. She was ready to give up and turn back when out of the corner of her eye, he appeared out of nowhere, sitting by the curb.

I've been in the suns too long.

A tuk-tuk approached. She cringed as it turned the corner. The dog waited until the vehicle passed, looked both ways, and crossed.

By the time Luna got across the street, the dog had cut into a gangway and vanished. Determined not to lose him again, she ran up the ramp to a courtyard where various animals lounged. She stopped at the sound of an angry voice.

"*Holera, psha koshch. Tso za kavawek....*" the grizzled man, hunkered over a motorcycle, snarled.

She did not know what the words meant, nor did she care so long as the words were not directed at her. What mattered was the bike was an honest-to-goodness, combustion engine-powered, two-wheeled motorcycle, just like the bikes featured in Biker Warrior. And this one had an attached sidecar.

Luna was so much a fan of the bikes of the era that she had convinced her Speeder Club friends to go on a field trip to a museum to see the real thing. Strolling through the aisles of glass-enclosed vehicles, the club had arrived in biker heaven, spending most of their time ogling motorcycles. Of all the bikes on display, the treaded rubber tires, spoke-rimmed wheels, and ruby-red color scheme made the Triumph Trophy her dream bike. And here she was, steps away from touching one.

The man got on the bike and gave the starter pedal a downward kick. The engine choked. His terrier grip on the throttle held tight. She stepped closer. The engine cleared its throat and evened up. Standing close enough to reach and touch it, the engine ran smoothly. The old man got off and scratched his head as the engine hummed.

"*Dobra dzievchynka,*" he said, patting the tank like a proud parent whose child had taken its first steps. The engine rejoiced as it ran.

From out of nowhere, she felt a poke at her bottom. She swatted whatever had bumped her butt. "Hey! Get out of there." She turned and saw nothing but a wagging tail.

"Is that an invisible dog?"

"Reuben is not invisible," he said gruffly. "Can't you see his tail?"

"Where's the rest?"

"Reuben is a canideleon."

"A what?"

The old man let out a long sigh. "A canine-chameleon, canideleon. Not invisible. Camouflaged."

"And his tail?"

"Dogs do not hide their feelings. Tails tell-all," he said with a frown.

Luna gasped. She could not help but point her finger. "It's you. You're the man from the transport, the bong improviser."

The old man nodded absently as he returned his attention to the bike.

Taken aback by the man's indifference, Luna took the nudging and wagging tail as signs of wanting to be petted. Despite being camouflaged, she figured out where the rest of him should be and scratched the place between his hips and the base of his tail. That sweet spot where fleas like to hang out and where dogs can't reach for themselves. *Did Calcus have bugs?*

With his back to her, Luna tried to come up with something savvy to say. 'Whatcha doing' did not seem the way to break the ice. The canideleon wiggled his heinie. "Reuben—is that your name? What a good boy." With every scratch, his hips, belly, chest, neck, and head gradually appeared.

She tapped the man on the shoulder. "Hello, I'm Luna. Remember me? You used my arm to save that–that beast," she said, putting out her hand.

He turned his head, looking none too pleased. "Beast?"

His eyebrows twitched like grasshopper antennae.

"You know, you know what I mean."

"No, I do not know what you mean," he said, leaning over the bike.

"The creature," she said, putting down her hand.

"Taurden, so?"

"That's what you call them?" *Did he refuse my hand because his were dirty?* Without a response, she went on. "I just started work-study at Xerxes. Back home, I worked in a stable. I know my way around animals. After graduating from high school, I was supposed to start pre-vet. That is until my scholarship got canceled."

The old man's focus on the bike did not waver. He shook his head and nodded to himself. Judging by the smooth sound of the engine, there was nothing to fix. Still, he crouched over the bike as if tending to a sick child. His face softened. He rubbed his chin.

"That was amazing what you did on the transport. Maybe I could tag along? Help out during my free time?" she asked hopefully. "Save some more taurdens?"

"Pick up that mallet...."

Luna found the hard rubber-headed hammer lying on the ground and offered it up.

"... and knock any such notion out of your head."

Crestfallen, Luna put down the mallet. Reuben's ears and tail drooped. She turned around and walked away. With each step down the gangway, the engine hesitated, then coughed, choked, and threatened to quit.

"Come back," he said.

Luna did an about-face, and with each step closer, the engine improved.

The old man pulled off a thin grimy layer of rub-on gloves to reveal clean hands and scratched behind his head. For the first time, he looked her straight in the face and asked, "What animals?"

"What do you mean?"

His right eyebrow raised. "Where you worked."

"Horses. There was a barn cat."

The motorcycle purred. From the exhaust, a light gray mist billowed. Without extending his hand, he said, "My name is Doctor Kairon—" He stopped mid-sentence as if catching himself. "People around here call me Kai. There is a patient that needs attention. You can tag along, that is if Reuben doesn't mind."

Reuben barked as if he understood. He ran in a circle, bouncing like a bunny, an energetic, twirling dervish, wagging his tail. Before anyone dared change their mind, he leaped into the sidecar.

Luna looked at the suns' overhead position and guessed the time to be about noon. *Why not?* Reuben fidgeted, hoarding most of the cramped seat. She pushed, shoved, and scooched him over enough to squeeze in. In the cramped compartment, the canid panted excitedly, seeming to relish the company.

Kai handed over a pair of tinted goggles. She questioned their small size as she raised them over her head. "Not for you. They're for him," he said, putting on a weather-beaten aviator's cap. "There might be another pair inside below." Reuben raised his chin, accepting the goggles like a knight suited in armor by a squire. Once the straps were tucked behind his ears, he relaxed.

Below where inside? She leaned over but could not reach down far enough. Reuben got an elbow. "Scoot over." The canid refused to yield. Using her foot as a hoe, she rummaged underneath and came up with a ratted pair of tinted goggles. "These?" she asked, blowing off dust and dog hair before placing them over her eyes. "No helmet?"

"No."

She was about to ask where they were going but found talking almost as difficult as riding in a tuk-tuk. Her butt buried deeper into the seat, and her arm reached around Reuben. Combing her fingers through his coat, she realized it had been too long since she felt the warmth of a shaggy coat. The view from the sidecar's vantage point provided another bonus. While a speeder's ride was smoother, how often does someone get to ride in an honest-to-goodness motorcycle sidecar with their arm around a canideleon? Her friends wouldn't believe it. If she wasn't right here, right now, she wasn't sure she would either.

Three pairs of goggles, a billowing speckled-gray beard, a broad smile, and a cold, wet nose cruised the countryside.

* * *

VALDEEZ'S OFFICE WAS the image of perfection. Something he considered of himself and demanded from others. He had it all: polished crystal chandeliers hung from the ceiling, the newest devices technology offered, and hand-woven oriental rugs on the floor. Awards, certificates of merit, and pictures of him shaking hands with celebrities and politicians adorned the walls. As someone known to accomplish the impossible, he made sure Xerxes never forgot it.

His polished shoes squeaked on the hardwood floors as he paced behind his oblong mahogany desk. His shirt's iridium buttons reflected the overhead lighting. Twirling the spiked metal sphere in his hand, his lip curled at the knock on the side door. "Come in."

The chief of Xerxes security entered and stood at attention. "I came as asked, Sir," he said.

"Dhiraj, you know the success of this mission depends on acquiring labor," Valdeez asked, glaring at the man. "On schedule."

"Yes, Sir," Dhiraj said. His eye twitched.

"You have approached the Calcans. No one, not one of them, will work the mines?"

Dhiraj cleared his throat. "The locals have been most obstinate, Sir." Dhiraj's shoulders sagged as sweat dripped from his temples. Sometimes the orders given were most unreasonable, he thought. How was he supposed to know how to communicate with alien humanoids? He had done as asked. No one could have done better.

"The bull was not supposed to arrive alive. How do you account for that?" Valdeez asked, lobbing the sphere in his hand.

"I only did as you directed, Sir. My best Calcan was on it. I engineered the piece myself. No one will suspect."

"I am well aware of what you did and did not." Valdeez put down the sphere and picked up a plastic cube from his desk. He peeked at a winged insect inside and tapped the cube. The bug rubbed its ribbed wings together, producing an audible 'click.' "Fascinating creature, Dhiraj, *Calcus cantankerous*. Small, and yet…." Not waiting for an answer, he said, "Floor. See what happens to those who disappoint me." A panel creaked, then separated the floor like an earthquake, dividing the space between them. "You might want to take a step back."

At their feet, the Plexiglas ceiling of an exposed room below allowed them to look down and see inside. The older, burgundy-haired Calcan from the transport lay spread-eagled, bound to the floor. He raised his chin and struggled against arm and leg restraints. His rantings muffled in the soundproofed room.

"Now let's see what your best has to offer." Valdeez opened the lid of a snuffbox and placed a pinch of the white powder at the base of his thumb. He sniffed, squeezed his nose, and closed his eyes. "Access."

A ceiling vent slid open. The captive's obscenities boomed from within.

"Now, now. You are hurting my ears," Valdeez said with a wicked smile. He tossed the cube in his hand, oblivious to the rage below. "This insect has an affinity for calcium, which makes mining this planet so profitable. Pity they do not thrive elsewhere. I would export them all over the galaxy."

Dhiraj's gaze transfixed on the man below. "Whatever you say, Sir," he said out of the corner of his mouth.

Valdeez's smile broadened. "Funny thing, they're attracted to vibration… and movement."

The Calcan froze in muted defiance. His eyes bulged, nostrils flared, and yet, his chin remained high.

Valdeez smirked at the Calcan's display and Dhiraj's unease. "For the longest time, we could not figure out why miners kept disappearing. We would find remnants of clothing and not much else. I do not mind saying it got to be a little embarrassing. So as not to scare off our employees, I informed corporate that a rogue band of scalers was kidnapping our men." Valdeez's nose twitched. The Calcan glared. "Your kind got the blame and helped fortify our security. For that, I am grateful. Greater presence, more investment. There is no way Xerxes can pull out now."

Dhiraj stepped away. His face turned pale.

Except for the Calcan's chest barely rising and falling, the native would have appeared as a petrified mass of flesh and bone.

"Hatch," Valdeez said, taking another pinch of snuff.

Above the Calcan, a hatch door opened.

"I tried to recruit your kind. Even offered generous wages. But no, you refused me." Valdeez pointed. "Look, Dhiraj. See what your best has to offer."

Dark brown insects crawled from the hatch.

The captive held his breath. His face turned a shade of purple. His cheeks, to the point of bursting, gradually released air. Bugs circled. His pulse raced. Lub dub, lub dub, lub dub.

"All except you. And then, you have the nerve to threaten me?" Valdeez stared, shaking his head, and flicked his wrist over the vent. Snuff drifted through the access hole like tiny snowflakes.

Dhiraj squeezed his eyes shut.

White particles wafted over the captive, covering his face. Ever so slowly, his chest raised, followed by 'achoo.'

Valdeez observed his security chief and said, "Dhiraj, if you want to continue as my head of security, you will turn your head and watch. If you are unable, leave now and keep going. I can always find someone who will."

Bugs scurried. 'Cicadic clicks' filled the room.

"Close access." The port door closed gradually, taking the screams along with it. "Dhiraj, how do you make people change their minds?"

"I don't know, Sir," he said, wincing at the carnage below.

"You give them zero other choices." Blood splattered the ceiling and walls.

"Is that all, Sir?" Dhiraj asked, shifting his weight.

"For now," Valdeez spoke as if he already knew the answer. "The new girl has decided to stay?"

"Yes, Sir."

"I do not intend to lose another."

Chapter 8

"The first condition of understanding a foreign country is to smell it."

—Rudyard Kipling

THE BIKE EASED into a soft curve and headed up a corral-fenced lane. Reuben trembled with excitement as his whimper grew into a whine. Nothing Luna could have imagined prepared her for what stood at the end of the driveway. Wide-eyed, her brows raised in awe, she felt like a little kid again, visiting the dead animal zoo part of the Museum of Natural History, pointing her finger at the platypus exhibit, and wondering what it was.

"Is that a duck's bill on a beaver?" she had asked.

Now, not fifty feet away and without a glass pane between them, her jaw dropped as it had back then. The animal they were there to see looked like a growth hormone-fed chicken on stilts.

As the bike slowed, Reuben's animated frenzy heightened. His nails clawed at anything within reach. His whining hit an all-time, ear-piercing screech. Luna muttered a slew of profanities as she pushed and shoved back to no effect. The bike mercifully squeaked to a stop.

"All right already," she said to the hyper-canid. With a heave, she half-hoisted, half-tossed him out.

Reuben hit the ground, running.

Kai dismounted the bike and rearranged his coat.

"I've never seen one of these before," Luna said, not doing a very good job of holding back her amazement. "It looks like…"

"A girastrich," Kai said, raising a brow as if to ask if she was coming, and walked away without waiting for a reply.

Alone in the sidecar, Luna found getting out harder than getting in. Lifting herself and raising a leg over, she watched Reuben head for a fence, sniff, leave a Post-It, and move on to the next one. *That's what all the fuss was about?* She rubbed her arms and legs, where Reuben had left scratch marks behind. *Next time, I'll wear long sleeves and pants.* "And make sure your nails are cut," she told the oblivious canid.

The patient had long pointy ears and button mushroom-shaped horns sprouting from the top of its head. It sported a collar around its long neck. The girastrich would have looked comical if it wasn't for a pointy beak, broad enough to chip ice, and beady eyes that followed her every step.

The Calcan, standing beside the animal, held the lead out at arm's length in one hand and, with his other, covered his nose in the crook of his elbow. One whiff and Luna understood why. The smell of rotten rag permeated the air. Her face soured like a shriveled prune. She had encountered some funky smells: stale urine at the barn, rotting garbage, and other general nastiness. But this took rank to a new height. Fly perfume. The dregs of a backed-up butcher's sewer could not have reeked any worse. No glass barrier. You asked for this, she reminded herself. *Good thing Xena doesn't serve big breakfasts.*

The bird's feathers were splotched in rectangular patterns varying in color from corn to cocoa. Its spindly, ruby-colored legs ended in two gnarly claws. Its knobby, yellow feet resembled something belonging to an oversize raptor. She did a double take. Half hidden, under the bird's wing, stood a young Calcan girl clutching the animal's leg.

Kai took the animal's presence in stride and spoke easily while the Calcan replied under the shroud of his arm. "The owner's name is Aapo," Kai said, translating over his shoulder. "His daughter, Teesa, and her pet, Hugo."

"Hi," Luna said, taking a half step closer. Aapo seemed locked in conversation with Kai, while, upon hearing her name, Teesa hid deeper under the bird's wing. *She's just shy*, Luna thought, resisting the urge to step away.

With a wave of his hand, Kai invited her closer. Showing no sign of sympathy for her olfactory discomfort, his facial expression remained neutral. "Hugo has been limping for the last two sauls and recently stopped eating," he said, barely loud enough to be heard.

Aapo cringed, holding the lead by the far end of its handle.

Luna stooped to the little girl's level and waved. When Teesa did not respond, Luna asked, "What's a girastritch?"

Kai put his hands in his coat pockets and looked at Hugo with the same intensity he had focused on the taurden back on the transport. "While Hugo and Reuben share mammalian characteristics, Hugo shows predominantly the avian, ostrich, rather than giraffe."

"Girastrich. Oh, I get it."

While Kai and Teesa appeared unfazed by the smell, Luna gulped, trying not to make it obvious that she was struggling to keep her cookies 'n''n cream breakfast from making a U-turn. "Where's that smell coming from?"

If it was possible for a girastrich to give someone the stink eye, that's what Hugo did.

"Did you see any lameness at the stable where you

worked?" Kai asked without answering her question.

"Sure, show-jumping horses go lame all the time."

"And how are they diagnosed?"

"With this type of problem, the vet would refer to an orthopedist who would send a technician to scan the leg. The specialist reviews the results, and if necessary, the meds are delivered, or someone comes back to treat."

Kai's eyebrows raised as he looked around the yard. "See any scanning equipment lying around? So, what now?"

"I dunno." *What did he mean, 'What now?'* She expected he wanted more of an answer, but his poker face gave no clue. *Was this a test? Was he angry, bored, or like this all the time?* "So, you mean, what are you going to do right now?" Luna asked, frowning.

He closed his eyes as if dredging for patience and exhaled slowly. "What have you noticed?" And then spoke to Aapo in what sounded like guttural Calcan slurs and sweeps.

Teesa stepped aside but kept a vigil on her pet.

Aapo looked relieved not to stand in place and led Hugo in a circle around them.

"Other than seeing a girastrich for the first time?" *Perhaps a shot of humor might help.* "Hmm, well, there's certainly a foul odor." Her eyebrows raised expectantly. When he did not react, she flapped her arms. "Fowl odor. Get it?"

Kai's expression matched Hugo's. He motioned Aapo to go ahead, and the Calcan trotted Hugo down the driveway.

Teesa's scrutiny did not waver.

"Close your eyes and tell me what you hear," Kai said.

No sense of humor. With her eyes closed, everything sounded the same. Aapo's footsteps mixed with Hugo's. *What did he expect her to say?* She scrunched her face to hear better. *Phoo*: *Phioo* "Um..." With each step, the differences became clearer. "Wait..."

Aapo, Teesa, and Hugo

"So?"

A rocking gait, like a pirate's peg leg. "They're different. No, wait. I'm hearing *flop-fliff*, like a scuba diver wearing different-sized fins."

"And what does that mean?"

Luna shrugged. "I dunno. Uh… one foot hits the ground harder than the other?"

"Okay, open your eyes." With a wave of his hand, Aapo jogged back. "If the healthy foot contacts the ground harder, which is the affected limb?"

Hugo's feet jumbled into a hodgepodge of contorted claws. He moved too fast to make out what was what. His wobbly legs looked like they belonged to an improperly assembled Erector Set more than anything found alive. His feet scrambled, his body leaned one way, and his neck curved the other.

Her chin raised in synch with each *fliff* and dropped with each *flop*. "The right one. No, wait. On the right side, but that's his left leg."

His gaze did not waver. "Asking or telling?"

"Telling," she said, squinting to make sure she was not mistaken. "Am I right?"

Aapo came to a stop alongside, heaving through his hand-covered nose.

A waft of funk slapped the air.

"Which part of the limb?" There was a glint in his eye as he stepped aside and said, "You will have to get closer."

Luna breathed through her mouth, hoping that teeth could filter odor. *If Teesa can stand it, so can I.* With eyes half closed, she dared herself not to look away and reached with her arms out, aiming for a thigh.

Hugo's beak swooped.

She ducked. A near miss.

"Uh-uh." Kai shook his head. "Outstretched grabby paws are no way to approach a patient. Dangerous, too." With a genteel wave, he stepped forward as if to say, "Allow me." His posture projected calm, and his eyes brightened. "Introduce yourself. Smile." With another 'right this way' wave, he said, "Try again."

Luna's eyes widened, and between stretched lips, her teeth gleamed.

"No. No, not like that. He will think you're a predator. Approach him the same way a beau would court a lady. Have you never been asked out?"

Luna nodded quickly and chuckled. The first time Arnie asked her on a date, he was so nervous that she did not know what was happening. Words fumbled from his mouth. It was so unlike him. At first, she thought he was ill or upset. He promptly turned red, did an about-face, and mumbled to himself as if repeating from a memorized script.

How hard could it be? She had approached new horses all the time, learned what not to do, and then remembered Bucephalus. *Hay bales are not going to save me this time.* She shrugged, stood straight, and took a deep breath. This time, she smiled through closed lips. Holding her hand at chest height and well out of pecking range, she flashed a palm in a jittery wave. "Hello Hugo, my name is Luna. How are you?"

Aapo peered over his elbow with a frown and a puzzled look.

Kai coughed twice and swiped his face as if wiping away tears, looking like he was doing everything to keep from bursting out laughing. He shook his head. "I pity the poor soul that comes to court you. Try again."

Aapo sighed.

Luna stepped closer. Hugo jerked his head. His beak plotted her course. Bit by bit, she reached for his smooth feathered body. Hugo flinched. She gradually moved beside him. Only then did her hand ease down his thigh. The oversized drumstick felt like a caveman's club.

"Now that you have made contact close your eyes and calm your breathing. When you do, your sense of touch will become amplified."

Luna did as asked and gently squeezed her fingers down the taut, sinewy tendons, muscles, and bone.

"As will your sense of smell."

Aapo juggled the lead while burying his face into his raised shoulder.

Luna's hands worked their way down toward the knobby foot. "Over here, below the uh… what is this, an ankle?"

"Tarsometatarsus, but close enough."

"Yes, I'm feeling tension and heat."

"Good. We can switch places," Kai said and spoke to Aapo, who did not look happy as he grabbed Hugo by the collar. Kai removed a tube from his coat pocket and squeezed a clear gel into his palms, wiping it over his fingers. He shook his hands, and a flexible clear film dried into instant gloves.

Kai nudged the bird's body with his arm, and Hugo shifted his weight onto the opposite leg. Kai tucked his shoulder under the raised lame leg and held the underside of the foot between his knees like a farrier shoeing a horse. The underside of Hugo's two toes looked surprisingly smooth, like a dog's pads, with the main toe offset by a smaller version of itself. Kai spread the toes, revealing a bubble of green pus.

Now unfazed by the smell, she leaned forward for a better view.

"A pebble has lodged into the primary toe to produce an abscess," Kai said, pulling a scalpel from another pocket.

Aapo's face turned a similar shade of green.

With a deft swipe of the scalpel, the pebble flicked, and pus exploded.

Hugo flinched.

Luna withdrew, but not in time to avoid a dollop of aquamarine-colored toothpaste-like pus from plopping onto her shoe. She gave her foot a flick, but the blob refused to budge.

Nasty.

"That was a good one. Festering for a while," Kai said, pulling a white tablet from another pocket. He placed the pill in the open palm of his hand as if serving it on a tray. "Well?"

Scraping the toe did nothing more than smear green ooze over the rest of her shoe.

I smell like Hugo.

Luna flicked her shoe again with the same effect and took the fit-for-a-horse-sized tablet. She offered the pill the same way Kai had presented it to her. Hugo had other ideas. Out of the corner of his eye, he sneered at her like he could not be bothered. When offering the tablet did not work, she tried to pop it into his mouth. It was a game of "catch me if you can," and Hugo's beak was winning. He parried her tablet thrusts with pecks of his own.

She tried once too often and shook her finger. Another cut.

"Birds do not have a refined sense of taste. So, what is the problem?"

"It won't take the pill?"

"The solution lies in asking the right question."

"Um, I can't get the pill in?"

"The question is, how to open the beak? Once you do that, the rest falls in place." Kai put his hands around Hugo's neck. "Get ready, aim…" Hugo gagged, and his beak opened. Luna tossed the pill for the score. Hugo swallowed.

Aapo leaned over and spoke to Kai.

"What did he say?"

"Nice shot." Kai peeled off his gloves, tied the ends into a knot, and put them in yet another one of his pockets. "Wait here," he said, turning around to join Aapo in leading the girastrich to the barn. Teesa skipped merrily behind, humming to herself.

Hugo's gait evened out. Luna sniffed while dragging her toe against the ground. It covered her shoes with dust, but the smell remained the same.

In minutes, Kai returned with a large sack, which he placed inside the sidecar. "Walk with me," he said. Reuben appeared to have completed his tasks and sniffed her shoe before deciding to tag along. The trio strolled around a corral filled with girastriches. Kai suddenly stopped and faced her. "Why are you here?"

"I like animals."

"Then go to a zoo."

"I have. This is different." While Luna had never been personally acquainted with a veterinarian, the ones she had met were helpful and outgoing. *Was he always this grumpy?* Unsure what to make of him, she lowered the leg of her shorts and quickened her pace to catch up.

The only change in his sullen face was a slight nod to acknowledge her reply. They continued their stroll.

"I've been meaning to ask. Back there with Hugo, how weren't you and Teesa affected? Couldn't you smell it?"

"If anything, taste and smell are heightened in Calcans. Teesa's concern for her pet outweighed any discomfort she may have felt. Which is more important? The need to change an infant's diaper or the person's reaction to doing it?"

Luna pondered this. *What happened to the smell while she was examining Hugo's leg? It was there; it just took a backseat. What the heck? This is as good a time as any.* "I have a problem."

"Most people do," He walked purposefully on. "How you manage your problems is the same as how you'll deal with that pus on your shoe."

"Which is?" Luna asked, fighting the urge to rub her knee.

"Leave your troubles behind. Forget, ignore, or let it fade away."

Luna cast her eyes at her shoe. "None of those will work. This is not the kind of problem that washes away." *What is he saying that I am not getting?* "Have you any other suggestions?"

"Put perfume on it. Mask the odor. Just as some people use alcohol or drugs to cope with their issues."

"Still won't make it go away."

Having circled around the corral, Kai leaned over the fence and watched the girastriches. She stepped to his opposite side, where her traumatized knee faced away. The birds mulled about, interacting with one another, and pecked in the feed trough. The animals seemed at ease. She glanced at Kai. Did he know something he wasn't telling? He could have been mulling over the mysteries of the universe for all his blank expression showed.

"Time to go," he said, breaking the silence and headed for the sidecar. Reuben wagged his tail.

"I'm going to smell all the way back to my pod," she said, shaking her shoe.

Kai picked up the sack from the sidecar. "Deal with the problem at hand," Kai said, opening the bag. "In the future, please stay clear of abscesses." He removed a pair of well-worn rubber boots. "At least the avoidable ones, and try these on for size."

"Thank you," Luna said, taken by surprise. Back home,

she had work boots for the barn, but they were too heavy and bulky to bring along. Besides, there was no need. Data entry could be done barefooted. She turned away to avoid letting him see her uncovered knee while she undid the laces of her tainted shoe and tried on a boot. Her foot slipped in too easily at first, but once she had the other one on and walked around, she gave a thumbs up.

"Hungry?"

"I'm starving." Luna tied her shoelaces to the back of the sidecar, hoping to keep her shoes downwind.

"Good. Be careful with the bag. It's got our lunch." Kai kick-started the bike, and the engine turned over and ran with no second kick. His brows jumped in amazement. "*Roksha kohana, swodka, najdrovsha,*" he said.

Luna's arms engulfed the bag. "Excuse me, what did you say?"

"The motorcycle's name is Rocinante. In Polish, that's *Roksha* for short. She is the best bike I have ever owned."

"I know that one. That's the name of Don Quixote's horse, right?"

He put on his aviator cap, tilted his head, and out of the corner of his mouth, said, "Asking or telling?" He gunned the engine without waiting for a reply, and they drove down the farm driveway, waving over their shoulders. Gray-colored exhaust puffed, and Reuben's ears flapped in the breeze.

From over her shoulder, Luna watched Aapo wave back; Teesa hugged her pet's neck while Hugo's head gave a fair impression of a woodpecker bobbing in and out of a feed bucket.

*   *   *

NO MATTER HOW often Jasmine told herself that forcing locals to work by eliminating animals was preposterous, she could not block the image of Luna's arm stuck inside the tube. The directive had to be true, or was it someone's idea of a cruel joke? Perhaps it was an attempt to ruin her father. Why bother with natives if robots eventually take over? The whole thing made no sense.

Jasmine inserted a tab in the collar of one of her father's pressed shirts while playing a game of chess in her head. She arranged it neatly inside a drawer and said, "Queen to G5."

"Bishop to B4," the Xerxes AI, Xena, responded. "Check."

Jasmine glanced at the ceiling. Where did the bishop come from? "Visualize b-board."

The game appeared virtually before her. "Is something the matter?" Xena asked in a concerned voice.

Jasmine covered her extended yawn. Reflexively, she said, "Excuse me." She had spent the night on her computer, monitoring the outpost's forums while searching for anything about labor acquisitions. No one on site had mentioned a directive, which was a good thing, but downed communications limited her search.

"Go back three moves," Jasmine said, finding it hard to believe she was about to lose another game and stuttering to an AI.

The game pieces returned to their previous positions.

She wiped the sleepiness from her face. *If I can't concentrate on a game, what else am I missing?* "Any forecasted MiPS activity?" Jasmine asked, crossing her fingers. *Luna is going to report the directive as soon as the shift happens. Could Xena block her from reporting it? Perhaps, but eventually, this is going to get out.*

"Nothing since yesterday's forty-seven tic glitch." Xena

cleared her throat. "Out of the last twelve games, you lost the last one and will lose this one in two moves. Would you like to play on or do something else?"

If the Federation finds out and Papa is involved, this could ruin him. "Good game. I resign. Close program."

"Are you certain there is nothing else I can do?" Xena asked. "A late breakfast or an early lunch, perhaps? Is there something you would like to talk about?"

Mum isn't here, and I can't complete a simple sentence in front of my own father. "No, no, thank you." She swiped a finger over a clean dresser top. *Even if I could comm out, all my friends ever want to do is talk about shopping, gossip, and boyfriends.*

Would Papa have preferred a son? She slammed a dresser drawer. *He hates me. What can I do? Therapy hasn't helped. The stutter keeps getting worse. Thank goodness, computer games and hacking do not require me to talk.*

Jasmine twisted her wrist bracelet on the way to the kitchen. *If I approach him with what we saw, can I keep Luna out of the conversation? I can imagine how it would go:*

"Papa, do you know anything about a plan to eliminate animals?"

"Where have you been?" he would say. "How did you come by this information? Who else knows?" Maybe send him an anonymous text? She bit her tongue. There was no way to keep Luna out of it.

While her father's favorite sushi pieces rehydrated, she hid her bracelet beneath the pickled ginger he never ate. *A girl needs her privacy. Am I going to go through with it?* While the fish regained its texture and shape, Jasmine changed her pajamas into something more befitting a visit with her father.

She stuck to the hallway walls, limiting her presence to the occasional nod, and listened for any hint of the directive. So far, so good. She turned a corner and was set upon by the head of personnel's wife. The woman blocked her path and took her aside. Under the guise of a conversation, she proceeded to rant and complain in a succession of run-on sentences. Jasmine responded with the correct facial expressions and nodded and shrugged at the appropriate times. *Must she speak so loudly? Can't she hear herself talk? Just because I stutter does not mean that I am hard of hearing.* When the woman stopped for air, Jasmine made her excuses and continued on.

Reigning in a stampede of mixed emotions, she smiled as an approaching mother walked a toddler by the hand. At first, she thought Luna's decision to stay had been a blessing. Finally, there was someone with things in common to talk to. Jasmine had to admire Luna's adventurous, albeit crazy, spirit. *Come here by myself? No way. Not even to fulfill a dream. I could never leave Papa.* Mum would want it this way. However, since the MiPS rotation, Jasmine had to consider her newfound friend as a potential threat.

She slid through the first set of security doors and slipped into her father's reception area. The plush carpet provided muffled footsteps, which aided her stealthy entrance. An attractive woman with radiant, toffee-colored skin sat behind a wall of flashing comm links. Startled, her father's secretary looked up.

"What a pleasant surprise. Jasmine, you have been a stranger for far too long." Feigning a pout, she said, "Don't you like me anymore?"

"Hello, Imani. As always, you are the most charming person to be around. How can I stay away?" *I completed a sentence.* Papa must be lonely without Mum, Jasmine thought. "Is he in, as if I need to ask?"

"Jasmine, you always know what to say. Let me have a

look at you. You've grown into a beautiful young woman. We should have lunch sometime. Give me a moment. I'll check." Imani flicked a finger over her comm. Flashing waves of muted buttons protested. "Jasmine is here to see you." She nodded. "Yes, I'll tell her." Imani frowned. "Sorry, something urgent has come up."

It always does.

"Can't tell how long he's going to be. If you like, why don't you leave a message? I'll pass it along."

"No thanks, I thought I'd just drop by. Oh! Did anything unusual happen during this last MiPS?"

"You mean besides something more for employees to complain about? And give me a stabbing headache in the process," Imani said, rubbing her temple. "No, not really. 'When will communications return?' they ask. Believe me, I wish I knew."

"I don't envy you." *The directive may have been limited to the tutorial.*

"Forgive me. I'm venting." Imani glanced at the flashing buttons and shrugged. "I'm sorry more work-study girls could not have stayed. It would be appropriate for you to be around more young women your age." Imani grinned like a cat with a feather sticking out of its mouth. "And a few boys, perhaps?"

Jasmine handed over the bento lunch box, feeling herself blush and unable to hold back a modest giggle.

Chapter 9

"If you reject the food, ignore the customs, fear the religion, and avoid the people, you might better stay at home."

—James Michener

IT STARTED WITH a whimper. Despite having Luna's arm wrapped around him, at the first sight of town, Reuben became agitated. His ears drooped, his shoulders tightened, and his whining steadily rose to a high-pitched squeal. She flattened him against the opposite wall. Chameleons were supposed to be mellow, quiet creatures. Petting, while telling him what a good boy he was, did no good. Canideleons, it seemed, were something else.

Kai shrugged, keeping his focus on the road.

Ask the right question, she reminded herself. *How do I close his mouth?*

Her grip around Reuben's neck tightened. He fussed and clawed, turning in the seat like a deranged spinning top. With one outstretched arm holding the entrusted sack out of reach, she fended him off with her other elbow. Whatever was inside had better be worth it, she thought. What could have such a rough surface, be so delicate, and yet be desirable enough to eat?

Nicholeta Dabija

Reuben at His Best

Cruising through town, Calcans stopped to wave. With her hands occupied and her shoulder pressed against the fidgety canid, she barely replied with a nod. Shrilly yelps rang in her ears. By the time they arrived inside the courtyard, she could not hear in one ear, her arm throbbed, and neither of the two could get out soon enough.

Before the brakes squeaked the bike to a stop, Luna handed over the cumbersome sack and raised herself up. Reuben jumped out, caught his hind paw on the sidecar edge, and in midair, corrected his balance.

"What is your problem?" Luna asked Reuben.

As soon as his four paws touched the ground, Reuben shook himself off and looked up expectantly.

"What? What now?" she asked.

Reuben's ears perked. His head tilted, and the tip of his tongue stuck out to the edge of his nose.

"Now, you're calm. You want to do something else?" she

asked in disbelief. "You've got to be kidding." Bewildered, she looked at Kai. "He's kidding, right?"

"That is the way he is," Kai said with an exasperated sigh. He peeled back the ends of the sack to reveal what looked like an over-inflated, pine-green-colored football with a shiny surface.

"That's lunch?" Luna scratched behind her ear. "Looks like a giant avocado. We're having guacamole?"

"Nope." He blinked with a smile. "Hope you are hungry. Lunch will be ready soon."

"Starving. Is there anything I can do?"

"No, not yet. Make yourself comfortable. Feel free to look around." He cradled their lunch in his arms and disappeared into the adjacent building.

Luna jumped at the chance to check out the bike up close. Her hand traced over the smooth gas tank, unscrewed the cap, sniffed, and wrinkled her nose at the odd volatile smell. Her fingers caressed the engine's nooks and crannies. She stepped back. Metal, rubber, cable, springs, bolts, tubes, and chrome combined to create a symphony of mechanical engineering. Why didn't they make them like this anymore?

The hot engine header tinkled.

In the open-air courtyard, hidden in the nooks and crannies, pairs of eyes followed her every step. Gravity-defying lizards clung to the side of walls, basking in the suns. Birds, in fruity colors, perched on trees. Woolly rodents lounged in the corner shade, and a stubby snoot peered out from inside a tin can. While the animals did not come in pairs, the menagerie would have impressed even Noah.

Luna could not resist giggling at the crusty furball wad-dling toward her. It came two steps closer and then stepped back. It spent more effort wavering side to side than progress-ing forward.

She outstretched her hand. "Come on, it's okay. I won't hurt you," she cooed, nodding with a bright smile. Its flat nose ventured close enough to nuzzle her leg. She petted its coarse back, and it rolled over. A soft, fuzzy, brown potbelly begged to be scratched. She could not resist and raised her voice loud enough to reach Kai inside. "What's the brown pudgy animal's name?"

On the other side of the partition, Kai gathered the utensils to prepare the key ingredient. He chipped away at the thick shell using a chisel and mallet like a marble sculptor.

"His name is Falafel. He's a molug," Kai said, popping off the top, breaking open the cap, and peeling back the transparent membrane. "Plenty for all of us," he said to himself.

Falafel's eyes sank, and he would have fallen asleep had Luna not finished with a pat on his belly before she got up to explore the rest of the yard. Against the building wall, a black furry creature with a white stripe along its back stretched in a slot among the shelves of motorcycle manuals, tools, and parts. The animal gazed from its booth as if seated in a box at the opera. A bushy tail wrapped luxuriously around its neck. A diamond necklace and earrings were all that was missing to match its tipped-up pink nose and jutted sharp chin.

"Gotta ask. What's with the skunk with attitude?"

"Gardenia is a skurrel. Careful. She does not appreciate being disturbed. Distressed, she can make your shoe seem fragrant."

On a potted tree branch, a flashy parrot with a long, wide beak squawked and intently groomed itself.

"That would be 'Tunisia,' the paracan," Kai said without peeking from behind the wall.

"Does she talk?"

The bird preened its feathers until Luna came closer, and

then the bird flew off.

"Nothing I can repeat."

A screech brought Luna's attention to the pile of rubble at the far end of the courtyard. "That would be 'Cheekee,' the monkagoo," Kai said.

Luna enjoyed watching the scrap-tossing antics of the pointy-faced monkey intent on getting to the bottom of the pile. He pawed furiously at whatever got in his way.

"Cheekee throws a fit when Baloney pulls his tail."

Kai must have X-ray vision, Luna thought, bending low enough to see a tube-shaped, smooth-skinned creature with a smirk. "What's the other one?"

"No one has the faintest idea what Baloney is made of."

As Luna stepped closer, Cheekee screeched and scampered off. He seemed willing to put his revenge on hold while Baloney safely waited before caterpillar-crawling away.

She blinked and did a double take. Between the rubble, the pleated aluminum folds of a motorcycle's heat-dispersing fins stuck out. While a real bike would not shoot its cannons, eject torpedoes, or release mines, no simulator could compete with the real thing. Could more of it be inside the pile? Of all the virtual motorcycles in Biker Warrior's game garage, Luna had selected the *Honda CR 250 Elsinore* most often. This one looked kind of like it.

She imitated Cheekee, throwing aside rusted mufflers, bent wheel rims, and twisted pipes. More and more of the bike became uncovered as she unwrapped it from its rubble prison. Caked-on dirt, broken plastic, dents, and rust did not matter. The engine had the 250-cc size stamp, the off-road design, and the original silver color scheme. She tugged on the rat bike's front forks and, spoke by spoke, freed it from the heap.

"What's with the bike?" she asked, catching her breath.

"Hasn't worked in years. Meant to throw it away. Never got around to it." Kai separated the yolk and poured the egg white into a mixing bowl. On the windowsill, potted plants labeled DUMAS, CERVANTES, SHAKESPEARE, CHEKOV, and TWAIN soaked in the rays of two midday suns.

Luna bounced on the balls of her feet as she pushed the intact bike away. It lacked a side panel, the handlebars wobbled, and the rolling knobby tires squished on the smooth floor. She closed her eyes and, as if making a wish, asked. "Mind if I try out the bike?" Her request came out louder than intended.

"Go ahead, but there's nothing to try."

Throwing her leg over the bike, the suspension creaked, and the seat flattened. Standing with the bike straddled between her knees, she rocked it from side to side. Fuel sloshed inside the tank. "Still has fuel in it."

"Could be." Kai beat the albumen with an oversize whisk and combined it with the yolk. "By now, the piston has probably seized."

The handlebars had the same shape as the simulators and speeders she rode in the game but lacked a control panel. "Where's the start button?"

"No button, kick start." The aerated egg mixture grew with each whip of the whisk, transforming it into a creamy orange sponge. "Do you read?" Kai asked, looking at the labeled pots.

She scrolled through her memories of movies featured by the Speeder Club. From the movie, *On Any Sunday*, she remembered that bikes from that era were kick-started. With a bit of poking and prodding, she figured it had to be some-where on the right side. She found the pedal beside the engine, extended it, and applied pressure with the heel of her shoe.

"Ever since Mom's bedtime stories, I read for fun before going to sleep."

Her foot pressed the pedal in a slow, downward arc. The piston inside the cylinder resisted but begrudgingly relented, as if fighting required more effort than the cast metal could bear. At least the piston hasn't frozen, she thought. After multiple kicks, the engine refused to start.

"Reading anything now?"

"There's the required stuff for school. However, I'm always on the lookout for a good book." She heaved a sigh. "Right now, I'm reading from a real hardcover, *Don Quixote*. The feel of a book in my hands helps put me deeper into the story. It's like I'm there, back then, along for the ride. Do you know what I mean?"

"Yes. Enjoying the book?"

"My favorite part is where Don Quixote jousts with windmills. Even if he thinks of them as evil giants, he takes them on with his frail self and nag of a horse, which qualifies him as a knight fulfilling a quest. Whether you consider him a hero or crazy, his successes as brave or failures as stupid, you have to admire his courage."

Kai pulled off two heart-shaped leaves from the Cervantes plant and ground them in a mortar bowl with a pestle. He removed a spice jar labeled 'ROWLING' from a cabinet and mixed the two. He sniffed the herbs, thought a moment, and plucked a leaf from another plant on the sill. "Twain is good with everything," he said to himself.

The sole of her shoe slipped off the pedal. "Ow." Releasing a long exhale, Luna wondered if she was doing something wrong. She balanced the bike between her legs and wiped her forehead. Looking down for clues, the exposed calf of her left leg brushed against the suns' reflected hot engine side case.

"Ow!" *That's going to leave a mark.* Perhaps something was missing? Did she dare ask? Was starting the bike worth the trouble?

Kai poured the frothy mixture into an oversized frying pan. The egg danced in the sizzling oil. "Any favorite classes?"

"Chemistry." Her knee shook, and the bottom of her foot hurt. Kick, grunk, grunk. Kick. Grunk, grunk, grunk. Nothing. Bupkis.

"We will dine alfresco. Would you mind setting the table?"

Luna got off the bike, thankful for the break, and laid it against the pile. *Maybe it is just another piece of junk.* At least she wouldn't need the treadmill today. She went to the table and wavered over the open book pages of veterinary illustrations and drawings of surgical procedures. Handwritten notes filled the margins. Leaving paper slips as bookmarks, she put aside the books and set the table, just like Mom had taught her: fork over napkin, plate, knife, and spoon.

Kai had exchanged his coat for an apron and came out with a sizzling skillet, setting the pan squarely in the middle of the table. He cut into their prepared lunch, ending with sixteen pieces of what looked like a green and red speckled omelet. The slice slid off a trowel and presented itself on Luna's plate like a generous slice of pie.

"Would you like something to drink?"

"That was a girastrich egg?" Luna's eyebrows raised at her portion size. "No thanks, not now. Looks good." There was a lot more on her plate than any meal bar vending machine ever served. Could she finish it? "This is all for me?"

Kai took a slice for himself. "It's extra fluffy." He looked at Reuben, who sat at his side, and said, "Pin, Reuben, pin."

Reuben leaped to his feet and scampered inside. Judging by the commotion, it sounded like teeth gnawing, a door opening, and a beverage container's '*whoosh*.' Reuben returned, wagging his tail and holding a can's tab between his teeth. His derriere shook, coming back with such vigor that a steady stream of soda trailed him to the table.

Kai pointed his finger at the floor, frowned, and shook his head. "What did you do?" His displeasure fooled only the four-footed waiter.

Reuben looked up wide-eyed, the picture of angelic canid innocence. His cherubic cheeks puckered as drool pooled in the corners of his upturned lips. His nose repeatedly poked Kai's leg.

Luna leaned over the side of the table and blinked a few times to make sure she wasn't seeing things.

Reuben released the tab. Judging by the sloshing inside, there might have been a few swallows left.

"Tells me it's the chameleon side that causes his lapses in comprehension. But sometimes, I'm not so sure."

Her brows raised, and her jaw fell. "For real?"

Kai spoke as if addressing an audience. "Because he for- gets to..." Kai pointed to the entranceway. "... close the door."

Reuben's ears drooped. Without making a sound, he got up slowly with his tail down and went back inside. A door slammed shut.

"How in the world?" She considered asking Kai if he could talk to animals like Dr. Dolittle but reminded herself that only was supposed to happen in children's books. Instead, hunger dictated, and she turned her attention to her plate. An unfamiliar but fragrant blend of herbs and spices welcomed her. "Oow, that smells good." She bit into the spongy texture, closed her eyes, and rolled the morsel in her mouth. Her taste buds opened like daffodil petals on the first sunny day of spring. As she swallowed, her shoulders sank in a freefall of delight.

"When I make an omelet for myself, the seasonings vary with my mood. This one is made especially for you."

"Oh, my gosh. This is sooo good. I've been eating engineered bars since I arrived." Luna took another laden forkful and, between bites, said, "Smells heavenly. So light it melts in your mouth. It's great."

"You can thank Aapo for the egg. The seasonings come from my garden. I'm glad you like it."

Reuben rested his chin on Kai's lap, and other than an occasional wave of his tail, he did not move or make a sound. Kai rewarded him with a smile, and a "Good boy" pat on the head. From Reuben's mouth, a slobber stalactite dangled, threatening to touch the floor. Kai cut the omelet into smaller portions and placed them in feeding bowls.

Falafel waddled to his meal as fast as his bowlegs could carry him and ate with such gusto that only his blunt snout prevented him from devouring the bowl.

As Kai doled out the omelet around the courtyard, he asked, "What is it about chemistry that interests you?"

"I love how chemicals interact at the molecular and physical levels," Luna said between bites. "How a molecule can change, dependent on what it comes in contact with. Take carbon. By itself, it's pretty much burnable charcoal. Add a molecule of oxygen, and you've got a deadly gas. Double the oxygen, and you're exhaling carbon dioxide. Exchange the oxygen for four hydrogen molecules, and you've got flammable methane. Or, add both hydrogen and oxygen, and you may have made something that is not only a solid but sweet. Neat."

"Uh, huh."

"I've been meaning to ask. How did you learn to speak it? You sound so fluent."

"Calcan? Like any other language. I listened, practiced, and my vocabulary grew. Took time. I am still learning. Reading and writing are the most difficult."

Between bites, the gnawing need for an answer disturbed an otherwise perfect meal. *You will keep your promise if you don't mention the directive,* she told herself. "Have you ever wondered about the metal sphere we took out of the taurden?" She put aside her fork. "And how he got it in his mouth?"

He stood, wavered, and, as if mulling over the answer, took the pan and said, "Yes." Then he turned around and went inside without saying another word.

When he added nothing more, she wondered how he would react to learning about the Xerxes Directive. Isolated and alone out here, there's not much anyone can do, she assured herself. Perhaps the MiPS has rotated, or Jazz has come up with something. She toyed with the last piece on her plate.

"What would Don Quixote do if he came across a giant but did not have a lance to fight with?" She held her breath, hoping for something that might prove insightful. "One-one thousand, two—"

"He would use a pebble," Kai said from the other side of the wall.

"Come again?"

"Ever hear the story of David, the little shepherd boy, who overcame the giant Goliath with a slingshot? He would find a pebble."

Luna pressed her chin into the cradle of her palm. "Even a boulder wouldn't work with this giant." And wiped her hand down her face, assured this line of questioning was going nowhere.

"Then untie a shoelace."

"This giant doesn't wear…."

"Ask the right question."

Luna closed her eyes and squeezed her fists, fighting the urge to blurt out what she and Jazz had found out. Biting her tongue, she gathered their plates. "Can I help with anything else?"

"No, thank you."

While she paced the courtyard, her eye kept straying to the bike. She wanted answers, not riddles. *Was it worth it?* Straddling the motorcycle, she asked herself, "Is anything worth the trouble?"

"Mind if I try the bike one more time?" And without waiting for an answer, she kicked the pedal. "Start you piece of junk." Less throttle, more kick. The engine awakened as if coughing up a hairball. The oil circulated as the piston moved up and down, lubricating multiple contact points. Within seconds, years of disuse spit out the exhaust with a green gring, cough, gring, gring, cough, gring, yawn. The challenged grinding of metal on metal smoothed into a resentful clack. The bike ran but sounded like a caffeine addict's search for morning coffee.

With a whoop, Luna air high-fived. She waited for Kai. When he did not come out, she fist-bumped the gas tank. Reuben picked up a pull toy and shook it like a pom-pom-waving cheerleader.

*   *   *

JASMINE WOULD RATHER be on her hands and knees, scrubbing corridor floors than do anything to anger her father. *Forget about it,* she scolded herself. *Don't do it. Play another game.*

Being found guilty of hacking Xerxes software carried a mandatory fine, jail time, and the revoking of computer access for life. The closer she got to their apartment, the more uncertain she became. "What are the odds?" she mumbled. "Of all the corporate communications, what is the chance Luna saw that one? Considering all the communiqués to come across since Xerxes arrived five tykes ago, average thirty communiqués per saul plus employee correspondence, that's almost 15,000 to one." She stood before their apartment entrance, rocking back and forth. *Turn around*, she told herself. *It's not too late. You have done nothing wrong.* Times the likelihood the directive piggy-backed onto the tutorial when we saw it— astronomical. *Yet.*

Even when the door had closed behind, she could not catch her breath. While she may not have had the best relationship with her father, she had never betrayed his trust. That was about to change. Luna wasn't the only one willing to go out on a limb. "*When the bough breaks, the cradle will fall, and down will come Jazz*...." She banged her head against the door as if that would put off the inevitable and stop her from doing anything dumb.

She entered the memorized code to her father's home office. *I've got to find out how deeply Papa is involved. If I don't do something, Luna may end up putting herself in danger.* The door slid open.

Though certain her father was at work, the thought of triggering a security sensor caused her fingers to tremble. Jasmine inserted a wallet-sized disk into the access port and activated the computer. While the electronic eye completed its cycle, she entered the prepared list of his most likely usernames and passwords. When none of them worked, she searched his desk.

A chess set and an assortment of worn wooden puzzle boxes took up most of a bottom drawer. *Maybe it's inside one of them.* She fondly remembered the solutions from childhood. When all the boxes had been opened and nothing found inside, she blindly reached the bottom of the drawer. Something poked her finger. Gently wrapping her hand around it, she raised a spiked sphere to the light. It was just as Luna described. *Papa must be involved.* She returned it to the same spot and discovered a dusty hardcover copy of *1001 Arabian Nights. Papa still had it after all these years.* She took out the book and fondly flipped through the familiar pages. *The same book Mum read to me.* She thumbed through the pictures and stopped at the dog-eared picture of Ali Baba hidden in the cave with the forty thieves. From between the pages, a microchip slipped out. On it, in tiny script 'Open Sesame 06-06-66,' she read and placed the chip into the computer port. For the username, she typed the words and smiled as she entered her mother's birthday as the password.

Green lines of script appeared on the monitor as Jazz chewed the ends of her hair. Using her Jazzy-script-generated access code to highlight the worm keys: Polyhedral and Avicenna. She entered the keywords—Directive, Labor, and Acquisition. She switched interfaces and searched multiple secret file directories—and found nothing. Most folders contained titles of routine operations. There were tons of memos and assignments, but not the directive. It was too risky to change search engines. Maybe the whole thing was someone's idea of a bad joke.

*　*　*

DHIRAJ WAS ON his own. For the first time in his life, unable to rely on family and friends, he felt very out of place. He disliked the role they sent him here to perform, the travel accommodations en route, and everything from the food to his living quarters. When they assigned him to Calcus, had they not considered that he was vegetarian? The dispensed meals were not fit for swine. What he yearned for was one of his wife's home-cooked meals. His mouth watered, remembering the evenings coming home to the smells of garam masala and curries. He recalled the wiggle of Priya's hips stirring the pan of palak paneer and delighted at the sound of his kids laughing and playing in the front room of their home. He had given all that up for this god-forsaken dung heap of a planet.

What had promised to be an exciting posting had turned into a living nightmare. It seemed like only yesterday when he came home to his wife with news of a promotion. He went so far as to buy flowers. Instead of being happy for him, Priya responded with doubts. What a killjoy.

"Why you? Why so far? Why so long? Don't they know you are a family man?" she asked. Question after question, she poked and prodded, never giving him a chance to respond.

Without a vase, the flowers wilted in his hand. For those brief moments when she had to catch her breath, he stood silent, bursting with resentment, unable to reply.

Instead of being happy for him, she ranted. "If it wasn't this Valdeez fellow who requested you, then who did?"

The mysterious recruiter had always gone through an intermediary. Since the promotion had to have come from someone with the position to authorize it, he reasoned, it had to be a board member.

Dhiraj had been contacted, instructed, and sent with the title of security chief in charge of technical analysis. So what if Priya made some valid points? He couldn't let her know that.

Better off changing the subject, he thought. "The contract stipulates only eight Calcan tykes, my love."

"What is this tyke? How am I supposed to know what you are talking about?"

Nothing he said satisfied her. Nothing he did seemed to please her. He felt that he could have gone and come back in the time it took to persuade her to let him go. "Perks come with promotion." He caressed her neck. "We'll be able to send the kids to that private school you always wanted." Her shoulders relaxed. "You will be able to redecorate the house just as you always dreamed." The tension in her muscles melted below his touch. "Don't worry. I'll be back before you've finished the house. Promoted, a big shot. You'll see."

Eight tykes out here might as well be an eight-year prison sentence. Pondering Priya's pointed questions, perhaps this was not the best career move after all. By his way of thinking, he figured a promotion hinged on what his assignment didn't say. On the surface, his mandated security presence was not enough to warrant a chief. Who needs security? The crew knew their job. The locals were harmless. What did it mean? "Carry out Valdeez's orders and report back?" "Report back" was just another way of saying "spy."

A technician approached from the far end of the hallway. With the new security chief's gaze focused ahead, only Dhiraj's shoe taps acknowledged the passerby.

Dhiraj had done as told, designed the untraceable sphere, and found the heathen to place it in the animal. Just following orders. And yet, as pressure mounted inside his chest, he cringed. The beast may have looked different from the cows back home, but as one of goddess Surabhi's creatures, it was his duty to protect, not kill. *I will have to make amends for my actions and hope karma does not punish me harshly in my next life.*

But not now.

Since the MiPS halted transmissions, he had lost contact with his source. This proved convenient since the disappearance of another miner and the loss of a native were hardly worth reporting. As Dhiraj saw it, there was only one way to get a first-class ticket out of there. He had to quit playing the role of pawn in other people's games. He needed leverage, such as information, to use to his advantage. His pulse slowed to the rate of the two soft blinking lights on his handheld tracker. He straightened his uniform and stood erect. Despite the best surveillance equipment available, Dhiraj always planted a good old-fashioned tracker on people of interest. Valdeez wanted his daughter's whereabouts monitored. *Fine. No problem. What is one more or less?* Two blips pinged Valdeez's main office on the tracking monitor. Dhiraj had waited too long to miss this opportunity. He needed electronic proof, and this was the place to get it. His lips parted into a crooked smile. How nice; father and daughter spending time together.

Dhiraj checked over his shoulder before attaching a cloning device to the residence keypad. While the circuit ran through its cycle, he wondered where a man of Valdeez's cunning would hide the information he needed. The man's daughter also bothered him. Jasmine was her name. While her communications tended to be typical teenage banter, why should a girl, and a disabled one at that, have such a sophisticated personal data security wall? Dhiraj grinned. What better place for Valdeez to hide something incriminating? Where is the last place anyone would look?

Chapter 10

***Repetitio mater studiorum est.* Repetition is the mother of learning.**

—Roman Saying

"You would rather stay indoors than risk getting hit by a snowball?" —Luna

"I've never been in the snow." —Jazz

NOT ONLY HAD the antique bike started, but the engine kept running. This is what it must have felt like, Luna thought, to be the first to take nuts and bolts and build the first spaceship to the moon. However, it did not take a rocket scientist to figure out that the real fun began when you got to ride it. Fingertips tapped impatiently on handlebars. Kai was still inside. A decision had to be made. *He didn't say I couldn't.* She revved the engine. Silence from the other side of the wall. Nothing to the contrary. But he had not given permission either. She closed her eyes. A coin flipped inside her head. *Heads, I win.* She twisted the throttle with the confidence of a Biker Warrior game wizard. Her pulse raced. The beating piston vied to catch up. The rumble of a real engine outpaced any simulated game. In harmony, her quivering hands, stomach, and legs shook with the bike.

Squeeze the clutch, press the gear lever, and let out—the

engine died. A red light appeared. Tap the gear shifter to the bottom, half-click to neutral, kick start, up click, and let out the clutch. The bike jerked. Like a jackhammer gone berserk, it whiplashed her back and forth. The engine hiccupped and gave out. She waited for criticism. Nope. Kai had not bothered to stick his head out. No reason not to try again, this time with more throttle. With concentrated effort and patience, the bike stuttered down the gangway. *I'm moving.* Upon entering the street, she looked both ways, squeezed the front brake, and stalled. Again: neutral, kick start, look both ways and ease forward. "I've got it," she told herself. Her face beamed with pride and shifted into second gear. *Damn.* From the beginning.

Every time the bike stalled, she pulled in the clutch, coasted off to the side, and began the process again. A rider has a lot more to deal with on the real thing. This one's front end wobbled at any speed over slow. The slightest touch of the brakes sent them off like squealing pigs. Fortunately, traffic was sparse, and the few Calcans she encountered were more patient than the drivers back home. She kept to the side streets and gained confidence with each passing block.

The learning process took its toll on her bottom. Sitting on a sawhorse would have been more comfortable. So what if the tires were low, and the handlebars shook? Luna had ridden it, and the bike's muffler heralded her return with a *green-gring-gring.* While Kai was not present to applaud, she performed a tight circle turn for the remaining courtyard animals, anyway. "I'm back," she shouted and turned off the engine.

She got off the bike, and before her swaggered second step touched the ground, the slam of metal on stone changed her cocky smirk to topple along with whatever fell behind. All forward motion slumped to a stop. Her ears reddened as she braced for an oncoming reprimand.

Rueben's bone dropped to a *clunk* as he looked up. Their eyes met.

"That bad, huh?"

Reuben leaned over far enough to look behind. He held that position as if deciding to comment and returned to the more important project between his two front paws.

Maybe it was something else. With one eye closed, she turned slowly. The downed motorcycle seemed to take up a disproportionate part of the courtyard. Never happened in the game. In an instant, her magic carpet had transformed back into a battered rug. The bike lay foundered and incapacitated. As if mortally wounded, fluids oozed from its side. Then it dawned on her. Old bikes don't put the stand down automatically.

Kai did not have to come outside for a look-see or even ask about the noise. He just knew.

Speeders went down all the time. No big deal. At the track, riders dropped them, taking curves too fast, hitting bumps at speed, and landing off balance on jumps. Testing the limits of their speeders, track surfaces, and their own abilities was part of learning. Falling made you better. You dusted yourself off, told everyone you were okay, righted the bike while fending off the jabs at your riding ability, and got back on.

Upright, a motorcycle was easy to maneuver. Lying on its side was like trying to raise the dead. When a player crashed or blew up in Biker Warrior, the game regenerated a new ride automatically. This bike weighed twice as much as she did and on its side was unwieldy to boot. Kai had not come out, and she was not about to ask for help. *Can I do it myself?*

"Got this," Luna said, loud enough to carry through the doorway. *At least, I hope I do.*

Reuben's gnawing teeth on bone agreed.

With her back to the seat, she bent her knees low enough to grab hold of the frame and stepped backward. With the load distributed between her arms and legs, her felled trophy steadily returned to its upright position. The bleeding engine trickled to a stop. The patient looked like it might live to run again.

Holding the bike upright with one hand, she bent over and poked around for the bashful kickstand.

"It's on the left, below the engine," Kai's voice said from inside.

He has got to have X-ray vision. And just like he said, there it was. The spring-loaded rod lowered with a sweep of her toe. A scrape scarred the engine case where it had hit the floor. Her moistened thumb rubbed, and her shirttail buffed, but the scuff would not come out.

"I scratched the—"

"It is not the only one, and you are not the first to drop it."

Luna exhaled a sigh of relief. She had dodged a big one. Not wishing to push the boundaries of her welcome, she settled for a seat while biting her lip and holding back an elated smile. *I got the bike started and rode it.*

"Pin, Reuben, pin."

Reuben took his time standing as if rheumatism had suddenly reached his joints. He arched his back and extended his front paws into an exaggerated stretch.

She repeated, "Pin, Reuben, pin."

He panted while his eyes darted back and forth.

"Come on, boy, you can do it."

His head tick-tocked between her and the doorway.

"That's it. You've got it."

Reuben's pendulum gaze hinged on the bone.

As if nothing had happened, Kai came out holding a wrapped package. Without looking down, he sidestepped Reuben's bone and kicked it from behind with his other foot. The chew landed in a bin in the corner.

Luna threw up her arms. "Goal!"

Reuben dashed after the bone as though it were a squirrel.

Kai's eyes swept the bike like a poker player holding a small pair.

"I'm sorry I scratched your bike," Luna said sheepishly.

"Thank you for telling me, but there was no harm done."

"Then you're not mad?"

His face provided no cues to the contrary.

"I was worried." Relieved, she flicked a piece of imaginary lint off her shirt, and her lips widened into a sheepish grin. "If it's all right, I'll have that soda now." She put up a finger. "Watch this. Pin, Reuben, pin."

Kai's shoulder barely moved enough to be considered a shrug.

"You can do it." Luna's eyes and finger pointed the way.

Reuben cocked his head and trotted uncertainly inside, followed by the sounds of a door opening and the swoosh of a can. Where he may have wavered going inside, he made up with a bouncy trot on the return. His tail wagged, and his hips wiggled as the pin dangled from his teeth. He sat in front of Kai with the opened can. Kai remained motionless. Reuben waited expectantly and cocked his head.

"Over here, boy. Give it to me," Luna said, extending a hand. Reuben complied. She patted him on the head. "Good boy. Now, close the door." When he did, she handed him the last piece of omelet and celebrated by chugging what remained in the can.

How many people can say they've rescued a taurden and a Honda?

147

Gardenia jumped off the shelf and peered into her bowl.

Luna's fingers tapped the table. The bike's wobble was troubling. She picked up her can and scanned the workbench. She fished a pair of tin snips from among the wrenches, sockets, and tools and cut a rectangular strip. On the way to the bike, she blasted a Barney 'BURP.'

Reuben woofed, and Falafel hid behind a potted plant. Gardenia frowned while the few other remaining animals scampered off.

"The last time I heard a sound like that, we had to put down the whole herd."

"Oops, excuse me," she said, covering her mouth. "I got carried away. I was about to fix the wobble." She slid the improvised shim along the bar gooseneck and turned the handlebars side to side. "Fixed."

Kai stood before the bike, stroking his beard as if giving a problem some thought. He crouched beside the bike, pulled a cable here, and bent lower to tap the spokes there. "I can give you a ride part of the way or arrange for someone to take you back if you like," he said, unscrewing a cap on the side of the engine.

The suns were well off the horizon. There was plenty of daylight left. "Thank you, but I think I'll walk or catch a tuk-tuk. I don't want to be any more of a bother." Luna kicked a tire. When no response came, she said, "Or maybe I was kind of hoping to borrow the bike. I would bring it back, of course," she said, hoping not to have overstepped.

"You can take the bike," Kai said, bringing out a metal tube with wooden handles. "It's yours. Consider it a gift."

"Thank you. That's very kind of you. But I can't accept. I'll bring it back."

Kai pulled a hose from the tube and attached it to the

front tire. He pulled and pushed repeatedly on its wooden handles. The tire gradually inflated.

"Can I help with anything?" The moment Kai shook his head, she rushed for her shoes.

Before she could slip out of the first boot, like he had eyes in the back of his head, Kai said, "Don't bother. Keep your boots on. Your shoe will air out better here than inside a pod."

That means I can come back, she thought with a smile. While on a roll, she felt compelled to ask. "I haven't seen anyone wearing a helmet." She walked over to the pile and picked up a metal bowl. The object she intended to improvise had a couple of holes, a large dent, and a wide lip. Once upon a time, it had served a purpose. Now, it was nothing more than a discarded piece of trash. She punched the inside and banged it on a pipe. Tough. She wiped the inside with her elbow and put the bowl on her head. "Mind if I take this too?" she asked, wiggling her head and tucking the back of her hair inside. "Kinda fits."

Kai gave a non-committal nod and switched to the rear tire. "You can find some cord in the workbench drawer."

She cut a length of rope, threaded it through two holes in the bowl, and fastened a bow under her chin. She gave the helmet a tap. "Check."

Reuben and Falafel sat next to each other, tilting their heads. Leaning over, side by side, they stared at her like at a circus curiosity.

"Thank you." She got on the bike. With the tires filled, it felt more stable, and without further complaint, the engine started on the first kick.

"No airbags," Kai warned, attaching a package to the back of the bike. "Take this. A local treat. Something for later. Have it for dessert. It is made from the Ail fruit."

She jolted upright. "What? Ale, like a beer?"

"As in, 'good for what ails you.' Try it. You'll like it."

She hung on down the driveway, riding a gas-powered, egg-beating, two-wheeled bucket of rust.

Don Quixote would approve.

Falafel's hind end jiggled, and Reuben's waving tail bid farewell.

*   *   *

WHILE JASMINE'S NIMBLE fingers combed, her eyes darted from one likely secure folder after another. Determined not to leave any potential hiding place unchecked, she widened her search to include financial reports, weather histories, social news, and trash folders. "This is taking too long," she berated herself. *Where would Papa hide a sensitive document?*

"S-search games."

"Repeat, please," the computer said.

Jasmine spoke up.

"What kind of game would you like to play?" the computer asked.

"Chess." A game board filled the screen. "Search game history." A list of her father's games appeared. Nothing there either. "Go to chess puzzles." A catalog popped up. "The Arabian Mate."

"White to win in five moves," the computer said.

She knew how the game was supposed to end. Getting there was the tricky part. Once she solved the puzzle, the 'Acquisition of Calcus Native Labor' file filled the screen.

It really does exist.

As she began to read, a rustle from outside the apartment wrenched her attention away. Someone intended to come in.

With no place to run or hide, her pulse raced while the rest of her froze.

Whoosh. The apartment door opened.

A muffled gulp slid down her throat. From the screen, SECRET gleamed in bold letters. Could it be Imani? She would never have come in uninvited unless Papa had told her to.

Footsteps. Too heavy to belong to a woman. Silence. Jazz closed her eyes and strained to hear beyond the regular beeps. Someone is tracking, and it's not Papa. She bit her lip. *Whoever it is, doesn't know I'm here.*

Her belly rumbled. The cerebral command to freeze had evidently not reached inside. She pressed her moist palms against her stomach. Snarling echoed like an alleyway tomcat proclaiming its turf.

Beyond the door, prowling footsteps paused.

Had he heard?

The beeps and footsteps continued toward her room.

Through measured breaths, she exhaled a relieved sigh. Her stomach disagreed. Perhaps it's a thief? Dare she confront him? She strained to hear. What's he doing?

Her closet drawers opened.

Some kind of perve?

Swish. Her personal computer turned on.

What does he want with that? *How did he get my password?* She leaned off the chair. *Squeak.*

Her room computer powered down in a dissolving *whoosh.*

He heard me!

The bedroom door closed.

She closed her eyes and held her breath. Her stomach grumblings did not comply.

Footsteps approached.

Stuck in limbo, holding her body weight just off the chair,

her arms cramped. *Could the screen glare reach under the door?*

The office security keypad blipped.

A dry swallow caught in her throat. *Can he get in?* As a series of high-pitched beeps came from the other side, she wilted into the chair.

His comm chirped, and his voice quickly answered. "Yes, yes, I will be right there," he mumbled.

The security chief. The main door closed. A stay of execution, or maybe not, she thought, trotting, then sprinting to the bathroom.

*   *   *

IT TAKES A lot more time and effort to ride a motorcycle than a speeder. Luna was caught off guard by how much coordination, balance, and strength were necessary to operate such a small bike. In the game version, all a player had to do was twist the throttle, lean side to side, and shoot. On this, going faster involved harmonizing easing off the throttle, squeezing the clutch, and tapping the shifter to change gears. Going faster in a higher gear, she re-engaged the clutch, giving only enough throttle to avoid over-revving the engine or depriving it of fuel. It was exhausting getting the hang of it all. However, the further and faster she went, the more adept she became, and it became increasingly more fun.

Cruising through town, Luna sang her favorite Corina song over the engine's twang. Never could she have imagined riding a real motorcycle with a bowl on her head, much less doing it in rubber boots and shorts. Her friends would crack up if they could see her now.

Polite stares and glowing smiles greeted her along the way through town. Mothers admonished their young children for pointing, while other adults could not hide their amusement. Luna smiled at the spectators. *Would she come across Ziggy? Wouldn't he be surprised?*

Tuk-tuks, coming from the opposite way, celebrated the bowl-helmeted girl with honks and cheers. She reached for the horn, but the bike shook convulsively, threatening to topple over.

Enough falling for one day.

A motorcycle raced past her. She twisted the throttle. The bike shook to the point she almost lost control. A page from *Don Quixote* came to mind. In the picture, a goateed old man sits in a chair surrounded by books. Knights in acts of chivalry adorn their covers. At Don Quixote's feet, a shield, sword, and lance await his beck and call. The imaginary head of a frightful giant and a dragon's tail lay before him. He holds up a dusty, dented helmet in one hand and its broken visor in the other. The caption at the bottom of the page reads, "Forget material things, for they will let you down. Put your trust in absolute truths, for only they can be relied upon." Luna slowed down. *Best leave well enough alone.*

Technically, she was not supposed to be outside Xerxes's walls without supervision. *Oops, too late now. Would Xena consider Ziggy or Kai to be authorized escorts if she found out? Probably not. What about Rizzo? Maybe he could vouch for her?* Sometimes, Luna cracked herself up.

The brim of her improvised helmet was not wide enough to keep the setting suns out, and the bowl was too heavy to keep from slipping over her eyes. Her chin raised to a sweet spot where she could see ahead without being blinded by the suns. Coming within sight of Xerxes, she squinted. Perhaps the suns were playing tricks again. The outline of the industrial plant, with its rows of smokestacks, made the complex look like an ominous castle. Wind-powered turbines and the arrange-ment of crisscrossed pipes appeared like the heads and arms of grimacing giants. The smoke from the towering exhaust might just as well have come from fire-breathing dragons.

Well, we're not in Kansas, and this isn't Disneyverse.

It occurred to her that she would need a place to leave the bike. She had forgotten to ask Kai how Calcans secured their vehicles. There was no place in the surrounding fields to hide it. She had seen no security measures since leaving Xerxes's walls. Back home, even junk like this risked being stolen or removed for recycling. Desperate not to explain how she lost the bike, she rode up to the taxi lot and recognized the haggling Calcan. She draped the bowl over a handlebar and tapped the man on the shoulder.

"Excuse me, sir. How much to park the bike?"

He did not bother to turn around.

Is this just him, or a Calcan thing?

As before, his hands raised like a thief caught in the act.

Is ten the going rate for everything? "Can you do five?" she asked, biting her lip, hoping her voice did not betray her need.

He turned and squinted, more out of curiosity than a de-sire to haggle. He glanced over her shoulder with a look of concern. "Kai?"

She nodded. "You know him?"

The Calcan smiled. "Certainly. My name is Nestor," he said matter-of-factly, walking over to the bike. "A pleasure to meet you. Any friend of Doctor Kai is a friend of mine. Allow me. I'll take care of it." He scrutinized her improvised bowl. "You can leave that too. They will be safe with me."

"Your English is very good," she said, handing over her helmet.

He removed Kai's package and handed it over. You don't

want to forget this."

"Thank you, thank you very much." The bike disappeared into the parking lot. There was nothing left to do but check in with Xena. *It's got to be getting late.*

Rizzo stepped in front of her with a boyish grin. "Did you like my sample?" His smile widened. "I have more. For you, make good price."

Luna shook her head.

He persisted.

She raised a forefinger and shook it like a mother scolding a child. Without saying a word, she snubbed him and walked purposefully toward the guards at the gate.

"Let down the drawbridge, fellas; I'm coming in."

The guards looked quizzically at one another as the dust-covered, rubber boots-wearing girl clunked past. One guard bowed at the waist and presented his hand. He winked at the other guard and said, "Right this way, Your Majesty."

*   *   *

LUNA TURNED A corner and found Jazz pacing the hallway.

"Where were you?" Jazz asked accusingly. Her stutter outed her concern. "Are you all right?"

"I'm fine. Tired is all. What time is it?"

Jazz shook her head as if caught by surprise. "Um, seven fortyish."

"Whoa. That late?"

Jazz relaxed enough to ask, "What's with the rubber boots?"

"Like them?" Luna did a toe twirl, extended her arms, and pressed out her heel like a shoe model. "My fashion statement. They'll be all the rage back home."

"No, really, I've been looking everywhere for you. I got worried."

"I was out, Mom," Luna said, reaching past her and through the pod door. "I have to check in with Big Sister."

Jazz stepped aside. "Okay, so maybe I overreacted."

"Have you been able to call out?" Luna slipped off a boot and tossed it in the tray. The whirring of the cleaning brushes sounded like they were working overtime.

"No, the magnetic poles have not shifted." Jazz shrugged. "You mean you were beyond the gate out?"

"I told you. I wasn't going to wait around. The promo said, 'Come to Calcus. See the sights,'" Luna said, putting her hands out as if that would help Jazz better understand. "That's all I did. Besides, the walls were closing in on me." Jazz's head bobbled as if weighing Luna's words. "Time flew. I didn't plan on spending so much time in town, is all."

"You went into town?" Jazz looked like she was going to have a stroke.

She's interrogating me like my mother, Luna thought and changed the subject. "I found the bong improviser guy. His name is Kai. I think he's the local vet."

"Wait," Jazz said, furrowing her brow. "There's a vet, and you talked to him? You didn't tell him, did you?"

"No, but I think he suspects," Luna said, waving her hand over the Xerxes monitor.

As Xena's presence materialized, Jazz ducked into the bathroom.

"Seven forty-six," Xena admonished. "You are fourteen mitts before your imposed curfew."

"Sorry, I forgot to check in."

"Would you like to continue where you left off?" The AI seemed appeased.

Inside the bathroom, Jazz stuck her head out so only Luna could see her, pointed to the screen, and slashed a finger over her throat.

Luna nodded to show she understood and turned to address Xena. "No, thank you, not tonight. Think I'll turn in early. Good night."

"Signing off." Xena's image dissolved.

"What's with the cloak and dagger?" Luna asked.

Jazz eased out from behind the door. "That was close. I'd rather security not know my whereabouts. We need to talk. Say tomorrow? Same place at the park?"

"Before you leave...." Luna brought out Kai's dessert. "... got time for a snack?"

Jazz swiped a hand over her stomach. "I'm famished. Uh, sure." She looked over the wrapper as if it were a bomb about to explode. "Okay, but what is it?"

"Ail Cake. As in, good for what ails you. I dunno. Never had it before." Luna peeled off the waxed paper to reveal a glistening apple red loaf and offered it to Jazz.

Jazz put up her hand and leaned away. "Not me... you first."

Luna tore off a gooey piece and gave it the sniff test. Tropical fruit aromas filled the citrus-scented air. "It's not poison. Besides, Snow White, it's your favorite color. How bad can it be?" Luna added, "Heh, heh, heh," like the Wicked Witch in the story. "Come, come, my pretty. Won't you take a bite?"

Jazz looked over as if giving weight to the dare. "Are you sure it's okay?" she asked with a frown and twisted off a morsel between her fingers. "It's sticky. I changed my mind. I don't want any."

Luna toyed with the piece in her hand.

Jazz watched closely as Luna took a bite.

Magical fireworks exploded over Luna's tongue. Sweet and

tangy, yet nothing like anything she had tasted before. She held her hands around her throat, gagged, overexaggerated a nasty face, and pointed a finger down her throat.

Jazz looked for a place to wipe her fingers. "What is this?" She recoiled with her hand held out. "Glue?"

Luna broke out laughing. "It's good. Yummy, even."

Jazz did not look convinced.

Luna smacked her fingers. "Go ahead, scaredy-cat."

Jazz shook her head.

"More for me if you don't."

Jazz reluctantly scrutinized the goo, sniffed it a few times, and placed a smidge to her lips. "Maybe I shouldn't?"

"Really? I've got leftover kibble if you want."

Jazz closed her eyes and barely opened her mouth. Her eyebrows raised, yet she held back any response. "Hmm, I guess it's okay. I've had better." She grabbed a hunk off the loaf, and just as her fingers reached her lips, Luna pushed Jazz's hand, causing the goo to smear over her face. Jazz's eyelids raised over her bulging eyes as red oozed from her mouth and chin.

Luna chortled, thinking the Ail cake made Jazz look like a deranged clown.

"I can't believe you did that." Jazz pushed out her hand, but Luna bobbed out of the way. Jazz jumped on the bed and grabbed a pillow. "You're... so going to get it."

"If it tastes so all right, how come you took such a big piece?" Luna took the bong from the side stand and used it like a sword, pretending to hold off the pillow.

Jazz raised the pillow over her head. "Now I've got you."

Luna shifted the bong to her armpit and held the pipe like a lance. In a deep, imperious voice, she quoted from the book. "I, Don Quixote de La Mancha, take on all giants..."

"You're talking about the character from the book?" Jazz raised the pillow higher above her head. "*Grrr.* Let's see what you've got, Doña Q."

Luna lowered her improvised lance, pointed at Jazz, and then to the mirror. "… and Calcan impersonators."

Refusing to get caught off guard, Jazz warily kept the pillow ready and peeked under her arm. In the mirror, dried, red crusts covered her mouth. "You shouldn't talk. Look at yourself, scaler."

In front of the mirror, they stood side by side, pointing fingers at one another. Both made faces, trying to outdo the other. Jazz wiped her chin and called for a time-out before going to the bathroom to wash her face and hands. Luna took off the pillowcase and tossed it in the laundry.

While Luna cleaned up, Jazz examined the book on the side stand. She flipped through the pages. "Let's make one thing clear, Don Quixote. I will not be Sancho in your version of the book."

"Rocinante, maybe?"

"Are you calling me an old nag?"

"If the shoe fits."

Jazz raised the remaining clean pillow.

"Okay. Okay. Truce, for now."

LATER THAT NIGHT, Luna opened the book to where she had dog-eared the page, read for a bit, and then put it down. "Xena?" The A.I. appeared. "How do you say thank you in Calcan?"

Xena acknowledged the question with a nod and paused. It took longer than the expected seconds for the AI to answer.

"*Spankuhn.*"

"*Spa-kuhn. Spakuhn,*" Luna said. "Thanks, Xena, *spakuhn.*"

Luna picked up where she had left off. "Don Quixote confesses that he hardly knows Dulcinea. Sancho is surprised that his master's ideal mistress is none other than the daughter of Lorenzo Corhuelo."

Chapter 11

Crisis = Danger + Opportunity

—Japanese kanji

JASMINE'S QUEEN-SIZED QUILT provided no comfort while she tossed and turned during the night. Sleeping with her face buried in a pillow, a courtroom battle waged inside her head, with frustration, worry, and doubt acting as witnesses for the prosecution.

It's not Luna's fault. She's here all by herself. Someone has to protect her.

"Good luck with that. You can't even finish a full sentence in front of your own father." She kicked the covers off her feet. "Send him a text."

Very funny.

"What if he finds out what you have been doing?"

I would lose his trust. I can't let that happen.

"He already considers you a failure. How much worse can it be?"

Her eyelids pressed into their sockets as if that would keep disaster from coming in. Finding no refuge in sleep, she threw off the covers, determined to bring up the directive. *I can't just spring it on him.* Not wishing to disturb a man who subsisted on four rays of sleep, she dressed quietly without turning on the light.

"I'll make him something for breakfast."

The man subsits on caffeine.

"Something he can't resist, like Mum used to make us from scratch."

He can't chew and talk at the same time.

She tip-toed into the kitchen and, just as she had predicted, found his bento box with his favorite sushi pieces missing without touching the pickled ginger. Retrieving her bracelet, she rinsed it off and placed it back on her wrist. *None the wiser.* She added a pinch of cinnamon to the coffeemaker and kneaded the breakfast loaf, according to her mother's recipe, before placing it in the oven. While the kitchen filled with the aromas and associated memories of past family Sunday brunches, she set the island table.

"Good morning, Papa," she rehearsed in her mind. "How are you this morning?" The words flowed eloquently.

"I'm fine," he'll say.

"Look what I made."

"You did? Smells good." He would smack his lips, anticipating the first bite. "Cut me a bigger slice, please."

Before he has a chance to swallow, I'll say, "We need to talk about something that happened during the last MiPS."

"What was that?" he would ask, savoring every bite.

"A top-secret document appeared while I was doing my speech exercises. Appeared out of nowhere." *Keep Luna out of it.* "If information about the labor acquisition directive were to get into the wrong hands, it might prove embarrassing. I have an idea about how to keep that from happening." *He would be so impressed that he would ask me to go on.*

"We'll sort this out together and be home before you know it," she said, imitating his voice.

The loaf is burning!

Reality stared her in the face. In a fight for her father's attention, his work was the champion. As the weak contender, Jazz hardly stood a chance. Cutting away the burned edges, she imagined Luna approaching him with the subject. "Murdered any more animals lately?"

Don't go there. You're not her.

His bedroom door opened. Jasmine braced while going through her speech therapy drill. Before saying a word, she closed her eyes, took a deep breath, and let the air out slowly. Her eyes opened. Valdeez entered the kitchen, hovered over his comm, and waved his hand over the coffeemaker without looking.

Jasmine cleared her throat. "G-good m-morning, P-P-P."

He jerked away as if being assaulted.

She took another deep breath. "I made it special," she said, sputtering splattered S's.

He frowned at the coffee. "You're up early." He pointed to the mug. "Is this for me?"

"Yes, Papa."

Who else would it be for? You know I don't drink coffee. Don't you?

She cut a generous slice from the middle. "I." *Just spit it out. No, don't do that.* Crumbs fell on the counter as she placed the piece on a serving plate. She moistened her lips, wanting to say, "I uncovered a secret," but it came out a broken version of, "I hope you like breakfast."

He swiped his comm between sips.

Should I be grateful that he looks in my direction every once in a while? The plate edged toward his elbow. *It's good. Just take a bite.* She cut a slice for herself, hoping he might get the hint.

"Is everything all right?" he asked as if three words were all he had to spare. "Something bothering you?"

Make that six.

"Made it special," she said, sliding her napkin over a trace of spittle.

"For me?" If the ends of his lips curved any lower, they would fall off his chin.

Your piece isn't burned. Her shoulders raised in a halfhearted shrug.

"What is it?" Like a spoiled child removed from the spotlight, his comm flashed in protest. "What's bothering you? Tell me."

Her finger flicked the edge of her plate. "I..." A hollow plea for understanding screamed silently within. Unable to tell if he was ready to pounce or storm off, her hands fell into her lap.

What have I done to make you so angry? Her tongue strangled any attempt at a coherent response.

"What? Has someone been bothering you? Tell me. Who is it? I'll assign security."

She twisted the bracelet around her wrist. *It isn't safety I need.* She shook her head. *You don't see me.* Her lips parted silently.

"Then what? What is it? Is there something you want?" He slammed the mug on the counter. "I don't understand. Tell me."

"Can't."

He crossed his arms with a scowl. "Can't what? Get through to your friends?" His gaze enveloped her like a shroud. "Yes. I get that. I have more important matters to deal with. Hold on a while longer. Quarterly reports and babysitting staff take up all my time. They're overwhelming Imani with complaints. Maybe you could...." He bit his lip and looked into his empty mug. "Don't worry. We won't be here long. Keep up with your speech exercises, and everything will work out fine."

"You promised the same thing last time. I want us to leave. I want to go home."

He slammed his hand on the counter. "We'll return when I say so." He looked at her like a detective grilling a guilty suspect. "Has someone put you up to this?"

"I miss home, and I miss—"

"Your friends. Yes, I know. You've said that. What about the new girl? Are the two of you getting along?" He squinted as if probing for a reaction. "Did she put you up to this?"

"Mum—I miss her." Her bitter smile could not lessen the sense of disappointment.

"Your mother. Yes, I do too." He patted her hand.

For all the good his attempt at conciliation had been, her hand might as well have been severed at the wrist. Resigned to another dead-end conversation, she said, "We should leave now."

His brow furrowed. "You are my daughter. Your place is with me. I'll hear no more of such nonsense. We'll leave when my work is done."

Her folded hands nestled limply in her lap.

"I don't like it here either, princess. As soon as I'm finished, we're going back home. This time, I promise, for good. No more outposts. Things will be better than ever." He looked at her and let out an exasperated sigh. "What? What is it now?"

"I'm worried." She looked him in the eye.

"About what? Me?" He looked confused and irritated. "We've talked about this."

"You talked—"

"Don't interrupt. The faster I wrap things up here, the sooner we'll be back home. As soon as I'm on the Council, you'll see." He pushed away the plate. "I'm late. Have to go."

He kissed her on top of her head. "Later, princess."

The door closed behind him. Two untouched breakfast dishes slammed into the sink. Jasmine sat at the island with her elbows on the counter and cradled her head in the cups of her hands. "I miss you, Mummy."

*　　*　　*

LUNA GOT UP well before Xena appeared and early enough to process the previous saul's figures as the data came in. "How do you say 'Hello,' in Calcan?" Luna asked before Xena could say a word.

"Would you please repeat that?" Xena asked, looking a bit confused. Luna repeated herself, and Xena answered, "*Ohenro.*"

"*Ohenro, spakuhn,*" Luna said.

"This is the second instance you have asked for a word to be translated into Calcan. Do you plan to converse with a native?" Xena waited. When no answer came, she said, "You are aware that you may not leave the premises without supervision. That has been specified in your contract. I have highlighted the paragraph's specific subsection. Shall I read it back to you?"

"That won't be necessary. The words might come in handy, um, for a sociology class." Xena was turning out to be like school detention, Mom's interrogations, and being grounded all at the same time. *A year of this?*

By mid-morning, the saul's data had been cataloged and analyzed.

"Will you be continuing with your classes?" Xena asked.

"I'm going for some exercise," Luna said, dressing in slacks. "I won't need directions. I know the way." As far as

Luna was concerned, the less Big Sister Xena knew, the better.

In the hallway, a passerby gaped as Luna clunked past in rubber boots. *Back home, these are going to be a hit.* At the park, she scoped the faces, saw no one unusual, and found a secluded spot. She peeked inside a wastebasket. A commotion startled her from behind. Shooting up straight, she turned to see Jazz standing right behind.

"My, you're jumpy. What are you d-doing?"

"Checking for cameras or microphones. Is the place wired?" She looked over Jazz's shoulder. "Shouldn't we be covering our mouths or something?"

"No, it's okay. Surveillance is off limits in here." Jazz looked Luna in the eye. "So, who else did you tell?"

Luna looked around and lowered her voice. "Come on, let's walk." Once well out of earshot, she continued. "I told you, I didn't tell anyone. I keep my promises."

"Wait. Hold up." Jazz tugged on Luna's arm. "Then how does this Kai know so much?"

"He happens to be the local veterinarian. That's what animal doctors do."

Jazz stepped back. "Calcus has a vet?"

"Come on, don't look so shocked. Haven't you been out-side? Don't you have the faintest idea what goes on beyond these walls?"

"I do not."

Luna cocked a probing eye.

"I don't care." Jazz raised her chin assuredly. "I wouldn't go out even if I was allowed to," she said, pouting.

"Aren't you a little curious? There's a whole world out there, waiting, no, begging to be explored. And the animals. Oh, my gosh, the animals alone are so worth it."

"It's not safe. Besides, Xerxes has no interest in anything

that does not pertain to mineral extraction. Once they leave, sub-contractors take over."

"I get that. Xerxes isn't interested in animals or anything else it doesn't control. But you aren't Xerxes."

"So what?" Jazz said with a shrug, quickening the pace. "You're going to play hero? What are you going to do—save the planet?"

"Wait up. The first time we met, you called me brave. I dunno." Luna grabbed Jazz by the elbow. "I've pounded my head, wondering how my life could have changed so fast. You're going along, living pretty much as planned." Luna snapped her fingers. "The next moment, you're playing 'what if' games in your head, wondering how things could go so wrong, so fast. You know what I mean?"

Jasmine raised her brows, searching the ceiling.

"You're right, of course. I'm just a girl in the middle of nowhere." Luna collapsed onto a bench.

"Then why are you here?"

Luna stared ahead. "Have you ever done something so dumb you can't let it go?"

"No, not really." Jazz shrugged and sat beside Luna. "Maybe."

"Well, I can't stop beating myself up about it." Luna reached into her boot and lifted her pant leg.

"Okay, sure."

"Back home, I messed up, big time. I'll never be able to take it back." Luna bit her tongue and shook her head. "I'd give anything to do it all over again. But I can't. That's why I'm here." Luna's pant leg raised higher. "Since it happened, working with this vet is the first time I've been able to put that aside." She turned to expose her knee. Angry, raw scrapes glared. "Get me?"

Jazz's eyes widened. "Wow. What happened?"

Luna lowered her pant leg. "Look. I'm a mess. I can't call home. Right now, my mother is probably freaking out. Well, at least I hope she is. And if that wasn't enough, we're in the middle of some sick scheme to kill animals."

Jazz elbowed Luna's arm. "Look, I admire you. I really do. I could never do whatever it is that you do out there."

Luna swiped her face. "And on top of all that, I'm homesick." She stood. "Come on, let's go."

"Well, how about this? I hacked into the system," Jazz said without a stutter.

"What? Look at you, taking all kinds of risks." Now it was her turn to be awed.

"Computers like me." Jazz put her hands on her hips. "What more can I say?"

"Oh, come on."

"Okay. Luck was part of it. During the MiPS, while reading the directive, I noticed a burned mark on the video."

"A what?"

"It's a piece of electronic signature that lets me figure out how to crack its code." Jazz answered as if reading Luna's mind. "No, I can't call out or get into the corporate mainframe, but I broke into their Calcan correspondence." Jazz laced her fingers, outstretched her arms, and put her hands behind her head.

Luna's brows raised. "So if nobody else knows, can you prove what we saw? Do you know who sent it?"

Jazz looked down with a bitter smile. "No, no luck there."

"Then how about this? We put a pebble in their operation."

"What? Put a what, where?"

"You know, like David and Goliath." Luna's step bounced.

The boots chugged along. "The shepherd boy with the slingshot."

"Yes. I know the story."

"Same idea. Only we don't need a rock to bring down Xerxes. All I'm asking is for you to stop them from killing more animals. Distract them for a while. Something like untying their shoelaces."

"I believe Goliath would have worn sandals, but I get your point. Yes, I can do that. Tie up security, change a few data points, plant a virus." Jazz raised a brow. "You know, you could stay and help."

Luna doggedly shook her head.

"You're going out again, aren't you?"

Luna's eyes lit up. "I haven't heard you stutter since you mentioned the hack. Gotta be a good sign. Right?" She huffed. "Stay here? No way."

Jazz looked down. "Figured as much. If shoes make the girl...."

"Only sometimes."

"Then I'd be worried if you were wearing stilettos."

Luna chuckled. She lifted the toe of her left boot to highlight where the gear shifter had worn through. "These come in a variety of colors, and I'm working on a version with an open toe."

Jazz shook her head. "Getting sent back home could be the least of your worries. Xerxes exerts a lot of influence throughout the galaxy. Especially back home. They can make your life miserable. Are you willing to pay the price?"

Luna nodded. "Are you? You're in this as deep as I am."

Jazz kept walking.

"Can you do your computer thing and cover for me?"

Jazz took off her bracelet. "Sure, but do me this favor," she said, placing it on Luna's wrist. "I want you to wear this outside."

Luna shook her arm. "I've never been big on jewelry. Bling gets in the way when you're mucking stalls."

"Well, you're not cleaning stalls now. Besides, it might get you out of a jam."

"Sure. Will you be okay without it?"

"How much trouble can a girl confined to four walls in a guarded outpost on a remote planet get into?"

"To quote Shakespeare, 'Let me count the ways.'"

"You're the one who better be careful."

*   *   *

MASSAGING HIS TEMPLES, Valdeez could do nothing more than wish his headache away. The arc of pop-up virtual screens surrounding his desk painted a dismal panoramic view. Red ink filled the bottom lines of raw data, and graphs spiraled out of control. The situation struck deeper than feared. Without a doubt, importing labor was proving to be costlier than expected. Employees could not work hard or long enough to justify the incentives, travel expenses, and wages. To make matters worse, two valuable members of the new mining crew had gone missing, and the rest were threatening to strike.

Damn planetary aberration, he cursed, making a mental note to contact the geological physics department about the possibility of controlling polar shifts.

The robot upgrades were going along ahead of schedule. In time, the process would complete itself. *Any fool can wait.* He was fully aware that Xerxes was not paying him to play it safe.

Success hinged on relieving insufficient supply. "Increase

the extraction of raw materials, and the rest would fall into place," he told himself. He rotated his shoulders, and his back cracked. If not, the project would be considered his failure, a blemish on an otherwise untarnished career. Furthermore, it irked him that a ready supply of able-bodied humanoids remained out of reach. Given a taste of a better life, he could not fathom why the locals refused to work. Lazy misfits who think of themselves as ranchers, he thought. As if anyone could consider those hybrid freaks of theirs to be animals.

Dhiraj stood outside the main office, monitoring his security controls and deciding whether to go inside or wait to be called. Having searched Valdeez's residence and found nothing useful, he felt satisfied to have planted a worm inside his daughter's software. While it was impossible to breach that much security in such a short period, the worm made it a simple matter of waiting before the fish began to bite.

The whereabouts of the new girl unsettled him, but that could be taken care of by planting a tracker on her as well. His head wobbled, asserting that there was no time like the present. He cleared his throat before pushing through the side entrance.

Valdeez rubbed the back of his neck, making no attempt to hide his displeasure at being interrupted. "Any news?"

The mottled sticker of a donkey contrasted with the helmet's white background and the tattered bits of material Dhiraj held in his hands. "We found what's left of one of the new miners. At least, we think it's him."

"So you cannot be certain?" Valdeez paused as if anything less than absolute certainty would cast doubt on the miner's disappearance.

Dhiraj opened his mouth to respond when the lights in the office and the wall-mounted monitor flashed.

"Yes! Finally!" Imani's voice screaked from outside. She rapped on the main door and peeked inside. "There's been a polar shift, Chief. Communications are back." She leaned against the door with a relieved smile. "Hello, Dhiraj. Finally, we can get some real work done."

Valdeez held up his finger. "Hold on." He checked his comm and read the text:

Note: A Federation inspector has infiltrated Calcus. Learned of incursion, last saul, your time. Make contact at twelve hundred rays. The Council will be in attendance. Take necessary precautions.

Dhiraj took the opportunity to read a version of the text sent from his source.

"Imani, thank you. I am aware of it. Disconnect all satellite comms. Nothing goes out. Keep us off-line." Valdeez looked at her as if nothing more needed to be said.

"But…." Her smile faded.

"Explain it as another temporary glitch," Valdeez said. "That is all." She shook her head and closed the door behind her. Addressing Dhiraj, Valdeez said, "At the moment, losing another miner is the least of our concerns."

"The agent can pose a threat, Sir. I will deal with it," Dhiraj said.

"Good. That's very good. I questioned your appointment, but now I see why you were chosen."

"No harm in playing both sides," Dhiraj said to himself. His chin raised ever so slightly. "I have taken the liberty of segregating the new group of miners from the others." Thanks to Priya's coaching, he knew how the game was played.

"It would embarrass the company if our actions were exposed." Valdeez looked directly into Dhiraj's eye. "Let's not forget it could ruin our careers."

Now it's 'our' careers. Dhiraj nodded, doing a poor job of holding back an expanding smile. "Shall we halt operations?" He felt obligated to go along with the charade, even if he knew the answer.

"No, increase pressure on the locals. Be discreet. Switch from breeding animals to entire herds." He pressed his hands onto the desk as if he were willing it to crash through the floor. "Damned scalers. I don't care what you do or how you do it. They must fold."

Growing rows of lights flashed on the comm console.

"Shut down all interplanetary connections. Nothing leaves this compound. Until I say otherwise, we are on lockdown. No exceptions. Increase security. Nobody leaves the premises. Do it now."

"They won't like it," Dhiraj said.

"I don't care. Deal with them however you see fit. Offer whatever it takes." Valdeez tapped off the comm link connection to Imani's office. "We cannot afford potential witnesses."

More like what 'Valdeez' cannot afford. I'm simply following your orders. "What do I say when they ask why? And they are going to ask." Dhiraj lowered his eyes, stymieing a smirk.

"Blame the scalers. They have an infection. We need to isolate everyone and take safety precautions. Whatever. Think up something. Increase recreational stipends. I don't care, but deal with it."

Dhiraj gathered the pieces of tattered cloth. "I'll get right on it. Shall I notify his family?"

"No, no leaks, and find that second miner." Valdeez paced before his desk. "And while you're at it, review all employee files. The Fed may be among them. When you find him, isolate him in the holding cell below."

"And if it's a woman?"

Valdeez's striking sideways glance was all the answer given.

*   *   *

JASMINE ENTERED HER apartment feeling as if she had been walking an emotional tightrope. With the MiPS burning behind, she balanced Luna's friendship with the threat she posed while trying to reach her father on the far side. "I have to know," she said to herself as she breached her father's home office for the second time.

She found the directive's electronic signature and systematically peeled back the layers to its source. It came as no surprise when she learned her father wrote it. He had to be involved. If not the author, then the one to implement it. Still, Xerxes had put him up to it. No wonder he was always upset, dealing with a financial crisis and a relentless flow of problems. So what if some Calcans lose a few animals? They will get compensated. In fact, the locals should be grateful. Xerxes has brought them out of the Dark Ages. If they work, they get a better life. *Papa and I return home, a win-win for everyone.*

Determined to be an asset in her father's life, Jasmine studied the Xerxes corporate world records and homed in on the workings of its inner circle. "So that's how it is," she said to herself. *This is the kind of information Papa will appreciate and what I need to bridge the distance between us. Not even a stutter can interfere with that.*

Feeling better than ever, Jasmine could not help wondering if it was the Calcans or the animals that bothered Luna so much. Two clockwise twists of her right hand and a pull of her left brought up Luna's personal history on-screen. Luna had been doing well in school, carried an after-school job, and still found time for extracurricular activities. All the things a university admittance board looks for in a candidate. While Jasmine had no interest in veterinary medicine, if things worked out, they might attend the same university next year and perhaps be roommates. Papa could arrange that.

While changing data points, Jasmine's fingers slid off the controls when a beep of her comm registered a signal. The planet's poles had shifted. Luna can call out, Jasmine thought with dread. Was she still within the compound, or had she already left? Ten blips later, the signal disappeared. The comm shook in her hand. Not long enough to send a message. Her heart beat down upon her stomach. Planetary poles were not supposed to revert like this? Or could they? With no time to spare, she closed the computer, intending to find out.

Down the halls, people voiced their dismay as they continually pressed their comm power buttons, shook, and stared, but nothing they did returned the outside signal.

Jasmine entered Imani's office with an exchange of nods. As usual, Imani maintained multiple conversations on her flashing panel of comm links. Her answers sounded the same. There had been a temporary shift, but comm links had not been restored. Out of politeness, Jasmine took a seat and rehearsed another conversation she imagined between herself and her father.

Imani looked up from her comm. "Did you say something?"

"I called ahead and left a message. He's expecting me," Jasmine said.

Imani muted the comm links. "I'm sure he's aware. But we're swamped right now. There's a lot going on."

"Please let him know I'm here. It's important."

As Imani raised a silent finger, asking her to hold, Jasmine walked straight for her father's office doors.

Imani dropped what she was doing and said, "Jazz, I could lose my job."

Two tall, lacquered oak barriers stood before Jasmine. Their ornate brass handles looked like mocking tongues sticking out, daring her to pass.

"He's got to eat sometime," Imani said. "Why don't you drop by with lunch, say, in a couple of rays?"

Jasmine released the handles and curled her fingers into fists.

*   *   *

LUNA WALKED PAST the otherwise unoccupied gate, only to be greeted by a flurry of people milling about across the road. Everyone at the market rushed exponentially faster than the day before. Rizzo looked to be conducting a brisk business. Techs and miners lined up anxiously before him, like at an ATM before a holiday. Without haggling, he robotically exchanged bills for plastic baggies.

Dust filled the air, kicked up by speeding vehicles. From what she could see across the road, market shelves emptied as fast as vendors could stock them. She stepped forward, coughed, and waved her hand across her face. Her shoulder pulled back as if mauled by a bear. Inches away, a dump truck flew by, honking its horn.

"Close one," the bear said in a throaty voice.

Luna placed her hand over hairy fingers and turned to see Ziggy's beaming face. "Thanks. That was a close one," she said, dusting herself off. "I thought Guardian Angels had wings."

"Not always." Ziggy rolled his shoulders. "Heads up where they drive on the opposite side of the road. Don't get flattened before you grow into those boots."

Behind them, security guards rushed to the gate, setting up a perimeter. Xerxes employees, laden with goods, walked past, while others, wanting to leave the complex, were prevented from leaving and directed to turn back.

Luna pointed over her shoulder. "What's that all about?"

"Word is, they're closing the gate. No one leaves. Looks like you and I are the last ones out." He pointed across the road and offered his elbow. "Shall we?" Arm in arm, the couple dodged across.

Safely on the other side, Ziggy asked. "Shopping or sightseeing?" He raised his hand, and a tuk-tuk magically appeared. "You're welcome to come with," he said, taking a seat and scooching over inside.

Luna could not help but think of how much Ziggy reminded her of her father. "No thanks. I've got my own wheels now," she yelled proudly over the sound of the tuk-tuk's engine. "I'd be willing to give you a ride, but I don't think we would make it."

Ziggy shrugged and tapped the driver on the shoulder. As the tuk-tuk drove off, Ziggy cupped his hand over his mouth, shouting, "Dan—sends his re—"

"What? I didn't catch that," Luna said. *Daniel is my father's name.* She thought she must have misheard.

In the parking area where she had left the bike, Nestor waved at her to look at something.

"*Ohenro*," she said.

Nestor's eyes sparkled at Luna's greeting. "Ah! *Ohenro*, Luna!"

Her jaw dropped as her eyes grew. Could she be mistaken?

This couldn't be the same bike. The one she dropped off was rusted, dented, and scraped.

"Yes, it's the same." He grinned so wide that the corners of his lips tested the boundaries of his cheeks. "It's missing a side panel. Maybe you should wait for a replacement," he teased.

"No way."

Her improvised helmet hung from the handlebar by a leather strap. The dent had been pounded out, the metal polished, and a liner placed inside. "Oh, my goodness. *Spakuhn. Spakuhn*, very much. How much do I owe you?" Luna pulled her wad of notes from a pants pocket.

"Kai," Nestor said, raising his hand. When she persisted, he shook his head. "Here, we do not charge the friends of friends." He mimicked putting on the helmet. "Go ahead, try it on."

Nestor must have garnered magic elves during the night to have gotten so much done in so short a time. She buckled the thick leather strap. *Helmet hair is a small price to pay for being safe.* "How in the world did you do it?" Now, her neck would not stiffen, holding her chin up. The polished inside lid reflected behind. Neat. A helmet with a rearview mirror built in.

He flicked his wrist, sending her on her way.

The first kick of the pedal awakened the primed engine. She tickled the throttle, and the muffler boomed. Nestor crossed his arms over his inflated chest. She let out the clutch and grabbed onto the grips. The rear tire spun, flinging gravel behind. *I could take on speeders on this.*

Heading for town, she shuffled her butt in the seat and noticed that her bottom had not complained. It must have been repadded. She weaved and leaned into corners, testing the tires' contact with the road. Checking the brakes, she squeezed the front grip and pressed her toe to the pedal, coming to a swift skidded stop. Unlike a speeder, this bike's speedometer's needle zipped like it never met a red line that it did not like.

In no time, she came upon Ziggy's tuk-tuk. "Did you say, 'Daniel,' as in my father?" she shouted over the noisy tuk-tuk's blaring exhaust. Ziggy cupped his hand to his ear and shrugged. He mouthed back words she did not understand. Another time, she thought with a wave. A squeeze of the throttle raised the front tire into a wheelie before the bike sped off.

Luna slowed as she approached town and drove up the clinic gangway. Spanish words uttered unflatteringly accompanied the sound of repeated kick-starts. Kai rested his foot on the pedal and shook his head in disgust. He reacted to her arrival without a response.

"Hello, Dr. Kai. It's me. I'm back. Check out the bike." He fiddled with his own motorcycle without turning around. Not the reaction she expected.

Reuben looked up from his spot, and Falafel rolled over, but Kai continued to pay her no notice.

"I've come back with your bike." She waited. *Maybe he can't hear me?* She spoke louder. "Do you have any patients today? I'd like to join you if that would be all right."

"Why are you working for Xerxes?"

Whiplashed by the question, she withdrew, not knowing how to answer. "I told you, work-study. So I can graduate and become a vet… like you." His body language provided no clues, and his silence became unsettling. What's made him so angry? Was it the bike? *Have I done something wrong?*

Reuben rested his head between his paws. His soulful eyes peeked up as if to ask the same questions.

"Don't you care about the company you keep?"

"How can I answer that?" What's got into him all of a sudden? Without saying anything more, she fumed. Her fingers fumbled as she tugged on the helmet's leather strap. She looked around for her shoes. "I'm sorry to have bothered you. You can have these back when you tell me where my shoes are."

"Got rid of them. They were stinking up the place." He turned to face her. "You still have that bowl on?"

Gardenia shuffled in her slot, taken aback.

"I'll cut this damned strap off if I have to," she said, rummaging among the tools on the bench. "Keep it, the boots, bike, whatever. They are all yours anyway." She worked the tin snips between the strap and her chin and got nowhere.

"How do I know you are who you say?"

"What?"

"You heard me. Answer the question."

"How am I supposed to prove who I am?" Why was he asking? Was this another test? Given the uncertainty, she asked herself, what would a pre-vet know? "Okay. Who else can recite that the product of uncertainty in position, times that of momentum, is greater than or equal to Planck's constant over four pi."

"You may know the exact position and how fast it's going, but not both at the same time. Heisenberg's Principle." He nodded to himself as if satisfied and said, "All right. Get in."

Reuben's ears pricked.

To whom is he talking? Seething through gritted teeth, she leaned down to take off her other boot when, without notice, her knee suddenly demanded attention. Too riled to comply with either, she readied herself to walk back barefoot. *I'll buy a pair of sandals along the way.*

"I had to be sure. I'm sorry. Keep the boots on." The bike

started on the first kick, and he extended his hand in an open invitation. "The helmet looks good on you," he said in a conceding voice.

Without her shoes and in no mood to argue, she wrangled alongside Reuben and, in a huff, wrapped her arms around her chest. *He needed to be sure of what?*

Reuben panted, urging them to get moving. Falafel watched, wagging his stubby tail with all the vigor it had to offer while Gardenia settled back in her throne.

Luna put on Reuben's goggles and found that her own fit better over the improvised helmet.

Kai steered the bike in the opposite direction of Xerxes. *Thank goodness. I'm not ready to go back.* She could not have been angrier, more confused, and also somehow relieved.

Reuben's ears and Kai's beard flapped in the breeze as he spoke lovingly to the bike. She recognized a few of the Spanish words.

"*Que Bonita, preciosa, linda, querida Roxana.*"

Chapter 12

Being cultured is not about how well you know your own, but the willingness to accept others.

—Unknown

TAURDENS GRAZED AIMLESSLY in the surrounding green hilly pastures. The road evened out, the engine hummed, and the bike's rhythmic rocking lulled. Reuben settled in, beckoning Luna to do the same. As if on cue, her eyelids drooped. Cares and worries blew away like the meadow breeze left in their wake.

The bike crested a hill. How long had she dozed? Her eyelid paused before raising. From afar, gray smokestacks and spinning turbines imposed upon the idyllic scene. The lurch of a pothole further interrupted her trance by causing her leg to tap against the sidecar's inner wall. Her aroused knee called out. Reuben turned to face her. Large, sympathetic, brown eyes filled his goggle lenses. His googly expression projected calmness and told her that everything would be all right. Her fingers shifted from the edge of her thigh to behind his ear. She was back on track.

The bike braked suddenly, sliding into a skid. Luna clutched the lopsided canid with one hand while holding on with the other. Reuben wasted no time before launching into another one of his 'we're here' frantic routines.

"D-duck," Kai said, doubling down on the Ds.

The bike careened into a row of shrubs. Despite wearing goggles, she closed her eyes, wrapped her arms around Reuben, and covered his head with her own. Branches scraped along the sidecar. Instead of crashing, the bike plowed through shrubbery onto a bumpy dirt road.

"Eyes up, heads down," Kai said, maintaining a warp-speed twist on the throttle. The turn incited Reuben further. His whining and shenanigans intensified. The next pothole sent his shrills an octave higher.

She wrestled him into a bear hug. "Settle down."

He subtly signaled submission by waning his whining and limiting his frenzy to an occasional tremor.

Lining the driveway, the occasional fence post stood out, surrounded by overgrown grass and weeds. Though splintered and peeling paint, they maintained their positions gallantly: tired sentries, relics of a bygone era, having endured while their fallen comrades withered by the wayside.

At the top of a hill, a rickety, hunchbacked old man dressed in a tattered suit greeted them in front of a dilapidated house. He waved a scaly hand, urging them closer. The scene was right from a *Mother Goose* poem. "There was a crooked man, and he walked a crooked mile. He bought a crooked cat that caught a crooked mouse. They all lived together in a little crooked house."

Were they here to see the cat, the mouse, or was it a combination of the two, a camouse?

Luna threw her hands up, grateful for the bike to come to a stop. Meanwhile, Reuben wasted no time before he scrambled out. On firm ground, he returned to his amiable self like a canid Jekyll and Hyde and commenced his inspection of the premises. He trotted off as if his previous behavior had been a terrible misunderstanding and was best left forgotten.

While Kai exchanged greetings with the Calcan, Luna scanned the premises. There was not that much to see. As the two men conversed, she nodded along at what appeared to be the appropriate times. The client's straight, gray hair matched the color of his scraggly beard. Pale scales filled the ruts left by rows of wrinkles. His suit, though neat and clean, bore patches and fraying cuffs. The bleached material had outworn its intended use.

Without warning, the man's open, scaly hand came toward her.

Unsure what to make of it, she hesitated.

Kai blinked.

Four swollen, bent fingers and a knobby thumb extended.

What am I waiting for?

His hand retracted.

She reached out with both hands and took it. As she shook his hand, her cheeks puffed, and her smile broadened. *My first physical contact with an alien.* His hand was firm, and though the palm was rough, the greeting was the same. He returned her grasp and shook.

"*Ohenro,*" she said.

"*Ah, ohenro,*" he replied and rumbled off a multitude of words.

She put up her hands and glanced at Kai for help. "Whoa! That's about all I know."

"He may not understand, but he hears you just fine," Kai said, standing back with his arms crossed like a referee, with no call to make.

She could tell Kai was pleased. Though his lips did not budge, the corners of his eyes betrayed the straight face. His crow's feet were dancing.

"That's about all I know." With outstretched open hands, she addressed the old man. She pointed to herself like a movie Jane talking to Tarzan and enunciated the two syllables. "Luna."

The old man nodded and repeated, "*Loo-Nah.*" He pointed to himself. "*Sachi.*" A come-along wave urged them to follow. He mimicked an exaggerated sneeze and, with pouted lips and soulful eyes, pointed around the house. "*Gina.*"

The patient looked nothing like the animals in the *Mother Goose* poem. Taller than a cow, with pink and black markings, Gina's cigar-shaped body ended in a long, thick tail. Limp mammary glands extended off her sides. She rested on her belly with four outstretched legs. Doe eyes, long, curly lashes, and a Muppet mouth accented her wedge-shaped head.

Gina sneezed. Thick, yellow mucus dripped from her nostrils. Ready with a handkerchief, Sachi scurried over and wiped her nose, looking as pitiful as his pet surely felt.

The love and attention paid to Gina brought back memories of the barn animals at school. *Was Daisy getting carrots? Did the other horses and Trulee miss her? Would Bucephalus give up sheltered stable life to spend one day with this old man?*

Kai walked around the patient, starting at the head and working around to the tail, he looked, listened, squeezed, and pressed. He pulled out a small, rubber-tipped mallet and what looked like a section of wooden rib from the back of a chair. *Tap tap* came the sound between Gina's ribs.

"What are you doing?"

"Percussion. The sound comes from…." He rapped the stick with the mallet along the length of Gina's chest and cocked an eyebrow. "What's that remind you of?" *Tap Tap Tap.*

"Sounds like a drum."

"Exactly. Think of the lungs as two air-filled drums." He continued backward, and just before the end of the ribs, the sound changed to *thud. Thud.*

"And that tells you?"

"Density of the lungs. Size of the heart, liver, and spleen."

Her eyebrows raised. "Just from?"

He pressed the back of his hand against Gina's ears and continued alongside the rest of her body.

"Why are you using the back of your hand?"

"More sensitive to temperature." He nodded to himself from time to time during the exam, much as he did when looking over a bike, but without having to stop to check the oil.

Gina sneezed and made an apologetic face. Sachi was right there with a handkerchief. Kai gently squeezed her throat, and the oversized lizard coughed. With a stethoscope over Gina's chest, Kai hovered over her heart, nodded again, and offered the earpiece to Luna. She recalled seeing an instrument like this on a museum website. She imitated placing the curved metal tips in her ears. She listened to the repeating '*pee-shoo*' beats and nodded. Then Kai took the end of the stethoscope and placed it on his chest. '*Lub dub.*'

Freshman biology came back. "The first sound, systole, is the closing of the—"

"Yes, yes. You have listened to two different heartbeats. They both pump blood, but they sound and circulate differently. Correct?" Before she could reply, he continued, "Amphibian and mammalian hearts differ—"

I know this one. "In that, the amphibian heart has three chambers instead of—"

"Okay. Which is better? Which would you rather have?"

Nicoleta Dabija
Sachi & Gina

The best has to be my own, was the first thing that came to mind. "The four-chambered one I've got?" Luna said, realizing she answered the question with a question.

His eye squinted. "So you're saying more is better?" Kai had that 'better get this right the first time' look again.

She let out an exasperated sigh. *Another trick question?*

"Four chambers are better than three?" She wondered if four was wrong but decided that was her answer. "I guess so." It sounded less convincing than intended.

"So if more is better, a darker pigmented skin is an improvement. Rough scales are preferable for sun protection and abrasions. Do I understand you correctly?"

"Yes." *Where is he going with this,* "Maybe."

"What if you were drowning? Then what?"

"The amphibian three-chambered heart. Because—"

"If you know that much, then you understand."

She did not get what skin and hearts had to do with anything. While she tried to decipher what she supposedly understood, Kai turned to Sachi.

"*She's been off her food for the last couple of sauls,*" Sachi said, sobbing. He related what the neighbors were saying about Gina. "*Since she stopped producing milk, they say she's a monster... should be done away with. Please help her, Doc. She's all I've got.*"

Kai squeezed Sachi's shoulder and looked him in the eye. "*There will be no such thing. She's not going anywhere.*"

"*She never hurt anybody, Doctor.*" Sachi raised his arm to cover his face.

"*I believe Gina has a cold and, with your proper care, should get better soon. But we have to keep her warm. What do you have to cover her?*"

Sachi nodded and, without saying another word, hobbled back as fast as his bowed legs could carry him. During Sachi's absence, Kai explained his findings while Luna petted the dejected patient.

"Gina is a jiliander, an herbivorous amphibian with reptilian skin and bovine, specifically dairy cow characteristics," Kai said.

"How is such a thing possible?" she asked, shaking her head.

"Hybrid mixes are rare. No one knows why this happens only on this part of the planet, but attempts to transport jilianders and other livestock have failed. They cannot survive anywhere else. Isolated, the way we are, word of their existence has not gotten out. For the rest of the universe, they do not exist." Kai scanned the open pasture. "Where has that canid disappeared to?"

"I saw him take off down the driveway," Luna said, scratching Gina's forehead.

Sachi teetered out with blankets enough to outfit a barracks. With outstretched arms, he balanced his tower off to the side one way, leaned around to see the other, and, all the while, half-blindly tapped his foot before taking each step.

Luna moved closer to help.

"*Aphloo.*" Bluish-green snot exploded from Gina's sneeze. The colors, arranged in a kindergartner's palette of green and yellow, added a glistening twinkle to the right side of Luna's otherwise unremarkable cream-colored shirt. Gina swung her head from side to side as if looking for someone to turn to. Hearing his pet's distress, Sachi peeked around the bundle, dropped his arms, and scurried inside.

"Ugh, yuck, ew," Luna said, flicking off the thick, slimy residue. "Gesundheit. That was disgusting." She raised a shoulder to wipe her neck and avoided getting any of it on her hands.

Kai pulled a glass slide from a pocket, slid it across Gina's nose, and held it to the suns.

Sachi returned, waving a folded, starched, embroidered handkerchief. He gestured, using it to wipe his face, and offered it for her to use.

The loving detail placed into every stitch of the elaborate needlepoint impressed Luna. "*Spakuhn,*" she said, accepting the handkerchief. She hesitated to use it. When Sachi turned to retrieve the blankets, she followed, tucking the hanky inside her clean cuff, and used the unscathed parts of her shirt to wipe herself off.

"Avoiding accidents applies not only to abscesses. At least you're making progress." In a lilting voice, Kai slapped his thigh and said, "You've got the right boots on."

"What's with Gina?" she asked, showing less concern about her appearance than for the patient. "Sachi seems really worried."

"Gina has a cold made worse by her amphibian difficulty regulating body temperature. However, with medication and Sachi's nursing, she should be back to her old self in no time."

Together, they helped Sachi bring what appeared to be every blanket in the house. Luna carried a down comforter, thinking it probably came from Sachi's bed. If he had a pillow big enough, he would have brought that out, too. They spread blankets over Gina like they were throwing tablecloths over a tall picnic table. Gina closed her eyes and rolled her shoulders. She obviously enjoyed being pampered.

Kai explained that the local pharmacist would drop by with her medication. Sachi nodded and appeared relieved. Covered fore and aft, Gina's tail thumped. Reuben appeared beside them and pulled the blanket over a partially exposed spot. He barked and pawed at his handiwork, praising a job well done.

Sachi reached into his pocket, but before he could remove his hand, Kai shook his head and placed his hand over Sachi's.

Luna offered to return the unsoiled handkerchief.

Sachi raised his hands, politely refusing, and gestured for her to keep it.

"Please translate," Luna said. "It's beautiful. I can't accept."

"His wife made it before she passed," Kai said. "It's more special than words can convey. That is why it is so important to him that you have it."

Luna skimmed the embroidery along the handkerchief's edges and held it close. Then she reached out, hugged the old man, and kissed his cheek.

Sachi waved her off, holding back what appeared to be a burst of tears. He shook off the emotional display, distracting himself by fussing over Gina. He retucked the nooks and crannies, even in places that did not need them. Gina let out a sigh, closed her eyes, and grinned with her wide mouth. Sachi hummed while Gina harmonized by cooing.

Before getting on the bike, Kai rearranged his coat pockets. Always the one to get in first, Reuben suddenly froze. His nose twitched. He ruffed in a huff. The source of his concern raced toward them. A middle school-aged Calcan girl riding a scooter stopped in front of Kai. Brush scrapes marred her Calcan arms and face. She sputtered her words between breaths, suspiciously keeping an eye on Luna as she spoke.

Kai nodded. "We're off," he said, donning his goggles. Luna squeezed in before Reuben had a chance to forget they shared a seat. Kai filled her in. "Anu's family operates an aarmadark ranch. Their animals have suddenly taken ill with unusual symptoms." Reuben's nose, like a car hood ornament, pointed full ahead.

Cool, more weird animals. If Luna had to guess, they were off to see dark-colored armadillos.

ON THE MAIN road toward Xerxes, Anu turned off onto a gravel road bordering a field of sheep-sized animals with long, rounded noses. It did not require a specialty in alien animal medicine to know that something was amiss. Most of the animals stood stunned, frozen in their tracks, while others looked to have keeled over. The three members of Anu's family hovered over a stricken animal, trying to get it to right itself.

Reuben did not hesitate. He jumped out and began his routine inspection. Kai cleared his throat and gave him 'the Ms. Watkins look.' The disillusioned canid trudged back, holding his head, ears, and tail down. He got back in, pressed his chin against the dash, and sulked.

"How long have the animals been like this?" Kai asked the aar-

madark rancher.

"Less than a ray," the father said. *"We sent Anu to find you as soon as we saw something was wrong."*

The animals appeared dazed. Luna followed as Kai stepped toward the closest aarmadark. He examined the animal, nodded, and, when finished, muttered as if conferring with himself. He walked the field and occasionally stopped to look at a particular plant. On closer inspection, he plucked it, spread its leaves, squeezed it between his fingers, sniffed, and, if having passed the previous tests, touched it to his lips.

These animals were dealing with something a lot more serious than Gina's cold, Luna thought. First off, there was no crud coming from their noses, and Gina did not have strands of saliva drooling from her mouth. These animals were not sneezing either. Some struggled to breathe. In fact, their blank stares and pin-sized pupils made them look like armor-coated, oversize stuffed toys. Whatever caused this, they all had the same thing.

Kai returned to the sidecar, pulling out glass tubes and a rubber stoppered bottle from a storage compartment.

So he doesn't keep everything in his pockets, Luna thought with a smirk. "I get the armadillo part, but with their armor plating and varied colors, I'm not sure where the dark comes from."

"Aarmadark is spelled with four a's," Kai said. "The other half comes from aardvark." From a glass bottle, he withdrew a striking red-colored liquid into a needled syringe.

"Wow. Same color as Ail cake."

"Distilled from the fruit. Calcans use it as a universal antidote." He demonstrated the technique, squeezed the syringe contents back into the bottle, and handed them over. "Your turn."

The syringe felt unwieldy in her hands while the exposed

needle tip threatened. She juggled the upside-down bottle in one hand while pulling the syringe plunger with the other. Xena's data tutorial had nothing compared to Kai's vigilant gaze. Her hands might as well have been asleep for the time it took to repeat the process.

"Fill the syringe more than halfway, slowly squeeze out the bubbles, and stop at the 1.5 ml line." Satisfied with the amount, he moved to the closest, sickest animal. "If this is going to work, we will find out soon enough."

Anu's father and brother held the animal upright while her mother held the aarmadark's head in her lap. Anu pulled the patient's sticky tongue and twisted it upside down.

While preparing the next syringe, Luna asked, "Why the tongue?"

Kai guided the needle into the slippery vein and pushed the plunger. "Ease of access. The armor plating covers all other accessible veins," Kai said. As the plunger slowly emptied, the thin-walled blood vessel brightened. Everyone held their breath.

The seconds passed. It seemed to take an eternity before the patient opened its eyes and took a deep breath. The aarmadark attempted to raise its head and snorted before pawing its hooves at the ground. It let out a 'bleat' and, with their help, rested on its chest before jumping up and scurrying away.

"What do you think caused it?"

"A central nervous system depressant. Probably a chemical poison. I have not come across any toxic plants."

Kai raised his eyes as if calculating in his head. "Based on the number of affected animals and the amount of antidote left," Kai said, "at this rate, there is enough for sixteen more."

"And the rest?"

Kai scowled. "The treatment will be rationed until gone."

Luna chewed her lip while Anu's family presented the next patient. Kai raised the emptied syringe over his shoulder. "I could ride back for more," Luna said.

"The antidote requires a lengthy distillation process. This is all there is." Kai's fingers reached back. "Still with us? Next syringe."

Careful of the needle, she exchanged syringes like a surgical nurse trading scalpels. "Could Blue Glass, I mean an amphetamine, work as an antidote?"

Kai pressed the syringe plunger. "It might, sure. Counter the poison's effect long enough to..." He looked over his shoulder at her through squinted eyes. Luna handed Anu the bottle and syringe. "Amphetamines? Where do you intend on—"

A fumbled apology blurted as she turned, grabbed her helmet, and dashed for the scooter. Getting it started was almost the same; however, the soft wet grass and loose gravel made steering and keeping her balance a lot more challenging. While a speeder hovered over uneven land surfaces, the bike squirmed and wiggled out of the ranch and onto the side road.

Anu, her family, and Reuben stood curiously, scrutinizing her hightailed exit.

*　*　*

AS TWELVE HUNDRED rays approached, Valdeez ran his fingers through his hair, checked his attire, and straightened his desk. The two doors leading to his office were secured. This call was too important to be interrupted. Besides, the fact communications had been purposely cut was on a need-to-know basis.

ON THE OTHER side of the main office door, Jasmine realized that if she could not get through Imani, she had no business attempting to stand up to her father. "Imani, you've been w-working for my father for a long time." Jasmine had Imani's full attention. The comm links flashed in protest.

"Yes, I have." She frowned. "Why do you ask?"

"You like working for him?"

Imani's casual tone switched to full alert. "Of course." She shifted in her chair. "Why do you ask?" The unattended calls remained unanswered.

Jasmine inhaled deeply and flexed her shoulders. "Sing the words before you speak," she told herself. "Was there a polar shift, or have communications been blocked?"

Imani hesitated. Her eyes narrowed as she sat back in her chair.

"Forget I asked. You've confirmed what I suspected."

Imani looked as if she had seen a ghost.

"But answer me this. Between the two of us, would you describe my father as being a reasonable man?"

Chapter 13

Necessity is the mother of invention.

—Plato

LUNA HAD TO act fast if the remaining aarmadarks were going to stand a chance. While her bike would have been faster, Anu's scooter on an open road would have to do. She leaned into the wind, filled with worry and dread. Déjà vu brought back memories of that rainy afternoon when rushing to Heiman's office, her mind filled with 'what if' questions. *What if Rizzo isn't there? What if he sold out? Would there be enough to treat the herd? What if it didn't work?* With the throttle maxed out, all she could do was hope for the best.

Her worst fears became real when she reached the Xerxes gate and found it, like the road, alarmingly deserted. The market was empty. The dust had settled. Only the turbine blades hummed their monotonous winged whir. She hopped off the scooter and hustled through the closest gravel-strewn aisle as fast as her clunky boots could take her. Searching stall by stall, she called out Rizzo's name. At the far end, she heard voices and took off in a galoshes-hobbled sprint.

At the far end, a dozen Calcans gathered in a corner. As Luna approached, they stopped mid-sentence. She scanned the Calcan faces, and, to her dismay, Rizzo was not among them. With her arms clutched to her sides, she heaved deeply before saying, "*Ohenro.*"

"*Ohenro,*" they replied in unison.

"Rizzo?" she asked, pointing to the market over her shoulder. "Would someone please tell me where I can find him?"

Muted, quizzical looks replied.

She repeated the name multiple times, using her best impressions of a Calcan accent. "Rizzo?" *I'm not returning empty-handed.* "Does anyone speak Terran?"

A young Calcan half raised his hand. He stepped timidly forward, prodded on by the others, as he shyly looked side to side. He gathered himself, stood straight, and said, "One, two, three, ten, twenty. You want to buy?"

Luna declined with a shake of her head and a wave. "No, thank you."

The young Calcan turned to the others for help.

She unstrapped her helmet and patted the back of her head. "The man with the bun in his hair. Blue crystals. Rizzo? Blue Glass."

Shrugs and blank stares responded.

She repeated Rizzo's name louder and caught herself flailing her hands as if that would help convey her meaning. *They must think I'm crazy.* "Nestor? Do you know where I can find him?"

Eyes brightened, and heads nodded enthusiastically. "*Tay-ya, tay-ya. Nestor tay-ya,*" they said excitedly. Everyone had their own idea as to the motorcycle mechanic's whereabouts. Arguments broke out, with fingers pointing every which way.

Great. Nobody knows where he is. A quick poll of pointed fingers directed to the opposite end of the market. "Over here?" She pointed to an unchecked aisle. Her Calcan entourage followed.

A hand-painted wooden bowl thrust toward her. "Ten," its vendor urged.

She brushed it aside. Another Calcan stepped in front and pointed in the opposite direction. Nestor was nowhere to be seen.

At the end of a far aisle, she found Rizzo huddled beneath a vendor's stall counter, squatting on a stool with a smoldering pipe in his lap and an ornate box by his side. He stared blankly, unaware of her presence and the eyes upon him. Dilated, black pupils replaced the color of his eyes, leaving a faint auburn rim. Rizzo, it seems, sampled his own wares.

Luna leaned over the counter. "It's me, the girl with the bong," she said, raising her voice. "Hello." Getting no response, she waved her hand in front of his bleary gaze. "Got any Blue Glass?"

His eyes rolled, and his smile grew. His expression was like a sleepy child's face getting up on Christmas morning. He put aside the pipe and teasingly toyed with the box lid before flicking it open. Bags of blue crystals filled the bottom half of the box. His smile morphed into a satisfied smirk. "Now you come to Rizzo. You like what Rizzo offers. Yes?"

She squeezed the countertop, resisting the urge to reach for the box. "Yes. Please, it's very important." *Swell. Nice way to come off nonchalant. This is going to cost more than a tuk-tuk ride.*

A crowd gathered. A tug on her sleeve urged her away. She shook it off.

"It always is." Rizzo's eyelids threatened to close as he pulled a plastic bag from the box. "For you, 100," he said, dangling the bag from his fingertips. He muttered to himself and laughed hysterically.

Calcan voices rattled in her ears.

Luna stepped away as if giving herself time to consider the price. *I can't leave empty-handed.* She turned to face Rizzo. "Not many buyers," she said casually.

"Perhaps not now, but they come back. Rizzo has patience. Rizzo can wait. Can you?"

She snatched the bag from his fingers, held it up, and shook it in the light. "How much for the whole box?"

Grumbling echoed behind.

Rizzo sat upright like he'd been zapped by a cattle prod. "Ninety-five," he said with a straight face. "Each."

"Oh, come on." Reflexively, she patted her pocket. If it cost that much, she had enough for almost ten bags. If she weighed about as much as an aarmadark and it took one bag to treat each one, that would not be nearly enough. "Bulk discount. Best price," she countered. Her eyes wandered. Doing her best impression of a disinterested customer, she shrugged and turned around. A few steps later, she realized walking away was not a price she was willing to pay.

Rizzo raised a brow.

A woman's hand tugged on her arm. Someone pulled on her shirt.

Luna pressed against the counter and leaned over.

Rizzo sifted through the box. "Four thousand."

"Your English is very good."

"Thank you. I have learned a long time. I hear you speak our language."

"I've picked up a few words," Luna said nonchalantly. "You never know when another language can come in handy, like *ohenro*, *spakuhn*, and… Oh, and how do you say, 'need this?'"

"*Shi-yao-tay*," Rizzo blurted, then checked himself. "Why you want so much?"

She closed her eyes and took a deep breath. *Ask the right question. Negotiate or go for it?*

When she did not answer straight away, he cocked his

head and squinted. "You want to work for Rizzo? Sell for me inside?"

Luna turned around and raised the bag to the crowd. "*Kai, shi-yao-toe. Shi-yao-tay, Kai.* Kai needs this." With looks of concern, the Calcans voiced among themselves. Discontent required no translation. If ever there was a time for Kai's name to work its charm, this was it. Luna waved the bag and pointed to the pasture. "*Anu, shi-yao-tay.*"

Rizzo winced. He did not appear to like where this was headed. All attention had shifted to him. And it wasn't the type of scrutiny he craved. "How much you got?" he asked, fuming.

She removed the notes from her pocket and turned the others inside out.

Rizzo grabbed the money out of her hand and thumbed through the bills. "Not enough. Three thousand more."

"I know it's not what you asked, but I can throw in my bike. The one Nestor fixed. It runs great." She may have had him over a barrel, but the aarmadarks could not wait. "It's not for me," Luna said. She spoke louder. "*Kai. Anu shi-yao-tay.*" Disgruntled voices behind her rose. She crossed her arms with a grin. "I'm going to hang around, follow you if I have to, and nag until you agree."

"Where is the bike?"

"I'll bring it as soon as I can." She took off the bracelet and held it out. "Okay? And trade you this for the pipe?"

Rizzo shook his head 'no,' while holding the box and pipe to his chest. "Pipe not for sale." He put the bracelet to his ear, shook it, and tossed it back. "What else?"

She patted herself down and raised her helmet. "I'll throw this in too."

"I have no use for pots. What else?"

"That's all I got. Please." Luna looked back at the crowd and raised the plastic bag for the Calcans to see. "*Shi-yao-tay Kai.*"

"Go." He reluctantly released his grip on the box.

"You won't need it," she said, tugging on the pipe. "I'll bring it back with the bike."

He let go. "Leave before I change my mind. And then, never come back. I do not want to see you again."

Luna did not need to be told twice. She sped off for the scooter, with the box, pipe, and helmet dangling from its strap while shouting, "*Spakuhn,*" over her shoulder.

*   *   *

ABSOLUTE SILENCE. ALL the doors to Valdeez's office were locked, and his internal messages were placed on hold. Having given Imani strict instructions that he was not to be disturbed, Valdeez straightened the few items on his desk and prepared for his conference comm. In a last-minute check, he straightened his cuffs, brushed off his suit, and flicked off a piece of lint. Promptly at twelve hundred rays, he sat erect in his custom leather chair and faced the wall screen. He opened a secure line, and the monitor filled with Council members seated at a conference table. They did not look pleased.

"We have reviewed your data," the CEO said, scrolling through his device. "You realize your future with this company depends on resolving the issue before us. While you have our full confidence and support, we will not hesitate to find a replacement if this post proves too much of a burden."

OUTSIDE HER FATHER'S office reception door, Jasmine did an about-face and tugged on the handles. "Open it," she said.

"Jazz, you can't. He's busy at the moment," Imani said.

"Open it." 'No' was no longer an option. "Do it."

"Jasmine, be reasonable. I could lose my job."

Jazz did not need to huff and puff to take on the persona of the Big Bad Wolf. "Do it, or I'll have you fired myself." In Jazz's version of *The Three Little Pigs*, wolves do not ask to be let inside. This wolf had a key.

Imani dragged her hand toward the security door lock as if her job, indeed her future, depended on what she did next.

VALDEEZ MAINTAINED HIS poker face, refusing to be intimidated. "Have I ever let you down?" The main door lock buzzed. His gaze slipped toward the reception door but otherwise disguised his irritation. The doors opened. Jazz marched through and stood by her father's side.

Jazz smiled at the screen and said, "C-cut the call, Papa," out of the side of her mouth.

"Get out, Jasmine," he whispered without moving his lips. "Leave now." Her presence warranted no more than a blink while he maintained his focus on the monitor.

On-screen, Council members leaned forward for a better view.

Valdeez did not so much as twitch in his seat as if that would show a loss of control. His flared nostrils, readymade fists, and glare may not have been evident on-screen but did bear down upon her teenage soul. She shuddered at what he might do if she came any closer. He may not breathe fire, but Jazz could feel the heat.

"No," she said, folding her arms defiantly, keeping her smile. "I'm not going anywhere until we talk." This time, she was going to be heard. A stutter was of no consequence.

The on-screen faces looked alarmed. Heads turned to one

another, and voices murmured.

Overheard by everyone, "If he can't handle his own daughter—" a female voice said.

When her father continued to ignore her, Jazz stood in front of him, just out of reach, with her back to the screen.

Council members peered to the side of their cameras, angling for a better view.

Valdeez stretched his neck to see around her, doing his best to maintain contact with the Council. While he concealed his emotion from them, she could hear him grind his teeth. Jasmine stepped closer, putting herself within his reach, effectively blocking his view. Instead of pushing her away, he stood, apologized to the Council, and abruptly canceled the session. "What's gotten into you?" He raised a finger and pointed it in her face.

Her eyes rose beyond the finger and met his glare. "Good one, Papa. Nice way to save face."

"I'll have you—"

"What?" she interrupted. "Neutralized as a potential witness while you continue your animal slaughter?"

His face and ears turned red. "How did you..." he blustered, then stammered.

"Find out?" She completed his sentence.

"Well, how did you?" His eyes shifted from side to side. "Tell me. Was it the new girl who put you up to this?" His eyes shot to the connecting reception door.

Without turning to follow his gaze, she said, "Yes, Papa, I closed the door. The fewer people that know about this, the better. Some things are best kept between us."

He flopped into his chair.

As if she could read his mind, she posed the next question. "If I know, who else knows, too?"

"Well?" he asked, holding his breath.

Within the cube's confined four walls, the insect flapped its wings.

*   *   *

KAI AND ANU'S family wound their way through a third of the field and came upon two aarmadarks, side by side, with rolled-back eyes and distended tongues. Kai scavenged the last drops of antidote, barely reaching the first line of the syringe. A decision had to be made.

"*This one is worse off than the other,*" Anu's father said, holding a younger, darker-colored animal's head in his arms. "*Doctor, which one do you want next?*"

"*The younger.*" Kai flipped the tongue and injected the contents. He flushed the syringe with the patient's blood and reinjected the contents. They stood back and, with nothing else to do, watched and prayed. Both animals' chests barely moved. Their tongues changed gradually from pink to lavender. Seconds turned to minutes. Anu's parents turned their heads.

Kai extended the younger aarmadark's neck. He pressed two hands rhythmically over the animal's heart. "*Yi yih, yi yih.*" After sixty counts, he leaned over and checked the tongue. The color stayed the same. After the third sequence, he closed the animal's mouth and puffed breaths into its snout. Anu's mother took Kai's place over the heart. "*Yi yih, yi yih,*" she repeated. Anu and her brother followed along with the older animal.

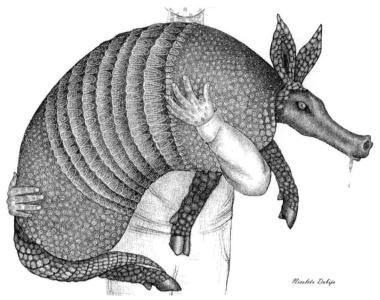

Aarmadark

After what seemed an eternity, the younger aarmadark gasped and twitched, struggling to clear its throat. Its eyes gradually opened. It took a breath and let out a pathetic bleat. Everyone sprang to help the animal right itself. On unsteady legs, it stumbled. Smiles perked until their attention turned to the remaining aarmadarks lying about the field.

BY THE TIME Luna reached the farm, all the remaining untreated animals lay on their sides. With the treasure stuck under her arm, she could not reach the hand brake in time and ended up taking the turn at speed. In the gravel curve, the rear tire slid. Its tire grooves clawed for grip on the uneven surface. One-handed, she pushed the handlebar grip; the bike over-corrected, pulled, straightened, and scrambled onto the field. Feet away from the treatment area, she stomped the brakes and skidded to a stop. Not bothering with the kick-stand, the scooter dropped beneath her.

"Got it," she said, opening the lid. "Crystallized ampheta-mine. Gotta be worth a try."

Without saying a word, Kai removed a tube of gel from a pocket and applied it to their hands. While Luna rubbed the evaporating goo around her fingers, the family continued doing CPR. Kai picked out a plastic bag like a pharmacist, filling a prescription.

"Administration, wind direction, and dosing are going to make this tricky," Kai said, all the while translating. "Getting any part of this wrong could have fatal consequences."

Maybe it sounds different in Calcan, Luna thought, but the edge in Kai's voice came off sounding like a rocket countdown. 'Ladies and gentlemen, we are ready for blast-off.' The aarmadark's nose and mouth were threaded through the pipe to form a tight seal.

Maybe Rizzo won't mind trading the taste of aarmadark breath for Orange Slide?

"Tap a pinch into the bowl," Kai said, stepping to the side. "We'll see soon enough." Before Luna opened the bag, the pipe extinguished. "Chest compression is not providing enough air to keep it lit."

While Anu's father went about relighting the pipe, Luna stepped away. Approaching Kai's bike, Reuben sat up with his ears perked. "Not yet." She twisted off the horn, and with every tug on the rubber bulb, it sounded like a congested goose. *He-yonk.* She handed it over to Kai, who immediately understood, attached the bulb over the pipe's access port, and squeezed.

The pipe smoldered, and when satisfied on which side to stand, Luna tapped a pinch of crystals into the bowl.

"Easy," Kai said. "We don't want to extinguish the em-bers."

Luna balanced the bag's opening over the port and gave the bag a tap, ever mindful of the breeze. A faint puff of blue billowed from the pipe's bowl. With the animal's head held upwind, they tried again, in sync, with Anu's mother releasing the chest and Anu squeezing the bulb. *He-yonk.* They watched and waited.

"Another pinch," Kai said, and the sequence repeated.

The older aarmadark responded slowly. Slower than those who had received the injection. But its eyelids fluttered, and its eyes twitched and eventually opened. The recuperation process repeated with a bleat and a struggle to get away.

With everyone aware of the wind's changing direction, they moved through the stricken animals. Kai held the bong and judged the amount by the animal's need; Luna dosed the crystals, Anu and her mother worked on CPR as a team, while her father and brother moved on to the next one. Between aarmadarks, Luna stretched from her crouched stance to watch the recovered animals graze.

Kai turned to the bike and whistled.

Reuben jumped out. "Away," Kai said. Reuben barked as he drove the feeding aarmadarks to the opposite corner of the field.

"What's that all about?" Luna asked. "Why is he herding them? They've recovered."

Kai blinked with a sigh. "I believe the water is the source of the problem."

Luna gasped and started to speak, but what was there to say?

The last aarmadark, found alive, lay at the pond's edge. It could barely keep its nose out of the water and had become too waterlogged to lift. It was rolled over and placed on its chest. Kai raised the aarmadark's front leg and checked its armpit for a pulse. Luna rummaged through the empty bags and scrounged for the few remaining crystals. They repeated the process, willing the pipe to keep burning. The blue puffs turned fainter, along with the animal's chance for survival.

The pipe extinguished. The chest compressions continued. Seconds turned to minutes before the patient started to show any signs of life. It raised its lids and sucked a breath through its mouth. Everyone pitched in and hefted the patient out of the muck.

Another one saved. Luna looked at herself. She could not remember when she had been so dirty—her shirt, pants, and boots were covered in mud—or felt so good. She knew it showed on her face and shrugged it off with a grin. Glances from Anu and her family confirmed with affirming nods. There would be laundry to do. Kai, on the other hand, looked like he had just come from a stroll in the park. How did he manage to keep his clothes so clean?

While Kai collected samples from the pond, the family returned silently, holding their heads down. She looked at them, confused, but said nothing. Only when handed a moist towel, did Luna reply with a somber, '*spakuhn*.' Kai joined them, placing the test tubes in his pocket. Anu's mother held her hand to her heart while Anu looked up at him with soft, glowing eyes. Her father and brother shook his hand and grasped his elbow. Their unspoken gratitude felt more effective than words could express. No wonder the mention of Kai's name brought so much attention. *Someday, I'd like to know what that feels like.*

Anu's mother spoke to her daughter. Anu replied by cupping her hand over her mother's ear and then reaching out and putting her arms around Luna's waist. The mother faced Luna and took a deep breath. The lady's lips struggled around the unnatural sounds. "Tank cue."

"You're welcome," Luna said, reciprocating Anu's hug. She glanced at Kai for something more to say. When none came, she left it at that.

Waving their farewells, Luna asked, "Why is everyone so glum? You saved most of them."

Kai started the bike. "We suspect the water has been poisoned."

"What'll that mean?"

"They will have to get rid of the animals. Eventually, abandon their home."

The bike's transmission kicked up a gear, and the engine growled.

The bummer of it all left Luna feeling like scrunching down to the bottom of her seat while Reuben's nose pointed the way with his chin propped on the sidecar's edge.

Chapter 14

A time to weep and a time to laugh; a time to mourn and a time to dance.

—Ecclesiastes 3:4 *Holy Bible:* King James Version

UPON ARRIVING AT the clinic courtyard, Kai handed over the test tubes and, without turning off the engine, said, "Take these inside, please." He got off the bike and bent down, squinting as if memorizing the position of every nut, screw, and bolt. His fingers hovered over the carburetor, ready to adjust the moment it misfired.

"What is it? What's wrong?" Luna asked, clutching the tubes in her hands.

Taken aback, he grinned as if caught coming too close to the Crown Jewels in a Do Not Touch display. "Have you noticed that small engines behave differently around you? Since you arrived, *Roksha* has never run so well." He held his hands behind his back, tiptoeing around the bike lest he disrupt her Feng Shui.

"Now that you mention it, since Nestor transformed my bike, not only does it run better, but it is more maneuverable than any speeder I've ever ridden. In fact, better than the bikes featured in the game, Biker Warrior." While the bike held Kai's attention, Luna used the moment to explore the secrets behind the mysterious wall.

Luna's idea of a laboratory was based on her science classes at school and in virtual museums. Without electricity, she could not imagine how an animal clinic could do without basic spectrophotometric analysis or digital ionic electrophoresis. Above, in the clear blue sky, a faint cloud whispered. Even the illustrious Doctor Frankenstein had to rely on lightning.

Before turning into the building entrance, a whiff of sweetness and fruity filled her nose. She thought it smelled like Bo's Orange Slide or a drink Arnie might sneak into class. Inside, cabinets, drawers, and shelves filled the pristine, skylight-lit room. On a black marble countertop, she recognized an antique microscope. Unlike the ones used in freshman biology, this one had no cables, no buttons to adjust, or an on/off switch. Even if there were, there were no outlets to plug it into. She leaned over, looked through the tube's single eyepiece, and saw an illuminated field. Where was the light coming from? Below the instrument's stage, a mirror slanted toward the ceiling. "Wow."

She looked around for a place to put the tubes before attempting to adjust the knobs and see what was on the glass slide. Trays and jars of floating animal body parts lined the wall. Attached to the counter, an instrument with four shiny metal tubes hanging out stood out. It looked more like a toy flying saucer than a piece of laboratory equipment. There were holes on top that could accommodate four test tubes, but they looked long enough to swallow them inside. A crank arm that came off its side made the gadget look even more avant-garde. *What's the worst that could happen?* Holding the six tubes in one hand, she looked over her shoulder and cranked the handle with the other. The chrome centrifuge tubes went flying, spinning like helicopter blades ready for lift-off. Luna let go, and the gear-driven tubes wound down.

Luna could have spent the rest of the day exploring inside. It was like having a museum all to yourself.

On the opposite wall, she ran her fingers over the weathered bindings of veterinary textbooks. Although she could not read the lettered script of all the titles, she recognized *Comparative Anatomy, Histology of Interplanetary Vertebrates, Physiology of Exotic Species, Microbiology, Space Veterinary Pharmacology, Internal Medicine of Non-Terran Species,* and *Surgery of Alien Life Forms.* Other shelves contained the words cardiology, gastroenterology, neurology, dermatology, toxicology, and theriogenology. She closed her eyes and tried to imagine herself applying the knowledge found in those books.

"You will find a test tube rack in the chemistry lab next to the distillation apparatus," Kai's voice stretched from outside.

Around the corner, a Bunsen burner boiled an opaque liquid inside a beaker. Cloudy gases floated through glass tubing, leading to a coiled, air-cooled condenser. Clear liquid dripped steadily into a stoppered collection flask. One sniff found the source of the sweet smell. She did not need to taste it to know what dripped at the far end. Just as Mr. White had gone over on distillation, this gave moonshine, firewater, and booze its kick—ethanol.

"I am experimenting with motorcycle fuel additives," Kai's voice said.

Luna cocked her head to see if he had come inside. How does he know what I'm looking at? *I don't remember clearing off a crystal ball from the table.*

On the shelves above, colored bottles like the ones featured in her virtual chem class were labeled: mineral spirits, toluene, iodine, methanol, and various acids and bases. "I could perform real chemistry experiments with the stuff you've got around here," she said loudly enough to carry outside. Luna picked up an open jar labeled red phosphorus and shook its powdery contents. "Right now, I'm studying phosphorus." The overwhelming smell of garlic ruffled her nose. Maybe it's a good thing that virtual chemistry can't replicate everything.

"You will find red phosphorus a plentiful resource around the planet. Farmers and ranchers use it as an insecticide and to fertilize pastures."

"X-ray vision, too," she whispered.

She plopped the tubes in a wooden rack at the sound of a scratching noise coming from outside. *Douch, douch, do, do…* When she left the lab and turned into the courtyard, she noticed a wound-up phonograph with an attached megaphone on the table. A vinyl record spun, playing a catchy, fast beat. She recognized the kind of music from Arnie's vintage Swing Era collection. Her eyes closed, and her chin bobbed. The first time she'd heard it was at one of Arnie's parties, and he had asked her to dance. Her shoulders dropped, and her hips swayed. Back then, she had found an excuse to decline. Told herself that she did not know Arnie well enough to dance with him. Without Kai's asking, she was not about to let a second chance pass her by.

While Luna could not name the steps that Kai danced to, she was impressed by how his body synchronized with the beat. Luna came onto the impromptu courtyard dance floor with a Running Man step. Reuben got up from his spot and pranced along. Although they moved to the same tempo, using different rhythm footsteps, they connected through the musical beat. Kai bopped and bounced around like a jacked-up penguin. At the same time, Luna shuffled, and Reuben alternated between jumping, twirling, and wagging.

Keeping in time to the beat, Kai reached for her hand, and she joined him in a three-step swing. They moved about to progressive twists and turns. Reuben woofed an approving bark. From her perch, Tunisia shifted her feet. Falafel hopped. Cheekee's tail sashayed. And Baloney rolled back and forth. The other animals looked more amused than curious. Gardenia, always on guard, observed, satisfied to reserve judgment from the comfort and privacy of her box shelf.

*   *   *

IN THE WAR to gain her father's respect, this was the battle Jazz could not afford to lose. No way was a stutter going to prevent her use of logic, common sense, and newly found knowledge to stand against his barrage of pointed questions. When he scrutinized, she ducked, deflected, and evaded with her own questions. Not a simple task since she talked a fine line between outright lying, impertinence, and evading the truth.

"Well? Does anyone else know?" Her father's eyes probed, as did his voice.

She wound her hair into a ponytail and wrapped it in front of her. "No one mentioned the directive on the way here, and there is no reference to it on the forums. Besides the two of us, your security chief probably knows since he will implement it. Am I right?" She looked him in the eye, effectively defusing his stare.

He remained poker-faced until he relinquished a nod as if having believed her.

"Why are you asking me? Isn't that supposed to be your security officer's job?"

"Never mind that," he said, tapping the desk. "How did you find out?"

"During MiPS, haven't electronic aberrations happened

before?" *Has his tone mellowed, or am I imagining it?*

"Yes." He drew out his answer as if deciding his next move.

She squinted, needing to remove the glaring image she had of him. In the new light, he was a hard-wired program with a piece of missing code. Given a little time, she could find and fix it. In the same calm voice her mother often used, she said, "Before we break for lunch, do you still believe the Council will let you inside their circle?"

He flinched as if surprised, opened his mouth to speak, but caught himself before replying. "A seat at the high table is what my career has been building toward. If I succeed here, they can't refuse me. Of that, I was assured." Valdeez paced the desk with his hands behind his back. "I have provided invaluable services for Xerxes. Time and time again, I succeed where others fail. They cannot replace me. I know too much. They will have to make an exception. I am sure of it."

"Certain enough to risk your future?" She would have gone on questioning his logic, but finding a solution to the Calcan crisis seemed more important than nitpicking company policy. "What will it take to break the native's resolve?"

"Xerxes's influence is everywhere. It goes beyond anything you could imagine," he said with a smile. "It may take a while, but eventually, they win. They always do."

"Out here, influence doesn't do you or them any good. Do you really think they can get away with it? What if the Federation intervened? They could put a stop to the entire project."

"Delay, perhaps. Might cause some unwanted attention."

"You're right. Not much teeth in that."

Valdeez balled his fist in front of his mouth to pause more than to ponder. "Embarrassment is a corporation's worst nightmare. Xerxes's strength lies in its image. A company cannot wield its power if that image is tarnished. Why do you think so much emphasis is put on branding and advertising?" He pulled a can of Elysium Sparkling Water from below his desk and pointed to the brand. "This is what people identify with. The logo, font, and colors are designed to catch and keep the customer's attention." He pulled the pin and sipped. "As long as a company does not noticeably change the contents, shoppers will keep coming back. It's my job to make sure they do."

Our job. "If labor is so expensive, why not charge more?"

"Competition forces us to stay in check."

"Didn't anyone consider that when they built this place?"

"No one could have imagined a polar shift's effect on electronics."

"So you're here because of poor planning? Looks like a setup to me."

"Maybe I am." He stroked his chin as if giving the notion some thought. "If it comes to that, I will deal with it. Right now, time is not on our side. Calcan resistance must be stopped. If we eliminate their livelihood, they will come to depend on us."

"And if word gets out?"

"It won't. I have taken the necessary precautions to make sure that doesn't happen. Don't worry."

She could not remember the last time it had happened, but now, not four feet away, her papa smiled.

"Then we're out of here. Home. Put this all behind us." He placed the frame and cube aside, clearing the space between them. "If I recall, you always wanted me to play chess with you. Here is your chance."

Shedding invisible tears, Jazz gave a sharp nod, while on

the inside, she boogied the Happy Dance.

There was a knock at the main door before Imani cautiously stuck her head inside. Seeing the coast was clear, she said, "Will you be having the same for lunch, Sir?"

Valdeez nodded.

Unsure how to proceed, Imani slipped toward them. "I assume you will want the same?"

Jazz returned the smile with a conciliatory wink. "No, thank you, I will have the Pasta Alfredo."

"Good choice," Imani said, nodding with a forgiving twinkle in her eye.

With a flick of his knee, a virtual chess set appeared on the desk. "I do my best thinking over a game," he said.

"White or black?"

"Since this is our first game, let's let the program decide."

"Works for me."

"Speed game?"

"That's up to you. You're the one with a schedule." The virtual board turned 180 degrees. Jazz had white. "Voice or manual?"

"No clock necessary. This won't take long. Computer: physical mode. I prefer to move the pieces manually."

Jazz rubbed her fingertips over her lips and considered her openings.

He sat with one arm clasped over the other. "You do know how to play, don't you?"

"I taught myself. Mum told me how the two of you used to play back in the day," she said, sliding her king's pawn forward.

The black king's pawn pressed its response.

She slipped her king's knight forward. The start of a basic opening.

He let out a sigh and pushed his queen's knight.

She slid over a bishop. He countered. The queen's pawn slammed on the black square. She pushed her other knight. The board looked like most beginning chess games, developing into the strategic middle. He wasted no time before his bishop attacked.

Jazz breathed steadily. She had studied his games. For once, she could talk without having her tongue get in the way. While she could have played this game with her eyes closed, she chose to watch his reactions. Instead of addressing his threat, she welcomed it and raised her knight forward, leaving her queen exposed.

Valdeez shook his head. "Didn't you see this?" he said, knocking her queen off the board. "I was expecting more of a game from you. Forfeit?" He tapped his fingers as if the clatter would cause her to crumble. His eyes gravitated toward the comm.

Losing her queen put Jazz at a major disadvantage, and yet, she showed no sign of defeat. Her eyes raised slowly from the pieces. He had gone for a quick kill, oblivious to the lurking danger. While the queen was a valuable piece, she was not essential to winning the game. At that moment, her caterpillar self morphed into a rising butterfly.

Checkmate in three moves.

*   *   *

KAI TOOK OFF his overcoat and carefully folded it over his chair. "I'm going to have Gina's medication prepared. You are welcome to come along if you wish." Curled up next to Falafel, and apparently without a ride in the bike involved, Reuben hardly raised his napping head.

Not much of a choice. Go back and do time, wait for the planet to shift, wait for Jazz, or… "Let's go." The last time she felt this excited about going somewhere was during one of her father's rare visits when the two of them went to the Animal Garden theme park.

While a trip to the pharmacist may not have been on the scale of computer hacking or planting viruses, it was an act of civil disobedience and another jab at Xerxes. She walked faster when Kai told her to keep close since their destination lay inside the central market. She was about to get a guided tour into the belly of the mysterious entranceway where the aromas came from. *Of course I'm going.*

Along the way, they came upon children laughing and playing in a blocked-off street. Judging by how they kicked the two balls between the makeshift goals, it looked like a Calcan version of soccer. A woman, her mother's age, played the midfield position, while a man, older than Kai, defended one of the goals. Luna could not help but smile at the fond but slightly embarrassing memories of her mom yelling at the top of her lungs from the stands during her grade school games. Here it seems, grownups got to play too.

As if he'd read her mind, Kai said, "Pocky uses two balls in the Calcan version of football. The idea is to get your team's colored ball into the opposing goal. This way, you're playing offense and defense at the same time."

"It looks like fun." Luna slowed to a stop. Having concluded that this was as good a time as any, she fumbled for the best way to say it. "I had to sell the bike. Otherwise, there would not have been enough to pay for the amphetamines. I'm sorry."

Kai turned to face her. "It was yours to do with as you please," he said as if Calcans routinely traded motorcycles for drugs.

"I couldn't have made the sale without mentioning you. Your name carries a lot of weight."

He watched the game and continued walking.

"They think highly of you," she said, catching up. "You've built a fine reputation."

A red ball came out of play, bouncing toward them. "A good reputation will take you as far as the next confrontation." Kai stepped into the ball's path and used the inside of his ankle to stop it. "A bad one will follow you around like an intruding shadow." He flipped the ball above his knee and popped it high enough to head-butt it back into play.

"Wow. You play too?"

"Everyone plays. Sometimes we even keep score."

A girl with pigtails ran up in time to catch the ball. "Ohen-ro, Doctor Kai." Other children caught up and repeated the greetings.

Kai spoke to them in Calcan and related. "They are asking if we would like to join in," he said, turning to Luna. "Would you like to play?"

"*Ohenro*, guys," Luna said, waving at them. "Not today, but thanks. Maybe another time, okay?"

The kids waved goodbye over their shoulders and returned to their game.

Moving on, they turned a corner, and she saw the market from a different angle. It looked like a giant circus tent surrounded by a row of weavers at their looms. Side by side, they moved their arms and feet in harmonic clickety-clack, with each weaver's creation contributing to a dazzling mosaic of colors, textures, and designs.

Kai passed between looms. "Don't stray," he said before slipping between canvas folds.

She passed her fingers over the loops and knots of a thick

pile rug and thought how great it would look hanging on her wall. Quickening her pace, she lifted the flap and blinked repeatedly, overwhelmed by its size. Overhead, the mammoth canopy dispersed the suns' rays. Her skin tingled as her eyes adjusted to the cool shadows. Nothing close to what it looked like from the outside. Goosebumps emerged from the temperature drop. She barely heard Kai's voice over the drone of echoing voices. Calcans ambled the crowded aisles the way shoppers do before an after-holiday sale, she thought. Vendors fervently hawked their wares, shouting and offering samples to anyone passing by. The last time Luna had seen so many animated people was when she waited in line for Struttle and Corina concert tickets. She leaned over. The aisle kept on going.

"Keep up," Kai's voice said from ahead.

Luna stepped around and passed the person in front of her about as well as a red blood cell's trek through a capillary. Her gaze swung left and right, obliged to linger at each stall. Metalsmiths polished copper utensils, and jewelers angled their trinkets to take advantage of the filtered light. She saw a bracelet her mom would like. There were rows of cut fruits, vegetables, and nuts in unusual shapes and sizes. The variety was mind-boggling. A vendor peeled fuchsia-colored fruit and offered her a sample.

She was about to accept when the words 'keep up' brought her back in line. Other tables featured bean-shaped fruits with peeled-back purple skins to reveal salmon flesh and teal-colored seeds. The last time Luna saw so many colors next to each other, she was at a cosmetics counter in an Amazon Department Store. Here, spice sellers touted their seasonings into spaced symmetrical cones, with every stand producing its unique savory blend.

Every time she checked, he got further ahead. Kai seemed to slalom through the aisle, like a fish swimming downstream, while she waded, bumping into tables and tripping in the shadows. She caught glimpses of him, here and there, talking to a vendor long enough for her to catch up. 'Hold up. Not so fast,' she wanted to shout. Before she knew it, 'poof' he vanished again. *Better learn to say 'excuse me' in Calcan.* In the crowded aisle, she felt terribly alone when she lost sight of Kai for the fifth time. *Too late to add 'where' and 'pharmacy' to my Calcan vocabulary.*

She stood off to the side and considered turning around and going back the same way they had come. They could meet up back at the clinic. Thinking better of it, she stepped into the aisle and ambled with the flow. Ahead, the shadows and obstacles parted like the Red Sea before Moses. She aimed for it, expecting to come out the other side of the market, and stumbled into a tranquil, open-air plaza.

Despite the chaos, she found a relaxed atmosphere in a courtyard bordered by shops and cafés, where Calcans strolled and jugglers performed. In the opposite corner, the backs of Calcans formed around the notes of an emanating flute.

She noticed Kai talking to a merchant. The apparent pharmacy stood off by itself, with rows of drawers making up three of its walls. On wooden shelves, glass jars of plant petals, roots, and leaves lined up for all to see. Luna's nose twitched. Golden fibrous roots squeezed and twisted, pushing against their clear confines. Their elongated hairs stretched as if feeling their way out despite being unable to break free.

As if he had expected her then, Kai said, "There you are. Galgani is putting the finishing touches on Gina's medication."

The pharmacist stirred the contents of a wide-mouthed bowl, using a long wooden spoon like a witch over a cauldron.

He wore a green conical hat that accented his facial scales and counterbalanced his chin's tapered beard. As Kai introduced them, Galgani paused only to nod while adding bits, pinches, and pieces before returning to the potion-churning task.

While the two men spoke, Luna stepped aside to look around. Peddlers, flower sellers, and musicians milled about, giving a medieval fair feel to the place. Her curiosity peaked at the Calcans gathered around the source of the flute. She craned her neck, bent over, and stood on tippy toes. From snippets, the flutist was a snake charmer, and indeed, there was a snake. This was not an ordinary cobra but the size of a python and had three swaying heads.

"Yama's a patient," Kai said, leaning over. She is cross-eyed. A severe case of triple strabismus. You can meet her if you like."

"Maybe next time," she said, stepping closer to the stand.

"You diagnosed Hugo using sight, hearing, smell, and touch," Kai said, pointing to the bowl. Her curiosity was piqued.

"Sometimes, it becomes necessary to use all your senses. Observe." Kai dipped his finger in the bowl and scooped up a schmear of yellow-brownish goop. He sniffed and, without hesitating, put his finger in his mouth and licked it clean.

Galgani winced. "Like a chef, your taste buds are a vital diagnostic tool." He smacked his lips and pointed to the bowl. "Your turn."

"Okay," Luna said, drawing out the word. "I'll give it a try." Her finger scooped out a gob of goo, closed her eyes, and sucked her finger. "Yuck." Her face scrunched at the bitter taste. She scraped her tongue with her teeth and wiped the rest off with her hand and sleeve. "That's disgusting." She took Galgani's offered napkin and wiped the taste out of her mouth.

Their stifled grins and belly laughs did not help.

"*Spakuhn*. That didn't help much."

"If you had—" Kai showed how he dipped his middle finger into the concoction but used his forefinger to taste it.

"You could have just told me."

Kai did a poor job of hiding his mirth. "To quote Sherlock Holmes, 'You see, but do not observe.' Care to try again?"

"Fool me once."

"Some lessons must be experienced. This is one you won't forget." Kai waved to a nearby vendor and brought over a candy-bar-sized package. "Can't hurt the taste." He unwrapped it. "I will take the first bite if you prefer."

Luna looked him in the eye and shook her head. "That won't be necessary," she said, reaching for the bar. "Even if there's another lesson in it, I'll bite," she said matter-of-factly. The mammoth-sized mouthful swirled and burst into sweet-tart goodness. "Oh, that's much better."

She held the bar and pointed to the bowl. "Gina might appreciate it," she said, shrugging a shoulder. "It can't hurt the taste."

Kai translated. Galgani nodded, and the bar dissolved into an orange paste. "Shall we continue?" he said, heading for the crowd. Luna walked by his side, keeping him between herself and the snake charmer. "Another lesson?"

"Learning cannot enter a closed mind," Kai said. As they approached a cobbler's shop, the woman behind the counter smiled cordially. She pulled out a pair of leather boots. Their polished tops and stitched bottoms looked like new except for the worn soles. Luna recognized them as her walking shoes, with the tops remade into ankle-high riding boots. "The same?" She could not believe it. "Oh, thank you, thank you very much. *Spakuhn*," she said and wrapped her arms around Kai.

"Act. Make the best of what you have." He patted her on the shoulder with a 'tut tut.' "They are broken in, to boot," Kai said, slapping a thigh, beaming and clearly pleased by his pun.

Luna could not wait to try them on. While Kai spoke to the cobbler, she slipped off a rubber boot and untied the new ones. Suddenly, Kai flew out the door.

Three men dressed in black Xerxes uniforms pushed their way into the courtyard. Holding up a tracking monitor, the man in front led the way. "Over there," he said, pointing at Kai. They charged while Kai sidestepped and dodged. In their rush to get him, the two bumped into each other. The closest grabbed Kai's wrist. "I've got him," he said.

Instead of resisting, Kai stood his ground. He grinned like the Cheshire Cat while placing his free hand over his attacker's and wrenched the man's wrist. The assailant groaned as his elbow and shoulder contorted. As if following Kai's lead, the rest of the attacker's body followed wherever his wrist led.

The other two came to their comrade's aid, but Kai moved back and forth, using his engaged partner as a shield.

"Uh uhhhh uhh," Kai said, leading with one hand while shaking a finger with the other.

The flute stopped playing.

The snake-charmed group turned.

Luna stood in her stocking foot. Before she could get to the door, the cobbler blocked her exit with an outstretched arm. "*Chechku*," she said, shaking her head. The sharp squint and tight lips stressed the intent. The curved leather-cutting knife clinging to the cobbler's side required no further translation.

The courtyard hushed.

Kai held the wristlock with one hand while pointing to the crowd with the other. "Gentlemen. I believe we have an audience. Do you have something to say, or did you come to dance?" Kai raised his hand, and the subdued man grunted. "We have a band." Kai chuckled, "On hand. Do you have any requests?"

The Xerxes guards looked at each other and split up.

The Calcans advanced.

Kai spoke in Calcan to the crowd. Luna recognized the word '*chechku.*'

The Calcans kept their distance.

The two men intended to come at Kai from each side.

"Calcans are peace-loving people," Kai said, lifting his hand and increasing pressure on the guard's wrist. The subdued man bent over and was dispatched with a knee. "Until they are not. Are you prepared for the consequences?"

The attackers rushed. Kai held his hands by his sides as each guard grabbed hold of one of his arms. "Come with us, and no one gets hurt," the bigger man threatened. He looked down at his fallen partner as he led Kai away. "Get up, Stu. Quit your sniveling."

Kai feigned submission but, doing so, side-kicked the opposite guard. The shorter attacker yelped, falling forward and grabbing his knee. The big man assumed a boxer's stance and raised his fists. "You're in for it now. Your ass is mine," he said, shuffling back and forth.

Holding his hands by his sides, Kai said, "Wouldn't you rather be helping your friends?"

"I'll settle for a piece of you, old man," the big man said, throwing a bulldozing punch to Kai's face.

Kai's torso twisted. The fist barely missed his ear. Kai counterpunched. A hollow '*thwop*' resonated off the man's chest. The big man winced, holding his hand to his side, and took short, labored breaths.

Kai stepped back with outstretched hands. "It's never too late to help a friend."

This only incensed the gorilla. He gritted his teeth, and his eyes narrowed. His nostrils flared as he gradually straightened. "Now you're gonna get it."

"If you get hit in the same place, your ribs will break," Kai said, putting up his hand, delaying the man's advance. The man dropped his elbow to cover his side. Kai switched stances. "On the other, breathing becomes painful." The thug tucked in both elbows. With his fists dropped Kai stepped in and openhandedly smacked the exposed head. *Thwack* echoed through the yard. When the assailant reached up, his ribs were left exposed, and Kai was there to exploit it, ever forcing the man to step back.

The man snorted and bore down, ready to charge. "You old coot, I'll take your head off."

Yama had left her basket and slithered to the scene. She rose to the occasion. Her inflated hoods, flicking tongues, and barred fangs were armed to strike. *Sssss.*

While facing the man, Kai leaned sideways and pointed. "Snake. B*iii*g snake."

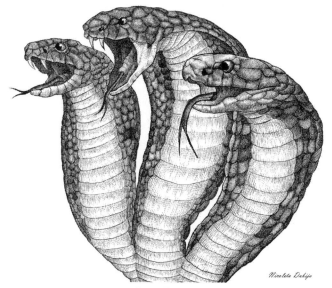

Yama Displeased

Unsure of what stood behind, the attacker turned. His eyes bulged, and his jaw dropped. Yama looked him eye to eye to eye to eye. Her serpentine smiles came within inches of a farewell kiss. He backpedaled, stumbled into Kai's arms, and took off running. Calcan heads turned to follow his retreat.

Yama bowed, which Kai returned, and then he turned his attention to the two remaining men. They cringed. On the ground, they were surrounded with their pants held below their knees. The cobbler's exposed blade glistened.

"*Dur!*" Kai said. The Calcans wavered.

One guard sat shaking, with his knees tucked to his chest. The other covered his groin with one hand while trying to raise his pants with the other.

"Do you gentlemen intend to have kids someday?" Kai asked.

The downed men cowered, too scared to reply.

Kai pointed to the cobbler's blade. "Do I have to spell it

out for you?"

One glance at the flashing knife was all it took for them to nod vigorously.

"And I am not just talking biological. Do you intend on being good fathers?" His raised eyebrows asked, but the choice was clear.

"Yes. Yes. Yessir," they said in unison.

Kai knelt beside them. The closest put up his hands and flinched at the slightest touch as Kai proceeded to massage the man's temple. "Quit your fussing, young man." The man leaned away like a child refusing medicine. "Hold still, or you will end up with a worse headache," Kai said and turned to the other. "My friend, Galgani here, has just the thing to fix you boys up," and pointed to the pharmacist. "No ligaments torn. Keep off it for a few days, and you will be walking fine in no time." The men nodded gratefully.

Kai spoke to the crowd and then to the men. "These good people will take it from here." He put up two fingers and pointed to the two men. "Gentlemen, as guests, I assume you will be on your best behavior."

The Calcans sprang into action, helping the downed men onto provided stools. Pitchers and glasses appeared out of nowhere, and musicians played. The snake charmer joined the ensemble, and Yama swayed along.

Luna leaned over, picked up the leader's dropped tracking monitor, and studied the flashing dot. In her stockinged foot, she hobbled over. "Are you all right? That was—"

"Grab your boots," Kai said. "Let's go."

Luna pointed to her new boots and repeated, *spakuhn* and thank-yous, till well out the cobbler's door. The knife-yielding woman simply nodded with a smile and waved her off.

On the way out of the market, a vendor approached Kai

with an overfilled fruit basket. They exchanged words, which he graciously accepted. Luna understood the words when Kai responded. "*Spakuhn, Evoo.*"

"Another fan?" Luna asked, carrying her rubber boots in tow. "Her name is Evoo, right?"

Kai drew his mouth into a straight line as he nodded curtly.

Walking out of the market, Luna asked, "How did you manage the big guy? His punch could have taken down a rhino."

Kai stepped faster without looking back. "A strike and a miss is not considered a hit."

"And how did you ever learn to fight like that?"

"No more difficult than hitting an aarmadark vein." He shrugged. "Simply a matter of knowing how and where."

Chapter 15

To fail to take the battle to the enemy when your back is to the wall is to perish."

—Sun Tzu

THE SACRIFICE OF her queen was essential if Jazz were to win the game and, if lucky enough to pull it off, capture her father's respect. True, there was no telling how he would react, but if he would stop long enough to listen to what she had to say, everyone could win. The reflex chess move would be to minimize her loss and take his bishop, but Jazz acted with a purpose. While his eyes strayed from the board, she raised her hand over her king. He stifled a yawn as he picked up his comm and scrolled. Instead of taking the bishop, she reached for her knight and moved it forward.

She crossed her arms and bided her time. There was a reason why, of all the real-time strategy games, Jazz had picked chess. This was the game her mother had introduced her to, the game they had played in the hospital, and, as a bonus, the game could be played by anyone, in any language, and required only one monosyllabic word. Used as a command, considered a full sentence. The moment had arrived to expose her real self. Like a butterfly, the word floated from her lips, fluttering over the checkered board pieces.

"Check."

He lowered his comm. The assured glint in his eyes shrank in concern. He pouted as if seeing something disdainful. His blasé smirk collapsed into a frown.

Message Received. Her face remained blank, though her chest swelled.

His eyebrows drew closer as he studied the board. He put his comm aside. There were two spaces for his king to move. Either ended in defeat.

She braced for an eruption. Would he take the loss personally? Was this to be their first and last game? She had made a statement that mattered. It was up to him to hear it. "See me," it said clearly.

His stare clung to the board. She took a deep breath. "Papa, how certain are you that the Council will give you a seat?" His head jerked back, looking as if he was hearing things. His eyes raised to meet hers. She could not be sure if he was more surprised by the question or that she had completed a full sentence. *Steady. Don't mess this up. Let him come to you.*

"Why do you doubt they will?"

"Ever since Xerxes first incorporated," she straightened in her seat, "its Council has only admitted descendants of the original founders." Two sentences in a row. Keep going.

Without questioning her further, he said, "Then I'll be the first."

"The Council is responsible to its shareholders and no one else. What if they rethink their offer?"

To come up with an answer, he cleared his throat.

She used the pause as a cue to reveal what she had learned from Xerxes's internal communiqués, the threats that faced him, and her plan to deal with them. He raised off his chair and slid his chair closer. If he asked an irrelevant question or veered off track, she reminded him of Dhiraj's indiscretion.

For the first time in her life, she was the embodiment of the princess, Scheherazade, charming the king with one of her tales in *1,001 Arabian Nights.*

He blinked repeatedly as if processing the information and asked, "How did you come to know this?"

The side door creaked, and Dhiraj slipped inside.

Before she came up with her prepared reply, her father raised his finger, effectively placing her on hold. He waved the security chief closer.

Dhiraj stood at attention and, with a sideward glance, leaned toward Valdeez. "Do you think it wise to involve her, Sir?"

Valdeez pressed his hands into the chair's armrests and, while he raised himself, brushed his leg against the side of the desk. In an instant, the chessboard disappeared. He waved his security chief closer and presented his hand palm side up, urging her to speak. "Go ahead, Jasmine. Tell him what you told me." He eased back down and leaned back in his chair. "Dhiraj, you will want to hear this."

"During the last MiPS, I read the labor acquisition protocol."

Dhiraj's jaw dropped, and his mouth formed a capital O. He shook off the shock and regained his composure. "Impossible."

Modeled after her father, Jazz sat back in her seat and raised an eyebrow. "Is it?"

"And if she knows, who else does too?" Valdeez frowned. He laced his fingers in front of him and tapped his thumbs.

"I will." Dhiraj blinked repeatedly. "Uh, look into it."

"See that you do." Valdeez squeezed his elbows into the sides of the chair. "And the next time you enter this room, knock."

Jazz tracked Dhiraj's footstep, and when he was almost at the door, she said matter-of-factly, "While you're at it, check your system's log. You'll find a hacker or hackers has penetrated security." Her eyes dwelled on the desktop family portrait. "A security system, if I recall, you designed."

"They have? How do you know this?" Dhiraj asked with a flushed face.

"If I've gathered this much information from my server's satellite network," she said, playing the part of a disinterested teenager and switching her attention to the curled fingernails in her palm, "think what someone who knew what they were doing might come up with." The tips of her manicured nails clicked like castanets. "I dunno... like a Federation agent, perhaps?"

Dhiraj slumped at the end of Valdeez's pointed finger. "You let this happen. Security is your responsibility. This is on you. If this gets out...." The recipient would have been dead and buried if her father's looks could kill.

"I will review our employee records and focus on the new arrivals. Maybe it is the new girl. I have watched her wandering about," Dhiraj said, spluttering. "Whoever it is, I will find them out and deal with it."

"You were not brought here for maybes. And as for the new girl, don't bother. We already know where she is. It isn't her," Valdeez said, rapping his fingers on the desk. "When she returns, bring her here."

"How, Sir? How can you be sure that it is not the girl?"

"Because we've used her as bait," Jazz said, scratching her bare wrist. "She might lure the real agent out for us." When Dhiraj's eyes met hers, she used the forefinger of her scratching hand to point out the absent bracelet.

"Do you have any idea who her father works for?" Valdeez seethed.

"You haven't been doing a good job keeping track of me," Jazz whispered out of the side of her mouth, waving her tracker monitor in front of him.

Dhiraj fumed and jerked the unit out of her hand.

"Do not give me another excuse to exercise my little friends," Valdeez said.

"Let us make it easier for you," Jazz said. "Find the missing miner."

Dhiraj's eyes darted back and forth in a confused look.

Valdeez cut in before Dhiraj could say anything else. "The other one."

Dhiraj left in a huff like he had been falsely accused of cheating at cards.

Jazz looked surprised. "Papa, you have friends?"

"Everyone has friends, princess."

＊　＊　＊

LUNA LACED UP her new boots and set the rubber ones beside the table. As much as she would like it to be true, "I'll come back," doubt crept inside her voice.

Kai's pursed lips and shrug showed otherwise.

"As soon as I'm able to." She pressed her thumb on the Honda's rear tire. "It's obvious that you're not Calcan and don't work for Xerxes. So, what's a Terran vet doing out here?"

Kai held the fruit basket in front of him as if weighing it but did not respond.

She took the air pump, unscrewed the tire's valve cap, screwed on the pump's nozzle, and worked the handle.

"You do not have to do that," Kai said, placing the basket aside.

"The rear seemed squishy coming over. The least I can do is return it in the best possible condition."

"Rizzo will get the bike. You do not have to return it yourself. Someone else can deliver it."

Luna picked up the pace. "This can't wait."

"Can't or won't? After what just happened, do you think that wise?"

"I gave my word. And I have my reasons."

"You saw the way those men came after me. They might report seeing you. Wouldn't staying away from Xerxes for a while be prudent?"

And miss my curfew? Sometimes Luna cracked herself up. "They weren't after you. Besides, the way those thugs emptied their glasses, I doubt they will report anything anytime soon." She took the tracker monitor from her pocket, pointed at her wrist, and showed the flashing blip. "I'm sorry. It was me they were after," she said, disconnecting the pump. "I swear. I didn't know I was being tracked." She squeezed the tire, "Close enough," and screwed the cap back on. "I'm responsible for bringing them here."

"That is of no concern," Kai said, chewing his lip. "One got away."

"I just have to," she said, giving the tire a kick.

"If ever you want to come back, a family can be arranged for you to stay with. You would be safe with them."

She shook her head in a conciliatory show of appreciation. "I've got to get a hold of my father." Her determination plowed deep into the furrows between her brows. Luna stooped over Falafel and rubbed his belly. His short paws begged for more. "As an officer in the Federation, he will be able to stop them." Reuben's chin and neck got obligatory scratches. "I love what you do. It's great. I have always dreamed of becoming a vet." The canid's head leaned into her hand, his eyes rolled back, and his rear leg kicked the floor. Thump, thump, thump. "But I can't wait for the next taurden to choke to death or more aarmadarks to get poisoned. I'm going to stop Xerxes. Or at least try to." Reuben licked her hand, and she bear-hugged him back.

Kai tugged on his beard but, other than that said nothing more.

"I appreciate your being worried about me," she said with a shrug. "What's the worst they can do? Kick me out? Ruin my life any more than it already is?"

He stared ahead, but unlike a totem pole, his arms were crossed.

"You know, I wasn't born with those marks on my knee. I did that to myself." Embarrassed yet feeling the desire to connect, she half extended her hand. *I've grown attached to you.* But did not step closer.

"Oh!" Don't want to forget this." She attached the pipe to the bike and, after fastening her helmet, waved Gardenia farewell. From a distance. "If this is the last we see of each other for a while, thank you. Thank you for everything. I'm going to miss you." She started her bike and revved the engine. "I will never forget you. All of you." And without looking back, she let out the clutch and drove down the gangway.

All that remained was a cloud of exhaust, and that vanished too soon.

*　　*　　*

REUBEN CHASED AFTER her, stopped at the sidewalk, and watched until the bike was well out of sight. Only when the sound of her muffler trailed off did he turn around and trudge back to the courtyard. He plopped his rear beside Kai, looked up, and released a grumbled sigh.

"Neither of us appreciates seeing her go," Kai said, glancing down at him. "Nothing I could say was going to stop her. She's stubborn, and that's all there is to it."

Reuben cocked his head.

"I was like her once. I understand," Kai said, nodding to himself. "Well, we're going to have to lie low for a while now that they know where we are."

Reuben looked at his toy box and shook as if he had just stepped out of the water.

"I don't want to leave, either." Kai hefted the fruit basket off the floor and placed it on the table. "She's bull-headed," he said, swallowing hard.

Reuben scratched himself behind the ear.

"You think we should go after her."

Gardenia screeched, announcing to all that it was time for lunch. She hopped off her shelf, jumped on a chair, and onto the table. In her rush to get to the basket, she knocked Luna's tracker monitor off the table. Tunisia squawked, and the other animals took off for the exits.

The canid yawned long and wide enough to sound like a roar.

"You think she's Daniel walking into a lion's den?" Kai picked up the device and watched the flashing dot advance through town. "She is right. They will come back. Kill more patients, destroy lives, and keep doing it until they get what they want."

Reuben uttered a guttural grunt.

"No one stops Xerxes by themselves. Do you think telling her how I tried and failed miserably would not have changed her mind?"

The canid's lips dipped into a canideleon frown.

"Neither do I. Still, we have to do something?"

Kai picked up Gardenia, held her in his arms, and stroked her silky fur. He closed his eyes as if searching for something inside. The skurrel peered into the basket with something else on her mind and squirmed to be released. Kai held her in one arm while he picked out a piece of jackfruit and put her down.

"Is she naive enough to think reporting Xerxes is enough to stop them?"

A breeze swept through the yard. Kai's nose twitched as he checked the basket. "Evoo added *dupcha* again," he said, shaking his head and turning away. "I don't have the heart to tell her that no one except Cheekee will come near it." Kai felt for the thorny fruit in the basket and placed it at the far end of the table.

THE FIRST TIME Kai sampled *dupcha*, he was the guest of a Calcan family. When it came to the fruit, he preferred it to be his last. A young Kai had never seen anything resembling the fruit before and, while curious, was more concerned with the odor circulating around the room. On the outside, it looked like a romantic encounter between a pineapple and a horned toad. Sitting at the dinner table, the host hacked at its spiny husk with a cleaver until it cracked open like a nut. The other guests looked on as if expecting a treat. Kai recoiled at the assault on his sense of smell. He looked both ways, repeatedly blinking to keep from holding his nose. Had someone farted? Was this a Calcan body function? No one else at the table seemed to notice. Inside the *dupcha's* husk, almond-sized seeds surrounded the sweaty skin of its peachy-colored flesh. The host's wife prodded with an elbow and showed how to eat it. The other guests ate with gusto, smacking their lips and wiping their chins to show how good it was. Kai scooped his fingers inside and came up with a larger chunk than intended. Everyone stopped to watch. Holding his hand out as if making an offering, Kai did not know if he should wipe it off or put it in his pocket. Juice from the stringy pulp dripped from his hand, down his arm, and soaked into his sleeve. Refusing to offend his hosts, he closed his eyes and breathed deeply. It was sweet. Definitely some kind of fruit. Tart and custardy. But, oh wow, the smell. When offered a second helping, he politely declined and rubbed his belly.

REUBEN'S NOSTRILS TWITCHED.

"What more would you have me do?"

Reuben turned his head from side to side, and his rear paw reached for his ear.

"Force them to leave. There is nothing that will make them do that."

As Reuben scratched his ear, his eyes sunk into canid ecstasy.

"Don't tell me to ask the right question."

When Gardenia slurped the last of the jackfruit, Kai replaced it with pieces of star and dragon fruits. She chirped delightedly.

Reuben sniffed the toes of the probing paw.

"If that's your idea, then it's not a very good one. David had lots of rocks to choose from and help, especially when it came time to find the right one."

In a huff, Reuben woofed.

"Don't argue. Just remember, this was your idea."

While Gardenia chomped greedily, Kai went to the far end of the table and, holding the *dupcha* at arm's length, took it to the workbench like a man with a mission. Between breaths, he finely chopped the fruit and collected the pieces into a glass container.

Reuben buried his muzzle between his paws and sank his nose into the floor.

When Gardenia finished feasting, Kai picked her up and placed her beside the *dupcha*-filled beaker. "This is for a good cause," he reminded her, raising her tail with one hand and squeezing her heinie with the other. A dark, oily discharge sprayed, coating the walls of the fruit-filled beaker. Gardenia squirmed while her anal glands emptied. Only then did Kai release her with a sincere apology.

Gardenia jumped off the bench in a huff.

With a clothespin clipped to his nose, Kai took the loaded beaker to the lab and topped it off with a rubber stopper. "Skunk and sewer gas," Kai reported, sounding like he had a cold. "This is a good start, but not nearly enough."

Reuben averted his eyes.

Kai reached for long-forgotten tubes, tins, bottles, and jars on an overhead shelf. He blew off cobwebs and wiped off the dust. He pinched, poured, and shook from containers labeled in combinations of symbols, letters, and numbers. Satisfied with the ingredients, he quickly attached the beaker to the distillation apparatus. Above the Bunsen burner, the liquid turned to gas. The contents churned, curled, and bubbled. The vapor evolved into fog and swirled around the glass walls. A mini tornado caught within a bottle. Higher and higher, the gases rose, turning murkier until they swooped into the condenser coils. Working around the glass spirals, the cooling effect devolved gas back to liquid. A clear droplet collected at the far side of the condenser lip, ready to be captured like a genie in a bottle.

Kai checked the tracker monitor and frowned. "David

needed more than a pebble to take on Goliath."

Reuben dozed by the table.

"That's all you've got?" Time was running out, and Kai had to come up with a slingshot.

*   *   *

THE HONDA ENGINE purred through the Calcan streets. *Prroom* echoed between the houses and shops. Lost in a mesh of thoughts and emotions, Luna looked around and realized nothing looked familiar. *I must have taken a wrong turn.* She reached for the clutch, shaking her wrist, and shifted to a lower gear. *Not only did I forget the monitor, but this tracker gives me something else to think about. If Jazz knew what was inside the bracelet, it would be the same as if she had placed a collar on me like some stray dog. Hopefully, she didn't.* Either way, Luna intended to find out.

Why can't things go smoothly like they do for everyone else? Why must life be so hard? If I had only done as told, I wouldn't be in this mess. Why bother getting out of bed? Every time I start something, it gets thrown back in my face and ends up hurting the people I care most about. The drumbeat of her heel, tapping against the footpeg, did a poor job of venting her growing angst. *I miss Mom. I miss home, Dad, and I miss my friends. I would do anything to have my old life back.*

Luna slowed to the side of the street. The sidewalks were deserted, and she could not recall the last time a vehicle had passed her by. None of the storefronts looked familiar, with their shutters closed. *This must be a Calcan holiday.* She turned around. Street after street, she searched for a familiar land-mark. A vehicle convoy approached. She slowed further until the lead driver stuck his arm out the window and pointed his finger. Their tires screeched. A glance at the rim of her bowl showed the lead vehicle breaking off and making a U-turn. A pickup truck swerved in front of her. Instead of stopping, she sped up and weaved around before it had her blocked in. The range of gunning exhausts spurred her throttle further. Her helmet confirmed. Luna was being chased.

After the assault at the market, it did not matter why they were after her. If it meant them pulling her over to find out, they were going to have to work for it. Luna assumed a racing stance with an arched back and relaxed elbows as the streets flew by. Time to find out what this bike could do.

Shrouded in its cylinder wall, the piston pounded revs while the engine riffed. The high-pitched crankshaft whirled, with sprockets, chain, and tires joining in. Luna glanced over her shoulder with a smile. "Catch me if you can, boys!"

Luna responded to a pickup's booming approach by cutting a sharp, right-hand turn into a narrow residential lane. The bike's brakes shuddered, and the tires skidded onto cobblestones. She knew she was in for the ride of her life when she could feel her heartbeat without checking for a pulse. The pickup driver slammed his brakes but overshot the turn. Too narrow for him to enter the alleyway, he pressed on, intending to cut her off on the other side. The Honda continued, filling the passage with a soprano *grüing*.

A four-wheeled ATV took up the chase where the pickup left off. It took the turn wide and sped down the corridor. Luna flew by doorways decorated with potted plants. Her front slithered on the uneven stone while the rear tire zig-zagged behind. The ATV's powerful engine and wide tires continued to close the gap between them. While Luna maneuvered the maze of concrete stairways jutting into the lane, the ATV took each stoop step with a bump. Flower pots fractured. Calcans yelled from doorways. Potting soil exploded into clouds of dust. Flowers burst into multicolored petal confetti. A particularly tall step tipped the ATV. The vehicle swerved, and a rear wheel scraped against the opposite wall, leaving plumes of sparks.

Further down the lane, feeding white-feathered chickeese squawked at the intrusion. Wings flapped, and feathers flew, avoiding the mechanized horde.

Before her, clothesline gauntlets of hanging laundry blocked her way. Luna eased off the throttle. The accelerating ATV edged within feet. She leaned over, grabbed a mop drying against a wall, and couched the handle in the pit of her left arm. Equipped like a knight with a lance, she jousted through lines of pillowcases, shirts, and sheets. Between pairs of hanging underwear, Luna noticed the lane end in a T. Having come close to ramming her from behind, the four-wheeled vehicle plowed blindly through. She tossed the mop, tapped the gearshift, counter-steered, and stomped the rear brake. Right before the wall, the ATV tapped her tire, sending the bike into the turn with an antsy swerve and her handlebar scraping against the brick.

The ATV driver's face, covered in tighty whities, never saw the oncoming wall.

After the crash, Luna slowed to a stop. The driver appeared shaken, not harmed. The ATV, or what was left of it, was not going anywhere. "One down," she said to herself. "Make a note to find out how to say, 'I'm sorry' and 'Where can I buy a mop?'" She rode on.

Light at the end of the alleyway meant leaving the safety of the row of houses and exposure to the street. Having decided that the best path forward lay ahead, she chose a narrow space between posts, guarding a fenced-in playing field. Back home, kids play soccer on fields like this.

She edged out of the lane, checked both ways, and revved

the engine. A honk of a pickup's horn alerted the others to her presence. *Great. My first game of pocky, and I'm the designated ball.* Without giving the turning around option any thought, Luna released the clutch.

On the two streets parallel to the field, two other vehicles joined the chase. Boxed in on three sides and with nowhere else to go, Luna pressed on. She jumped the curb, landed hard, tucked in her elbows, and aimed for the playing field entrance. The handlebars slipped between the wooden posts, with molecules left to spare. Just when Luna thought she had the field to herself, a monster pickup rammed the barrier behind, hauling posts, barbed wire, and kicking up the turf. Luna was used to Arnie coming up on her tail, but he could never pass her, nor did he try to run her over.

Actions must be taken to minimize potential witnesses, she remembered. Were these guys serious? The two trucks racing on each side of her blasted their horns. She sprinted for a grassy mound on the far side of a goal. *Can't stop, have to warn Jazz.* Coming from behind, the pickup's massive frame hurled closer, blasting its horn.

Speeder racing meant not fooling yourself into thinking an accident won't happen but asking yourself if today was your unlucky day. Speeder tracks back home, designed for rider safety, required special gear. Those courses were built for soft, controlled landings; even then, sprains and fractures were bound to happen.

Calcans had added the grassy knoll behind the goalposts to provide spectators with a better view, not for motorcycle jumping. Luna would have to launch high enough off the mound to clear the fence and curb to land safely. *If this ends badly, I will need more than a metal helmet.* She hated being trapped and taunted more than anything else, so she ripped the throttle.

*   *   *

WITH THE COCKTAIL brewing, Kai needed something to fire it with. He recalled that once upon a time, ladies used squeeze atomizers in perfume bottles long before pump sprays came along. In those days, a gentle squeeze of the bulb was enough to spritz a fine mist. Unfortunately, the device he required had to disperse a specific amount and be compact enough to hide and deliver his concoction at a precise moment.

Kai paced the courtyard, searching for a solution until distracted by a fit of nasal rasps. Falafel snorted in a corner, his back arched, trying to catch his breath. When Kai and Reuben came to his rescue, the molug managed to cough out a meatball-sized hairball. While Reuben licked his friend's face, Falafel's bout of choking gave Kai an idea. All he had to do now was find it.

Although Kai had looked at the scrap heap every day, now that he needed something from it, he found it hard to believe how large the junk pile had grown. It resembled a beaver dam built of pipes, tubes, and engine parts. He climbed toward the top, tossing aside the larger pieces. Reuben naturally pitched in. What Kai pulled aside, Reuben took over and pawed out of their way. Falafel placed his front paws on a muffler tailpipe at the base of the pile, and since his paws were too short to do much else, he encouraged them on. Kai twisted, slid, and pulled at the tubes like solving a giant metal wire puzzle. When a thingamajig came up with potential, he shook it and, if found unfixable, pitched it. Reuben did not care; he just liked to dig.

From his vantage point, Kai found what he needed among the bric-à-brac making up Baloney's nest. Unfortunately, the mechanical part was beyond his reach, and time was running out. Left with no other option, he pointed inside and told Reuben to fetch. The canid worked his way between the ends and edges of jutted metal with the intensity of a game show contestant. He placed his mouth around the mechanical part and, without room to turn around, shimmied his way out like a cork in a bottle.

"Good boy," Kai said, wiping off slobber from the fist-sized carburetor. He checked the choke and then flicked the butterfly valve open and closed. "This will do,"

Given how Reuben's tail was wagging, he seemed to agree.

From his workbench shelves, Kai pulled a toy-sized fan motor and a wind-up spring from an antique clock. He wound the spring. "Yup." He tinkered with the spring, attached it to the fan, and squeezed the assembly into the carburetor's throat. With a twist, he released the spring's catch, and a steady breeze streamed through the carb's output flange. Supercharged, all that remained was loading it.

Kai replaced the clothespin on his nose and donned an apron and rubber gloves before entering the laboratory. Reuben preferred to stay outside. With a syringe, Kai took a deep breath, loaded the carburetor's fuel bowl, and stoppered the bottle. "Oof," Kai said, placing the carb into a sealed glass jar. With the smell contained, he grabbed his coat. That was all the prompt Reuben needed to twirl.

"Whoa," Kai said.

Reuben froze.

"Not this time."

Reuben's eyelids and lips drooped. The canid looked up with a 'you can't leave without me' frown.

Kai carefully slid the jar inside his pocket, raised his coattails, and swung a leg over his bike.

Reuben whined.

"Sorry, boy."

The bike started without rebuke.

*　　*　　*

ON THE FIELD side of the mound, Luna's engine responded to her throttle's prompt. The two Xerxes trucks turned their respective corners. On a collision course, they sped up, closing in, and aimed to cut her off. Luna had to nail an Evel Knievel jump if she was going to escape. Beyond the point of no return, she said to herself, "A projectile travels farthest when the angular position of a vector, theta equals 45 degrees," and aimed for the mound's highest point.

Coming into town like a bat out of hell, a tuk-tuk drove toward Luna's landing zone from the opposite side of the mound.

Behind her, the pickup kicked into high gear, with the driver banging his hand on the panel door.

The bike, a glutton for punishment and equally able to dish it out, devoured the turf below its treads. Luna hit the mound and soared like a motorized Mary Poppins over and beyond the fence. Midair, her eyes met the startled tuk-tuk driver's eyes below.

With the Jack-in-the-box of all surprises coming at him from above, the tuk-tuk driver panicked. With two trucks closing in from both sides and a two-wheeled torpedo hurling above, he swerved. Luna's tires slammed onto the tuk-tuk's roof and landed with a resounding *tha-thunk*. The tuk-tuk's brakes screeched, and its tin roof puckered from the shock. She braked and trampolined with a bunny hop off. Two dents in the roof remained.

The tuk-tuk bounced off the curb and tilted off the walk.

The trucks skidded toward each other.

Both of her bike's tires bounded off the asphalt. Her bent knees and elbows absorbed the shock's brunt. The suspension bottomed out. She winced at the sound of metal scraping on metal, like ground cavity-riddled teeth.

Behind her, the monster pickup skid past the mound with enough height to clear the barbed wire and miss the tuk-tuk. However, the dragged fencing caught the goalpost. In a recipe for a vehicular layered crash cake, the pickup landed on top of the two Xerxes vehicles' hoods, providing a metallic frosting.

"Add the words, 'body shop,'" she said to herself as the bike's rear end fishtailed it out of town in a biker's farewell salute.

Chapter 16

"They're funny things, Accidents. You never have them till you're having them."

—A.A. Milne, 'Eeyore' *The House on Pooh Corner*

AT EVERY BUMP in the road, the small bike's suspension bottomed, and its wheel bearings rattled. Luna avoided potholes, clasped the shaking handlebars, and tightly squeezed the fuel tank between her knees to avoid falling over. Despite those efforts, she frequently peeked up at her visor lid and double-checked over her shoulder. Having made it this far, she did not feel the Honda had enough to withstand another round. Only when certain the road remained clear, both ways, did her pulse slow to where her heart no longer threatened to leave her chest. "You did great," she told the bike. "I don't care what shape you're in. If you were mine, I'd bring you home."

Finding the Xerxes entrance deserted and unwilling to push her luck, Luna turned off the ignition and coasted to the market. With no one around to leave the bike, she parked in the aisle where she had last seen Rizzo. She laid the pipe on the counter and considered leaving her helmet as she unfastened the strap. *If I decide to keep the bowl, something else will have to be left behind. Takes up as much space as a pipe,* she thought, balancing it in her hands. *It means a lot more to me than it does to anyone else.* She gave the bike a last look before tapping the tire. *For you,* and again, *for me. We're going to need it.*

Luna kept a low profile as she advanced toward the unattended gate. On the alert, nothing more than rustling vents and swishing pipes met her at the entrance. With her back plastered against a deserted corridor wall, a hand came out of nowhere and grabbed her by the collar.

"Brat," a gruff male voice said from the shadows. A fist belonging to the security thug from the courtyard shook in her face. Up close, he looked even more terrifying with his broad shoulders, deep-set eyes, and unshaven scowl.

"What's your problem, dude?" Luna reached behind and wrenched at his fingers, but his grip held tight. She stepped back as her shirt came half over her neck. Holding a Babe Ruth grip on the helmet strap and choking from the collar stuck under her chin, she wound up and let loose with a swing. It was hard enough to knock one out of the park, and she connected with his kisser. Metal banged on jaw, ringing a gong-sounding echo through the hall. Heavy-heeled footsteps rushed to answer.

The big guy grabbed his chin, shook off the blow, and lunged at her throat.

She ducked, sidestepped, and swung again.

"Umph." He fell to his knees and keeled over.

Gray-colored uniformed guards stormed from both ends of the hall. "Are you all right, Bill?" one of them bent over and asked.

Doors remained silent and closed. With nowhere to run and no place to hide, Luna backed against a cold wall's hard surface. *Fear wants to dance. If I agree, which of us is going to take the lead?*

She stepped closer, holding the helmet behind her back,

and peered over Bill like a curious bystander. Her voice rose as she shook her head. "I don't think so. Looks like his ribs are broken."

Bill winced between breaths as his arm raised gradually, and he pointed his finger. "It's-ugh-her."

Glaring frowns poked from above.

This would be the part where David goes on to find himself facing multiple Goliaths and fresh out of stones. "Your guy kinda overreacted. I was just trying to find a place to comm out," she blurted, looking around as if lost. "I'm new here. I must have taken a wrong turn."

None of them seemed convinced.

"Maybe, one of you guys could show me how to comm out?" she asked, batting her lashes. The helmet swung daintily in her hand, like Little Red Riding Hood's basket on the way to Grandma's house.

They shook their heads.

"Don't get me wrong. I understand you have to follow orders, but your guy grabbed me."

One by one, she met their glares. Fred Leary, his uniform badge read, tapped the Taser on his hip as if looking for an excuse to use it. *No sympathy there.* Henry Chow, a frowning steamroller of a man, crossed his arms across his broad chest. His uniform buttons strained to hold back his ample girth. He had the physique of an offensive lineman with a 'there never was a dessert I didn't like' attitude. Standing next to Henry, Trip Noel might have been his comical sidekick, with a beanpole physique and a fuzzy upper lip. "What was I supposed to do?" She raised her collar to prove her point. "Come on. Help me out here."

Trip leaned in and squinted for a closer look at her frayed collar.

"You know how some people tend to overreact. Is Bill that kind of guy?" Her doe eyes reached out with a touch of concern. "You really don't have to go through all this bother. Now, if you just point me toward my pod." She stepped backward, pointing over her shoulder. "Is this the way? Don't want to be a bother. I can make it from here."

Fred blocked her exit. "I'll take that," he said, grabbing the helmet.

"Sure. Check it," Luna said, rolling her eyes. "It could be loaded." She looked back at Bill as he was being helped to his feet. "Sorree."

They formed a column down the hall. *Untie their shoelaces.* She placed her wrists together and raised them over her head. "If it makes you feel safer, why don't you cuff me?"

"Knock it off," Fred said with a shove.

"Hey! Take it easy back there, Freddy. Watch the hands." She looked side to side. "Which one of you is supposed to be the Big Bad Wolf, 'cause this certainly is not the way to Grandma's house?"

Their blank faces were having none of it.

"Oh, well then. Take me to your leader."

They turned a corner and picked up the pace. *I'm just getting started.* She rocked her shoulders, stomped in sync with the echoed boot steps, and added the occasional double step. *Too, too, chi choo. Oh, what the heck.* She hummed the "Imperial March" from *Star Wars.* "Dum, dum, dum...."

Her stormtrooper escort looked at her and then looked over at the other and shrugged. Behind, Fred clenched her helmet in his fist.

"Be careful with that, Freddy. Imma gonna wanna receipt." When that got her nowhere, she addressed young Trip. "Cat got your tongue? Too bashful to talk to girls?"

Henry smirked.

She turned her attention to the other side. "Isn't black supposed to be slimming, Hank? Do the girls where you come from really go for the belly-bursting buttons look?" Her elbow nudged Trip. "Think your partner is getting too chubby for that uniform?"

"Hear that, Henry?" the younger guard said. "I think she just called you fat."

Hank sucked in his stomach.

"Don't they come in bigger sizes?" She looked over and winked. "Bet he can't stay away from the snack bar."

The young guard smirked while Henry fumed.

"Just saying," she said over her shoulder. "Your buddies don't look too bright. Is that the best they can do around here?"

Another shove.

"They're probably the reason they put instructions on food wrappers. Not that Henry seems to have any problems."

Stifled snickers followed.

By the time they reached the main office, Fred was flushed, the veins in Henry's neck were throbbing, and Trip had a hard time refraining from laughing his head off.

The receptionist gave Luna little more than a sideward glance before they passed through the oak doors. This is how Princess Leia must have felt entering the Death Star.

Her escort stopped to stand at attention.

Doesn't look like any principal's office I've ever been in.

Nothing alarming about two men talking over a desk. Unless they were willing to poison water and eliminate potential witnesses. Though the man in the uniform stood a shade taller, the man in charge did not need to stand to exude confidence. His presence, like his voice, projected well. He wore his suit like a fashion model and had the movie-star good looks to go along with it. *The evil side of the Force?*

Remember why you came back. She scratched the back of her neck as if reaching for a jedi light saber. Without covering her mouth, she yawned loud enough to wake a wookiee and interrupt their conversation. "Is this where I register a complaint?"

Her guards looked like they wanted to distance themselves but remained where they were and settled for closing their eyes and shaking their heads.

The two men at the desk continued without pause, though she caught the fleeting gleam of the man's eye.

Adverse to showing fear, she remained defiant like a brittle bone bleaching in the sun. She cleared her throat over their voices. "Your men tried to run me over."

"Chief, take care of it," the man in charge said without acknowledging and then turned his attention to her escort. "You may leave, gentlemen." He sent them off with a wave of his hand. His eyes latched onto hers. "You must be mistaken, young lady. We rescued you." He extended his arm without offering his hand and sat as if inviting her to do the same. "We have not been introduced. My name is Valdeez."

Luna took measured steps closer, thinking that while better looking, he was a lot more threatening than Heiman.

"As the person in charge, I am responsible for your welfare and safety," he said.

Filled with dread, she eased into the chair. *This is not your first trip to the principal's office. Breathe. Sit up straight. Mimic his posture.* With her shoulders back and chin raised, her eyes met his. "My name is—"

"I know who you are." His pitch-black eyes probed. The lines of his jaw prodded.

Luna met his gaze with crossed arms and responded with a smirk. Instead of his hard look, there were three pairs of serpentine eyes in her mind. Without fangs, Valdeez had nothing on Yama. "Your idea of a rescue is to have your men try to kill me?"

"We cannot permit minors to wander off," he said, shaking his head while maintaining his gaze. "You must be mistaken."

They stared at each other like opposing bookends. Determined not to blink first, Luna furrowed her brows and locked her eyes on his. Sizing each other up in a contest of wills, neither flinched.

"Your scores are impressive, Ms. Auer," Valdeez said, breaking the impasse. On the wall behind him, her school records appeared.

Luna blinked. There was something vaguely familiar about the way he spoke.

"Xerxes has not only provided you with an opportunity to continue your education but has also agreed to pay you. Why do you disrespect us?" He sounded as if her actions had offended his sense of right and wrong. "Don't you care? Don't you want to better yourself?" Valdeez scrolled on without waiting for a response. "Judging by your on-site data reports, you have adjusted to our work schedule and are current with your academic assignments. Good." As he spoke, her teacher reviews appeared on-screen. "You have shown an interest in the sciences and stated that you want to become a veterinarian. Is that correct?" Again, without waiting for a reply, he said, "I have a proposition for you."

She tried to swallow, but it sounded like a gulp.

"Luna, I believe we are wasting your talents here. How would you like to return to Rockwood? The Xerxes Corporation has uses for veterinarians. I might be convinced to help a willing, capable veterinary prospect like yourself."

Back where I started.

"You would be on the next transport in time for the first semester of your senior year. I can arrange that." Valdeez turned in his chair and faced the screen, giving her time to consider.

She raised her hands as if praying and pressed them against her lips. *Mom would be so relieved. I'd be back with my friends. Right where I was supposed to be before Heiman ripped me off.*

Valdeez drummed and rolled his fingers on the armrest.

No one to turn to. No place to hide. On the desk, a buzz came from the insect stuck inside the cube. "And if I refuse?"

His chair swung around. With an incredulous stare, he raised a brow. "You have left the premises without permission and put your safety at risk. You don't seem happy here. I'm giving you a way out." His frown turned to a scowl. "It would be foolish not to accept."

Luna gritted her teeth.

With another flick of his wrist, the wall screen displayed a horse jumping competition. A mounted chestnut-colored horse entered the riding arena. Luna immediately recognized the announcer's voice. She was the rider. Inside, an emotional tub of doubt, grief, and guilt overflowed. Her hand inched toward her knee.

The announcer's voice said, "Riding Sancho, substituting for his owner, is Luna Auer." On-screen, the horse and rider went smoothly through their jumps. "Nice up and over. This is this junior rider's first competition, ladies and gentlemen." There was a round of applause. The horse and rider moved effortlessly, without fault, and on track to beat the clock. They sped to the last series of jumps.

"You were riding well." Valdeez's smile broadened. "Until."

"Stop! Turn it off," she pleaded.

Valdeez did not blink. The gleam in his eyes laughed at her discomfort.

"And faultless, coming into the final combination." Approaching the last jump, Sancho stumbled. Horse and rider toppled in a horrific mass of grunts, limbs, and shrieks. The audience gasped. The video paused.

Luna dug her nails into her thigh.

"Shame about the horse. Ended up putting him down." Valdeez's smug grin widened. "Didn't they?" Behind him, the camera zoomed in on Sancho's thrashing limbs. With her leg pinned below, Luna struggled to clear herself. Officials ran to help.

Hearing Sancho's pitiful neighs again broke her heart. At that moment, she would have done anything to crawl inside herself, fall asleep, and never wake up.

Her personal bank history replaced half the screen. "Was it guilt that prompted you to empty your savings account? Did it make you feel better?"

The accent. She pinched herself. *I've been so stupid.*

On-screen, officials freed Luna while Sancho struggled.

"Answer me. What if I refuse?"

Valdeez showed indifference with a shrug. The screen filled with a camera feed of Luna in the market, holding up a bag of blue crystals. "Selling drugs is a crime. It is my duty to report it." Valdeez let out a long sigh. "Dhiraj, you can come in now."

By this time, Luna had guessed who was in the picture inside the frame standing next to the cube. The wall screen changed to Luna speaking to Ziggy by the side of the road. She undid the bracelet clasp and tossed it on the desk.

Without even a show of concern, he asked, "Perhaps you

can tell me where we can find this man?"

Luna stood and looked around. "Where is she? I know you're here, Jazz."

Valdeez raised his eyes quizzically.

"Come out, Jazz, or should I say Judas? Come out, or are you too much of a coward?"

Jazz tip-toed through the side door, followed by three uniformed security men.

Luna stared incredulously. "Did you know they were trying to kill me?" she asked. "How could you?"

Jazz froze. "I'm so sorry." Her words came out as a strangled sob. "That was never s-supposed to happen." With open arms, she stepped closer apologetically.

"Talk to the hand," Luna's outstretched palm said. "Don't you dare come closer."

Jazz stood where she was and leaned back as if insulted.

"Don't look at me like you don't know what I'm talking about," Luna said contemptuously.

Valdeez and Dhiraj looked on, amused.

"You're better than this," Luna said.

"Think this through," Jazz said, holding her hands on her hips. "Quit playing the martyr. You'll get what you came for. Just go. Forget you were ever here."

Luna's fingers clenched. "I don't forgive or forget."

"Really?" Jazz said harshly. "Grow up, Luna. The rest of your life depends on what you do next."

Valdeez sat back, watching the girls with a bemused smile.

"Forget the animals they have already killed. Easy for you, not for me. Allow them to keep poisoning more animals and possibly kill someone?" Luna would have preferred expressing herself differently but settled on dismissing Jazz with a wave. "No way."

Jazz glanced at her father and shook her head. "You give him no choice."

Valdeez portrayed the sympathy of granite.

"He'll ruin you."

Luna shook her hands in frustration. "Don't you get it?" Luna said, trying to get through her ex-friend's thick skull. "This isn't about Xerxes or your father. This is all on you."

"He'll do it."

Luna might as well have snarled. "And he'll go down with me."

Jazz looked at her father. "Help her understand, Papa," she implored.

"Take her to security," Valdeez said and nodded to Dhiraj. "Below."

Dhiraj gestured for Luna to follow him. When she refused, he pulled her arm.

The main doors swung open. A blurred presence stumbled into the office, supported by the arms of two guards. When Henry and Trip released the hunched-over figure, he teetered. Luna might not have recognized Kai were he not wearing his coat.

"What did you do to him?" She pulled away from Dhiraj's hold on her arm. "Let go of me."

"We didn't touch him," Henry said defensively.

The security chief's grip tightened on her arm.

Kai writhed side to side, flexing his torso. He transformed before their eyes, like a snake outgrowing its skin, until he stood at his full height and slowly raised his head to reveal his face. "Let the girl go."

Dhiraj pointed. "That's Kaironowski."

"Doctor Kaironowski to you," Kai said indignantly, readjusting his coat.

"The vet?" Jazz asked, edging closer to her father.

"He's a wanted criminal," Valdeez said, shaking his head. "Didn't any of you know? Why do we bother posting a list of wanted criminals?"

Dhiraj hoisted Luna out of the chair and placed her opposite Kai. "Why did you bring him here?" he asked the guards.

The three security men squirmed as they looked at one another. Trip blurted, "We found him wandering the halls."

"He showed us your tracking monitor. We just brought him here to return it," Henry added hopefully.

To corroborate their story, Fred held out the device. Their location blipped on the monitor.

"Did you search him?" Dhiraj asked.

Luna pulled away. When that failed to work, her nails raked his arm. Dhiraj slapped her face and yanked her toward the exit.

"P-p-p…" Jazz stuttered, holding onto her father's sleeve.

Kai reached inside his coat.

When plant and animal tissue rots, the protein matter of which such tissue is composed breaks down, releasing an airborne blend of putrid chemicals. In the same way, our noses turn away from rotten eggs, and our body has evolved to avoid certain smells. Way before decayed matter enters our mouths, those compounds float up our nostrils and activate the odor center in our brains. Nausea emerges. Add a splash of Gardenia's gift and a dollop of *dupcha,* and one close whiff will trigger the stomach to propel anything inside-outside.

Trip lifted his elbow and sniffed under his arm. Henry shook his head as he fanned the air in front of his face.

"The old coot reeks," Fred said, reaching to restrain Kai while pinching his nose.

"P U," Trip said.

A hint of queasiness crept through the air.

Sweat dripped from Henry's temples. His cheeks reddened, rising into ruby puffs. He pressed his fist over his mouth. He looked ready to burst.

"Ugh. Restrain him," Valdeez said between breaths. Jazz paled as she pressed her face into her father's back.

"The old, *urp* guy, *urp*, seemed harmless enough," Fred said in their defense. Henry and Trip covered their faces as they backpedaled for the door.

Luna kicked Dhiraj in the shin. "Let go of me."

Dhiraj grunted through face-covering fingers.

His security team looked uneasily at each other and then at the floor. A guard leaned over. "I think I'm going to pu—"

"Don't say it," another said. Their eyes frantically searched the floor as if looking for a place to splash down.

As Dhiraj bent over, Luna bit his arm hard. He let her go and—

"No!" Valdeez exclaimed, "Not the r-r...."

Kai held out the carb, looking pleased, not embarrassed. However, as Luna dashed toward him, she had to wonder if he had, in fact, soiled himself.

A volcanic chain erupted, spewing forth fountains of rainbow-colored fluids. The room's circulating ventilation system could not compete. The oriental rug's symmetrical lines reappeared as a backdrop to a Jackson Pollock canvas.

Kai winked. "If Hugo was the appetizer." His eyes watered as he waved her behind.

"Whoa," she said, putting out her hand and giving him a wide berth.

"This is the main course."

Bill's attending guard entered from the side door with his Taser drawn. "Oh, my."

"This man is a wanted criminal," Valdeez raged, wiping his mouth with his suit sleeve. "This isn't just vandalism anymore, Kaironowski."

Kai waved the carb. "Time to vacate the premises," he said as if serving an eviction notice. "We're leaving, and I suggest you do the same."

"This time, I'll put you away for good," Valdeez said, pointing to the guards. "Get them! A bonus for whoever arrests them."

"Uh, uh, uhhhh." Kai stepped backward, waving the carb like a garlic strand, fending off vampires. With one hand pinching her nose, Luna grabbed his coattail and guided him out the door. The guard rushed with an arm over his face, slid on the slick gastric slip and slide, and sent his Taser sailing in a pool of puke.

Once past the side office, Kai and Luna took off running down the hall. Kai slowed suddenly as they approached a large vent.

"What? Why are you stopping?" Luna asked. Heavy-heeled footsteps echoed through the halls.

"Check it."

"Check for what?"

"Intake or exhaust."

Placing her hand over the duct, she felt a sucking breeze. Intake."

With his back to her and keeping a lookout, he said, "Good. Now pry off the cover."

Grommet by grommet, she worked around the edges. Booted footsteps approached. A side pried off until the entire frame popped off.

"Get ready to run. Go for my bike." Shouting joined the chaos. "Stop for no one. Get Roxy started. And leave," Kai said.

"But—"

"No buts. You can do it. Don't wait for me. Now go."

Luna took off in a sprint.

KAI TOOK A deep breath before opening the butterfly valve and tossing the makeshift carburetor inside the ventilation duct. A steady stream of vapor spread fumes throughout the complex. He wasted no time, darting for the exit, and did so with a pack of rabid guards behind.

LUNA GOT ON the bike. Higher, wide seat, thick handlebars. Compared to the Honda, Roxy felt like getting aboard a tractor. Starting one bike has to be the same as another, she hoped. She kicked the pedal. The piston raised, increasing the pressure within the combustion chamber. The valves closed like the compression phase of the heart. The spark ignited the fuel: air mixture. Without enough force to turn over, the engine kicked back. Her knee took the brunt of the force. From her view of the entrance, Kai came running down the hallway faster than anyone thought possible.

"Take off," he huffed, with capture closing on his heels.

With her full weight on the pedal, she kicked with all her might. Steps away, Kai bounded and, in a Superman dive, launched with his coattails flapping like a cape. The bike sprang to life. He landed inside the sidecar with a thud. Luna twisted the throttle and popped the clutch. The bike lunged.

Fred made a running leap and grabbed the edge of Kai's coat. Upside down, Kai squirmed. The guard should have known. You don't yank, much less hold on to a superhero's cape. A forward thrust threw Kai back and toward the middle of the bike. The guard's feet dragged. Those left behind choked on dust. With the additional weight, the bike tilted to

Luna's side, causing the third wheel to rise. Forward momentum, and Kai's kicking rocked the bike. The whole thing
threatened to topple over. Luna cranked the throttle. The
engine jerked. Fred's shoes dragged until he released his grip.
Three wheels touched down and took off, spinning.

Luna didn't look back as the bike sped away, threatening
to veer off the road. Like an escape artist in a straitjacket, Kai
kicked and twisted inside the sidecar. Down to her last fumes
of keeping it together, Luna trembled.

A flying insect smacked her in the face. Stinging from the
slap, she squeezed the handlebar grips to keep from losing it
while bug guts smeared across her cheek.

Kai righted himself and checked behind. "It's okay. You
can slow down."

Ooze dripped off her lip.

He put his hand over the throttle. "They won't follow."

"How can you be sure?"

"I let the air out of their tires," he said calmly.

The bike slowed and evened out. "What else did you do?"

"Something that should have been done long ago. Fought
fire with fire. Xerxes has polluted this planet long enough.
Poisoning the water was the last straw."

"That's not what I mean. What did you do, that you're a
wanted man?"

"This isn't my first run-in with Xerxes."

"They'll come after you."

"Won't be the first time."

Kai raised his coat collar, sniffed, and turned his head.

"Will the smell last long?" she asked, trying to keep her
eyes on the road.

"Not long enough to read *War and Peace*, but long enough
to cause a stink back home."

"And I thought I was in trouble," Luna said, working up a chuckle.

He pointed off to the side. "Over here, let's pull over."

She stopped, rolled off the bike, and staggered to an embankment at the edge of a field. In the distant pasture, Taurdens grazed before them. "I've made a mess of things," she said. Kai stood behind and off to the side. He held his hands behind his back and affirmed with a muted nod. She picked up a handful of pebbles at her feet and threw them, one at a time. "If I hadn't gotten you into this...."

"You did not get me into anything. You could say that I've been a pain." Kai took a breath. "Problem for them since before you were born. Today, I simply took it up a notch."

"I should never have come," Luna said, shaking her head.

"And miss the Calcus experience?" Kai's grin highlighted his waving eyebrows.

"You sound like a Xena promo. You know what I mean. Coming here, the whole thing was a big mistake."

"You have negotiated, fixed, diagnosed, treated, and saved. You're a menace, all right."

"You don't get it. The real reason I came had nothing to do with funding my education." Luna blinked. "I came to pay for what I did."

Kai stared blankly at the field and nodded.

"I'm responsible for the death of a friend. For saying yes, when I...."

Kai stepped closer.

Luna dug her booted toe into the loose soil. "I'd been partying the night before. Maybe drank more than I should." At that moment, she wished to dig a hole deep enough to crawl inside. "How was I supposed to know that the horse's owner would come down with the flu the next day? I was

Sancho's groomer, walker, and exercise rider. We'd gone through the jumps dozens of times. I'd never been in a sanctioned event. So, when offered the chance to take her place, I didn't think. And now he's gone." The hollow swallow stuck in her throat. "And I'm to blame."

"You figured to punish yourself by coming here?"

Tears rolled down her cheeks. "That was the idea. It seemed like the right thing to do at the time. Now, I'm not so sure. Everything's a mess." She looked at him, shaking her head. "We are so screwed."

Kai picked a pebble from Luna's hand and, with the elastic band from his goggles, used it as a slingshot. The pebble flew over the ditch into the pasture. Luna grabbed hold of him and received his arm around her shoulder in return. She sniffed. "You know, you could take that coat off."

"A doctor shouldn't administer anything he is not prepared to take himself."

"Still." She turned her nose away but held on.

"Like the taste of Gina's medicine, you'll never forget that horse. But you need to find a way to forgive yourself." He patted her on the back. "We'll get you there."

"Mind if we start off headed upwind?" she asked with her best attempt at humor.

Kai nodded. "You're asking the right questions."

They broke into wide smiles, then Luna screeched. She dropped the pebbles as she saw the end of a bug burrow into her finger. Blood seeped. Kai took hold of her hand and, in one fell swoop, twisted it out.

"Eww. Gross," she said, sucking her finger.

Kai squashed the insect between his fingernails and showed her the goopy remains. "Meet Calcus cantankerous. They're attracted to vibration and sound. Painful by themselves, in numbers, deadly."

"I saw one, just like this, on Valdeez's desk."

"That would explain the local evacuation," Kai said, nodding. "Valdeez must have disrupted the swarm."

"So that's why Calcans won't work for Xerxes."

"Nature keeps insects in check. Mining has changed that." Kai removed a tube of antiseptic from his coat and applied it to Luna's cut. "Let's head back."

When he offered to bandage her finger, she declined, thinking the smell had also permeated the gauze. She checked the direction of the wind. "I'll drive, that is, if it's okay with you." She got on before he could answer, appreciating the feeling of being in control. "I could use a good copilot."

"Whatever you say." Kai sniffed his lapel and wrinkled his nose. He left coattails hanging out the sides.

Luna momentarily lifted her hand off the grip to suck her finger. *What was it with this place?*

Chapter 17

If in doubt at a fork in the road, check for the path least taken

—Luna

AS THE MOTORCYCLE approached the town, the engine's hum harmonized with its whirring tires. However, as Luna rapped her knee against the tank, reality, fear, and doubt comprised her improvised riff. "Kai was right," she told herself. "The past couple of days have been rewarding." Great while they lasted, she realized with a shrug. *For all the trouble I've caused, has it been worth it?*

At a glance, anyone who did not know Kai better might have thought he was vacationing, lying back, and catching some sun. *He is probably asking himself the right questions. I wouldn't know where to begin.*

Kai remained detached within the sidecar as empty streets, boarded-up windows, and closed doors left her with a sense of impending doom. While grateful for the distraction of her throbbing finger, she found it hard to fathom how, under the circumstances, he could remain so calm. She rubbed her forefinger against the grip and shuddered to think what more than one bug might do.

As they approached the pocky field, Luna steered away from the tangled web of posts, wire, and vehicles strewn across the street. Kai turned to face her. Without attempting to hide her involvement, she focused ahead. She did sneak a peek at the wreckage and, to her relief, found the tuk-tuk absent from the pile. Its roof would be another thing best left for another day.

Absent were the smells emanating from the market. Stalls and looms stood still. Mothers and daughters no longer walked arm in arm, exchanging secrets. Gone were the cheering children scoring on their goal-keeping fathers.

Her intuition proved right as the bike turned into the gangway and found the courtyard in shambles. Everything that once stood was overturned. Anything that had not been nailed down littered the ground. The unpleasant smell coming from the lab hinted at the disaster awaiting inside.

As Kai righted the table, Luna called out Reuben and Falafel's names until she heard the erratic thump of a tail near the metal pile. She found them huddled beside each other and panicked when neither tried to rise. Before she could say something, Kai had scooped Falafel into his arms and placed him on the table. Reuben pawed the floor, anxiously scrambling to stand.

"Hold on there," Luna said, kneeling. "Let me help you." He groaned as she righted him onto three unsteady legs. "Take it easy. He'll be okay. Just let me look at you." Reuben leaned unsteadily on her shoulder while keeping Falafel in sight. "Calm down, big guy." Supporting him with one arm, she gently pressed his raised paw's toes and worked her way up in the same fashion she had used on Hugo. He winced when she pulled his elbow. "What am I going to do with you?" Luna asked, shaking her head. "Big boy like you, standing up for his little brother." She repeated the process with her hand held higher, and when he flinched, she said, "I think it's his shoulder. Maybe kicked or something. Nothing broken, as far as I can tell."

Something had to be terribly wrong if Kai did not respond, and all she heard was the sound of repeated huffing. As she stood and edged closer, Reuben hobbled after. Kai's hands pressed rhythmically over the molug's chest. Falafel gasped. The CPR pace quickened and then alarmingly stopped.

Reuben let out a mournful howl.

The courtyard dimmed as if a candle had gone out, leaving behind a trail of smoke. Kai's head bowed, and his shoulders sank. Reuben placed his front paws and chin on the table and nuzzled his furry friend. In a somber farewell, Kai fondly stroked his pet's head, which would no longer feel the tenderness of his master's touch. In shrouded, somber steps, Luna inched closer. She felt a part of his burden and tried futilely to relieve him as best she could. Kai's chin quivered. His lips wrenched into a sad smile. Luna blinked repeatedly, but the tears kept flowing. *Just because vets see death all the time does not make them immune to it*, she thought, placing her arm around Kai's waist.

"I have to go," he said, wiping his eyes. "Stay with Reuben. The two of you will be better off here. Don't worry. Someone will come for you soon."

"What? Who?" Rattled, his words made no sense. "Where are you going?"

"There's an emergency." He handed her a slip of paper.

"What's this?" The Calcan script carried no meaning. "I want to come with."

"A message left by the table. I can't take you," he said, patting his coat. "You have already been exposed to enough danger."

Reuben hobbled to the sidecar, and before Kai could stop

him, he jumped inside and landed with a yelp.

"Not you, too," Kai said, shaking his head.

"What emergency?" Luna asked. Kai's unwavering stance was beginning to piss her off. "Dagnabbit, answer me."

He pressed his lips together as if covering his grief with urgency.

Before Kai could say otherwise, she got on the back of the bike and clung to the passenger rail. "You men and your emergencies. My father always had an excuse for leaving my mother and me. 'Fed emergency,' he used to say, right before he shot out the door." Her knuckles blanched from holding the rail so tight. "And now you? I already have daddy issues, and you're not helping right now."

"Bloating requires immediate attention," Kai said, kneeling between the bike and the sidecar. "It may already be too late."

"No way are you going to leave us," she said, squeezing her thighs into the bike's fender.

He started to untwist the sidecar coupler. "Calcus cantankerous can't reach here. Both of you will be safer if you remain." He nodded to himself and pointed toward the rear of the bike. "Pull out that pin, please. There is no time to lose."

"You take me with, or we're going to end up walking. Either way, where you go, I go." She peered into the sidecar and pointed a thumb. "And so should he." Reuben had wasted no time curling up and settling in.

"Don't make this any more difficult." Kai closed his eyes as if summoning strength. "You don't have to come along." He wavered as if arguing with himself and then shook his head. "Nor should you. This trip could put yourself, as well as all of us, in danger."

She looked him in the eye and stuck out her chin.

"All right, but stay close, and for once, do as I say." He re-tightened the coupler and started the bike. She put her arms around him for a second, backed away, and turned her head, ruffling her nose. *Did he have only one coat?*

With the sidecar to himself, Reuben yawned and let the rocking do the rest.

"Bloat?" Kai asked over his shoulder. "Are you acquainted with the term?"

"A horse got into the grain room once and came down with it," Luna hollered back. "Must have been awfully painful from how he acted and sounded." Once they were well underway, her grip relaxed on the rail. Her nostrils did not.

"The taurden has a series of stomachs where bacteria, protozoa, and fungi break down plant cellulose."

"Yeah," Luna said, "I know what a ruminant is." So long as she just listened, the smell wasn't so bad, so she wiggled her tush to the far edge of the pillion seat and leaned back as far as she could.

"New pasture growth can produce excessive fermentation in the rumen. If the animal cannot expel sufficient gas by belching or flatulence, it builds up, like a balloon."

Feeling no need to comment further, Luna drifted away, preferring to admire the scenery. Sachi, leading Gina into a distant field, caught Luna's attention. She lifted a hand to wave but preferred to hold on with both hands. Galgani's med works fast, she thought, smiling as Gina leisurely chomped away, looking ravishing in her improvised comforter wrap.

Kai turned onto a lane leading to a farm that appeared to be deserted except for a few taurdens grazing and chewing their cud in the immediate pasture. "Stay," he said to Reuben before turning off the engine. Kai called out a few times before they left the bike parked between the barn and a storage shed filled with powdery red dust-covered sacks. The garlicky smell reminded Luna of phosphorus. Reuben's nose twitched. Reuben grunted before curling up and disappearing in the sidecar's lining.

*   *   *

IF KAI HAD a fairy godmother that could grant him one wish, she did not disappoint. In case he wanted to stir up havoc, she'd tossed in the wand and plenty of fairy dust. While Cinderella's dress, coach, and horses may have disappeared at midnight, Kai's concoction lingered. The odious combination swirled into the deepest crevices of the mine and out the facility gates. Its invisible, putrid aerosol streamed along pipes, cables, and corridors through vents, pods, and shafts.

Despite being outside and against her father's objections, Jazz continued to wear a gas mask with the same resolve she clutched her family picture frame. She stood by the gate, watching her father direct technicians and their families to awaiting vehicles. Not only was her father at his cordial best, but he looked perfectly groomed without a hair out of place or a wrinkle in his suit. People, leaving the premises, responded to him like sheep to a shepherd. Irate employees approached him with complaints, and by the time they parted, one would have thought he had rescued them from certain death.

A woman, her father's age, stepped up and looked at him starry-eyed. She patted him on the arm and nodded like he had this contingency plan in place the whole time. *He's good, really good,* Jazz thought. *Something else I could never get away with and a trait I did not inherit.*

Furthermore, she could not get over Luna's refusal of the generous offer. *The way Luna had told it,* Jazz thought, *becoming a veterinarian was the most important thing in her life. Maybe she did not want it as badly as she had let on.*

Valdeez stepped aside during a break in the exodus. "Take off that mask," he said, smiling through gritted teeth. "You're causing a scene."

Jazz preferred to further distance herself and stand aside to watch a little boy wrestle free of his mother's hand. *Run for it, little boy!* Not a problem for the youngster since his mother refused to release her comm from shielding her nose. *I'd like to run away, too.* The boy took off toward a group of playing children.

"Pee ewe, you stink, Hunter," a little girl teased, pointing at the boy.

While most adult employees remained in her father's trance, others grimaced. *Not everyone gets caught up in my father's spell.* Women winced while fanning their clothing. Concerned technicians came out, shedding their masks in search of their families. They were not greeted with open arms but with frowns of disapproval.

"There you are," Hunter's mother said to her husband. His eyes evaded. "Can we leave this hell hole now, once and for all?"

He sniffed his lab coat and nodded. "You'll get no argument from me."

"Finally, we agree on something," she said, shaking her head and extending her hand to her son. "Come along, Hunter, we're leaving."

Hunter pouted. "Oh, Mom, I was just having fun."

Employees and their families lined up to fill a convoy of awaiting SUVs, buses, and trucks. Hunter's mother's frown extended out of the side of her mouth as she contorted to fit inside the back of the last pickup truck. "I'm going to smell like this all the way to Terra."

"We're not going back for my toys?" Hunter asked with a look of surprise.

"No, Hunter. We're going home," she said. "Now, hold on to me."

"Xerxes can send for our things," Hunter's father said, ruffling his son's hair.

While a tech relinquished his place to Hunter's mom, he said, "Xerxes can replace everything for all I care. We're never coming back."

"And pay for it all," Hunter's father chimed.

"Ready?" the vehicle driver asked.

The adults nodded. They closed their eyes and settled in for the ride.

The overloaded truck's suspension heaved as it prodded forward. Hunter put out his hand to catch the breeze. He's just like any other kid, Jazz thought, imagining his hand as a *StarCraft* Cruiser. Kicking up dust, the last vehicle pulled out of the lot and joined the others. Hunter looked to be having the time of his life.

Startled, Jazz felt a tap on her shoulder.

"That is the last of them," her father said. "We can leave now."

The mask's buckle slipped between her fingers.

"Here, let me." His hands shook, reaching out to relieve her of the frame.

Jazz pulled away. "I'll do it myself."

"Then use both hands," he grumbled. "Follow me when you're finished," he said, marching off.

"I've thought of Papa as being unreachable," she said to herself, taking off the mask and wiping her brow, "but never as a bully." She followed around the side of the complex to a loading dock where a lone truck with an extended cab remained. It looked like a dump truck, and although it sounded like its engine was off, its walls shook, humming like a tuning fork.

He placed his hand on the side of the truck and gave it a gentle tap. His grin widened.

"What's inside?" Jazz asked.

From behind, Dhiraj came out of nowhere. Out of breath, he tore off his mask and sputtered, "It was your daughter. She was the one." He pointed at her accusingly, even though it was obvious who 'she' was. "She hacked our system."

Papa will kill me.

In a fit of rage, Valdeez turned to her and raised his hand.

Prepared to take the blow, she did not blink. *So do it already.* "Go ahead, Papa. If that's what you want to do."

He hesitated.

"Do it. Do it if it makes you feel better." *Spoken without a stutter.* She smiled.

Dhiraj smirked. He looked to be enjoying this.

Her father turned solemnly. He slipped a Taser from his sleeve and calmly faced Dhiraj. Without so much as a hint of emotion, he thrust the device at Dhiraj's chest. The security chief crumpled into a mass of fits and tremors. Valdeez continued pressing the wand long after Dhiraj lost consciousness.

Jazz pulled on her father's arm. "Papa, stop! You'll hurt him."

Valdeez brushed away her hand and straightened his suit. "Grab his feet," he said. "Help me get him inside."

Stunned, she froze with her mouth agape.

"Don't just stand there. Do as you are told. You want to go home, don't you?"

Chapter 18

"I am a slow walker, but I never look back."

—Abraham Lincoln

LOW-PITCHED BELLOWS GREW louder as Kai flipped the barn latch and slid open the oversize door. A welcome wave of freshly cut grass filled Luna's nose as her eyes adjusted in the dim light to the familiar sight of wooden beams and stalls. She slid the door closed and cupped her hand to the side of her mouth. *"Ohenro.* Hello. Is anybody here?" she yelled. The taurden replied with grunted *moo-ahs.*

In the middle of the straw-covered floor, a taurden, lying on her side, constantly bawled while she struggled to right herself. The cow's distended left flank looked ready to burst.

"The farmer must have been in a hurry to leave," she said.

So immersed was Kai in treating the patient that he barely blinked as his hand reached inside his coat and retrieved a shiny scalpel.

How deep do those pockets go?

Kai pressed his thumb and forefinger against the cow's hide behind the last rib and sliced open the skin with a slash of the scalpel. Luna flinched. Parting through the layers of cherry-red muscle, an expanding balloon popped through. The taurden kept bawling without missing a beat. Blood trickled from the incision, down the sides, and cascaded to the floor into crimson pools. Dust and hay mixed with the metallic smell of blood.

From an opposite outside pocket, Kai pulled a sheathed steel dagger.

Does that coat come in my size? The supposed instrument looked like a sheathed knife with its tip sticking out. "What's the dagger thingy?" she hollered over the taurden's cries.

"A trocar."

The blade's exposed tip looked more like it belonged to a bayonet.

Reuben began barking, not one of his usual, which added to the commotion. Luna found it hard to think, her ears drowning in booming bellows. Brakes screeched, adding to the infernal racket.

"Think of it as a pin," Kai said.

"You're going to pop it?"

"Asking or telling?" Kai's smile resembled an upturned rainbow.

The flooding red pools on the floor conjoined as though clotting lakes.

"There's the bike," a man's voice hollered.

Luna stepped around the cow's flailing hooves, combing the open stalls, and boarded walls for an exit.

The sounds of booted footsteps approached. "Shut that dog up," a gruff voice said.

"I already looked. Didn't see anything," another voice said. The barn door slammed open, and three uniformed men pushed their way inside. Luna recognized Fred, Henry, and Trip.

"Bark, bark, bark."

"*Moooooooah, oooah.*" The cow's insides rose like oven-baking dough.

"When I say the word…" Kai said between grunts. His eyes dipped toward the floor.

Luna acknowledged with a nod.

"Well, if it isn't the Stinkmeister and his sidekick, Jokerette," Fred said with a smirk.

Henry nudged. "Trip, will you get a look at the hump on that—?"

"It's a lopsided camel," Trip said, elbowing back.

"Knock it off," Fred said to the others. Reuben's barking persisted, and the taurden's bellowed mooing crescendoed. "We've been ordered to bring you in. You are both under arrest."

While the taurden's distress captivated Henry's and Trips' attention, Kai raised the dagger over his head. The two guards' expressions changed to concern. Luna stepped further back.

"What do you think you're going to do with that, Mr. Funny Man?" Fred asked, waving his pistol.

"We're ready for you this time," Henry said, pulling out a Taser. Trip fumbled with his holster and, as soon as he got his Taser out, pressed the switch to the sound of a powered lightsaber.

"You've caused us a lot of trouble, old man," Fred said. "Just give me an excuse."

Kai looked comical, holding the sheathed dagger. "Did you forget to take the cover off?" Luna whispered.

"You're not so funny anymore," Trip said, holding out his Taser.

"Cannula."

"I couldn't hear. What did he say?" Henry asked.

"Canola. I don't know. I can't hear a thing with all this racket," Trip said.

"Don't take any chances, fellas. Set them to full power. Zap 'em. I've got you covered," Fred said.

"What's he holding?" Trip asked, adjusting his Taser.

"Crazy old fool. Serves him right, coming to a gunfight with a knife."

"This isn't a knife." Kai held a lighter and pointed to the trocar. "I use it to pin the tail on donkeys." In one fell swoop, Kai stabbed the trocar into the taurden's side. The trocar pierced between the layers of skin, past the layers of muscle, and into the rumen.

Luna gasped.

Trip flinched.

The taurden let out a lengthy grunt. Gas hissed, but nothing else.

Somehow, expecting more, she leaned toward Kai and whispered, "Did you miss?"

The guards nodded to each other. "Rush him," Fred said.

"Duck," Kai said.

Luna dropped.

The men rushed with buzzing Tasers.

Kai flicked the lighter with one hand while pulling the trocar out with the other. *Whoosh.* Sparks ignited methane into a steady, blue, fiery stream. The heat of the blaze reached the back of Luna's neck. Using the cannula as a nozzle, Kai aimed it like a flamethrower, lighting the men's clothes ablaze. They shielded their faces, dropped their weapons, and threw themselves to the ground, rolling and patting themselves out. Kai extinguished the flames with his thumb and directed the remaining gas away until it fizzled. The rumen shrank, the hump disappeared, and the cow let out a relieved moo.

"That's so cool."

"Take their Tasers," Kai said, kneeling beside Fred. He

unloaded the pistol and handed it over to Luna. "Take care of these."

"I know just the place," she said.

Kai helped the men peel off the charred parts of their clothing and applied ointment, from a tin produced from another pocket to Fred's singed eyebrows and exposed parts of their hands.

They deserve a good taste of Gina's tonic.

Fred's ruby-red face looked like he had been in the suns too long, she noticed as she passed. With parts of their underwear scorched through, she closed her eyes for modesty's sake.

Luna peered into the sidecar. *Where's Reuben?* A wagging tail appeared.

*   *   *

"HE'S WAKING UP," Jazz said, pointing to the seat behind them. The truck's tires screeched. "Why are we stopping?"

Valdeez threw the gear shift in reverse and backed off the side of the road. He pressed the accelerator further. "Finishing what I started."

"Papa, can't we just leave?" They drove, in reverse, deeper into a field. "Are you listening to me? Stop!"

Valdeez slammed the brakes and, without shutting off the engine, put the truck in neutral. Her flushed face and pursed lips response required an explanation. "You don't get it. That vet and your little friend have given us a way out. Their stunt has played right into my hands."

"What are you talking about?"

"Sabotage. They caused a natural disaster. Livestock will disappear. Xerxes will end up with more workers than they know what to do with."

"What disaster?"

"Stay here," he said, getting out. He pulled semiconscious Dhiraj from the back, and before she could react, he locked the doors. She raised the handle, but it refused to open. The rumble from the rear of the truck muted her shouts of protest and window pounding in the closed cab. Breathing hard, Valdeez climbed back inside and, between breaths, spoke down to her as if speaking to a misbehaving child. "Calm yourself."

"What are you doing?"

"Make sure your window and vents are closed." He tapped his own vent and, once satisfied, turned off the engine. "One day, you will thank me," he said, pulling a CAUTION-labeled red lever. Gears whirled, the tailgate creaked, and the truck shook. A gray, rolling haze drifted out from the gap below the rear gate.

Jazz shoved her shoulder into the passenger door. "What did you do? Let me out."

"Quit that."

In their rearview mirrors, the fog turned darker.

"I can't." Valdeez squeezed her arm. "Keep still."

Dhiraj shook his head, raised up on his elbows, and struggled to sit up.

"If you leave, we die."

*　　*　　*

FROM THEIR VIEW outside the barn door, Kai and Luna had watched a Xerxes truck break through a fence at the far end of the pasture. They recognized Valdeez as he pulled out his security chief and laid him on the ground before getting back inside.

"What's he up to?" Luna asked.

An expanding haze arose from the vehicle's rear. The man beside the truck pushed himself off the ground and steadied himself as he wobbled alongside the truck. He pounded on the driver's cab. He yanked on the handle. The door remained shut. The driver pointed to the rear of the truck. The haze had grown into an ashen mist.

"Valdeez has gone mad," Kai said, shaking his head. "He intends to release an arachnidian plague."

"What plague?"

"What you see is a swarm of insects that penetrated your finger. Take Reuben. Go back to the clinic. Get away from here as fast as you can," he said, turning for the barn.

Luna tugged on his coat. "Come with."

"Someone has to tend to the men."

"I'll wait for you."

"Don't worry. We'll be right behind."

"How?"

Reuben nudged her with his nose. Before she could react, Kai slipped inside the barn and slammed the door. "No time to explain," he said, locking the latch.

She pulled on the handle. "We'll wait until you come out." Reuben pawed the door. Frustrated by his lack of response, she leaned against the wooden slats, wrinkled her nose, and checked her shirt. *That's not it.* "We're not going anywhere without you," she said, turning her attention to the truck.

Sachi and Gina, oblivious to the unfolding danger, had wandered to the edge of the field. The truck wobbled as the emerging mist changed to dense fog.

Luna yelled, jumped, and waved her arms.

Out of range of her calls, Sachi tucked in the collar of Gina's wrap with his back turned to the truck.

The security chief looked behind and took off, running. He stumbled on the uneven grass. The buzzing, spherical mass hovered over the vehicle before pursuing the fleeing form. Dhiraj tripped, fell, got to his feet, and dashed toward the field's edge.

"Sachi and Gina are in trouble," Luna said, bolting for the bike. Reuben limped after. She tapped the tank. Almost empty. Screwed off the gas cap and said, "Pin, Reuben, pin." The canid stood on three legs, watching as she untwisted the sidecar coupler. "Come on, Ruben. You can do it. Pin," she called repeatedly over her shoulder as she dashed for the shed.

Reuben cocked his head. His ear raised as he gawked.

Luna clawed at the closest bag, tore open a corner, and scooped out a handful of red powder. "Pin, Reuben, pin."

The canid stuck out his nose and sniffed the link attaching the sidecar to the bike. Luna darted back with one hand cupped over the other. "Pin, boy, pin. You can do it."

Reuben nudged the pin with his nose and placed the pin's ring between his teeth. He shook his head and, in doing so, lost his balance. He went at it again, wrestling the tab in a battle of tug-of-war.

"What's taking so long?" Kai's voice came from inside. "Get out of here!"

Red phosphorus is used in fertilizers, gas additives, and insecticides. When mixed with ethanol, it forms phosphine gas in the presence of heat. Better work, Luna thought. *Not too much, not too little.* She sifted the fine powder between her palms, funneling it into the tank. *Goldilocks, just right.*

"Leave now," Kai's voice commanded. The door latch came undone. *I should, but…* Luna shook her head. *Sachi needs me. Gina needs me. I've got to try.* She jump-kicked the starter. "Take Reuben inside."

Reuben's rear legs kicked in. With a yank, he fell on his haunches, with the pin left dangling out the side of his mouth.

The bike separated from the sidecar and tilted away. Trying to hold the bike upright, Luna's sole slipped on the loose gravel. The more the bike leaned, the greater the pressure on her leg. The edge of her boot dug in. *If I let go, the bike will fall.* Luna closed her eyes and heaved. The bike continued its downward slant. *If I force my leg closer and don't slip, I can push off. But if it falls on top of me...*

The barn door opened.

The insect cloud erupted into a storm.

Luna's boot heel edged closer. Her knee crunched. Traction gained. She twisted the throttle and popped the clutch. The engine coughed and grumbled. Spark inside the combustion chamber exploded. The crankshaft turned. The sprocket devoured the chain's slack. The rear tire spun. The rear end slid, and the fuel inside the tank swished.

Kai peered out the door.

The insect horde surrounded the running man. In one fell swoop, it engulfed him as he let out a sheared shriek before his clothes dissolved into shreds. The blob contorted into a giant mitotic cell, engulfing, twisting, and pulling.

The bike surged in spurts and stalls.

Sachi hummed as he scratched Gina behind her ear. Her tail thumped along.

The flying mass bulged in multiple directions. The far side struck toward the starting truck, while the near side tugged toward the pasture's edge.

Kai rushed out. "No."

Luna gunned the throttle. The engine faltered.

The truck drove off, leaving the field, and headed back onto the road.

The swarm pulled on itself, back and forth and side to side as if trying to decide which way to go.

What do you say, Professor Heisenberg? Let's toss chaos into the inevitable.

The bike engine cleared its throat. "Roxie, if Lil' Sancho can do it, so can you," she coaxed. "Time to do your stuff." The motorcycle took off in an ascending roar.

The insect mass aimed toward Gina's tail. Luna steered a course to intersect the insects' path. Gray exhaust turned a shade lighter. The bike sped up.

Luna cupped her free hand and called out, "Sachi!" The insects maintained their course. Sachi must have heard. He stepped away from Gina and raised his hand until he turned behind and noticed the buzzing cloud. His eyes grew wide, and his eyebrows raised. He furiously waved the bike away, scurried back to Gina, and covered her eyes with his embrace.

Kai watched in dismay while Reuben stood next to him with saliva dripping from the corner of his mouth. Kai looked at the canid wagging his tail. "Drop it." Spit and pin slobbered to the ground.

Gina's tail thumped as Sachi closed his eyes and held his breath.

Trumpeting her charge, Luna squeezed the horn. *Hee-yonk. Hee-yonk.* The swarm strayed. Within feet of colliding, Luna put down her foot, slammed the brake, and skidded into a one-eighty. The tire slashed turf into the whirring mass. A deliberate invitation to play catch.

The bike's bugle taunted: *hee-yonk.* Luna rose off the seat like a meerkat on the lookout. The buggies took the bait. Satisfied that the chase was on, she blitzed for a rolling hill. The swarm picked up the pace in a deadly game of fox and hounds.

Unhindered by terrain and taurden cowpies, the insect throng caught up. Roxie has a tail.

Luna throttled the bike at the base of the hill, and the front wheel rose. The exhaust turned into a plume of phantom pink. At the top, the motorcycle took off in a Grande Jeté, floating in the air like a ballerina defying gravity, leaving behind a rose-colored miasma. The swarm closed in on the muffler and kissed the spinning tire. The treads dissolved. The bike landed and bounced, with its bald tire sliding in bugs.

The swarm stuttered. Unable to flap their wings, those flying in front dropped like flies. Those unaffected caught up with a vengeance.

A breeze picked up. The red contrail spread. Luna chose a serpentine track around the grazing taurdens. Not willing to risk crossing through the poisonous gas, she headed for an untainted slot toward the barn.

Kai, sensing her direction, grabbed Reuben by the collar and rushed inside.

The bike swerved, skidded, and barely missed slamming into the barn. She rode on till the fence line ended, the insects dwindled, and the exhaust funnel turned pink and finally disappeared. The smooth rear tire ran low, leaving only a trail of littered insects behind.

The bike sputtered, surged, and backfired. She pulled the clutch, and the engine died. "You did all right, Roxie," she said, coasting toward Xerxes and a crowd of awaiting red dust-covered Calcans. Before coming to a full stop, a chant of "Luna, Luna. *Achadempai* Luna" met her. Nastor, Ziggy, and other miners were there, leading the crowd. Aapo, Teesa, Anu, her family, and even Rizzo were among them, cheering along.

Before Luna could put down the kickstand, she was hoisted

on shoulders and surrounded by celebrants. From her vantage point, it looked like every Calcan in the vicinity was there, celebrating a Holi Festival—Calcan style, in her honor. "*Spakuhn*," she repeated with waves and smiles while turning her head back furtively toward the barn.

Ziggy got close enough to reach over and hand her a can. "Ginger ale, right?"

"Daniel? You know my dad?" Luna yelled over the cheering voices. She couldn't make out his reply, but reading his lips and nod confirmed it.

Rizzo tugged on her pant leg. He pointed over the crowd to where she had left Lil' Sancho. "Yours."

"*Spakuhn*." Luna raised her voice again in Ziggy's direction. "I left a friend back there. I have to go back."

"What? I can't hear you." Ziggy shook his head as the parade passed, waving her on. "Enjoy the ride," he said, more to himself than she could hear.

With a pat on a Calcan shoulder and wiggling to be put down, Luna stood immersed in well-wishers and smelling of red phosphorus-covered congratulations, vigorous handshakes, Calcan accented thank-yous, and pats on the back. By the time the queue wound down, she was covered in red, resembling every other celebrant.

"Care for a ride?" Ziggy shouted, standing out the side of a tuk-tuk.

Luna wasted no time getting in.

From the driver's seat, "For you, only four," Nastor said with a wink.

"Yes, I work for the Federation, and your father sent me," Ziggy said, looking pleased. "Your father and I have been friends for a long time. He asked me to keep an eye on you."

"You are one hell of a babysitter."

"The first time I saw you, before you got on the transport and fell on your butt, I was set on sending you home." He shook his head with a grin. "I'm glad I didn't."

" 'Cause it would have blown your cover?"

"There's that. But when I saw the way you handled yourself in front of that beast—"

"Taurden."

"Taurden. I knew you were your father's daughter."

Pride rose within, and she pressed her lips together, sealing the feeling inside.

Drawing his eyebrows together, he said, "I'm glad your parents weren't around to witness that motorcycle display. You nearly gave me a heart attack." Satisfied with her conspiratorial response, he continued. "Let's keep that part between us."

Arriving at the farm, the tuk-tuk's tires crunched on the insect carapaces. In the distant pasture, Sachi waved as Gina and the taurdens grazed. Luna returned the wave before Nastor cut the engine.

"Kai. Dr. Kaironowski," they yelled. "Reuben, here, boy."

Silence.

What if the bugs got to him, or I poisoned him?

Nastor slid open the barn door. Kai, Reuben, the three men, and the taurden were missing. Dead bugs squashed below their feet. Lumped where she had last seen him, tatters of Kai's coat, remnants of charred uniforms, and a lumpy tarp strewn on the floor were all that remained.

"Exhaust would not have caused them to disappear," Ziggy said.

"I should have—" Luna said, catching herself.

"You did what you could," Nastor said.

Luna wept. "Not enough," she said, with shreds of Kai's

coat clutched in her arms.

Nastor placed his hand on her shoulder. "It's okay."

Ziggy led her out of the barn. As Nastor slid the door closed, a breeze caught a corner of the tarp. It rose and fell back again.

Chapter 19

A teenager reserves the right not to take an adult's word for it.

VALDEEZ PACED THE institutional green corridor like a first-time father in the days before husbands were allowed inside the delivery room. He held his hands clenched behind his back, shook his head, and mumbled. The scuffed swish-swoosh of his soft-soled shoes echoed through the empty hall. Beyond the casement windows, the south wall cast a long shadow into the landscaped yard. Manicured lawns and pink impatiens lined the surrounding walk. He came to an abrupt halt and straightened out his shirt as the clicks of heeled footsteps approached. Father and daughter embraced with punctuated pecks on the cheek.

"Let me look at you," Valdeez said, stepping back. "All grown up and more beautiful each time I see you."

"Oh, come on, Papa, it hasn't been that long."

"I'm telling you. You are the picture image of your mother." He squared his shoulders and, with a nod, judged the decision final. "She would be very proud of who you have become."

Jazz blushed.

"I worry about you," Valdeez said, shrugging his shoulders. "When you weren't on time, I thought something might have happened."

"I'm sorry. My partner was late getting to the closing, and the lawyers took longer than expected," Jazz said. "You know how it is with work and commitments. These things take time." She placed her hand against his cheek. "Are you okay? You look pale. Are you eating all right?"

"I'm fine, really. Don't trouble yourself."

She took him by the arm. "Come on, then. Let's go for a walk."

He patted her hand and headed down the walkway. His footsteps scuffed in harmony with the tap of her leather-heeled soles. "Tell me you're not working for them," he said, maintaining a forward gaze.

Jasmine snickered and squeezed her father's arm. "I don't work for anybody." She squeezed tighter. "As of today, I am self-employed."

"Then what was that closing business about?"

"Xerxes did offer me the security chief posting on Algernon." She looked up with a grin, and before his frown could respond, she said, "Which I immediately turned down. I can't very well be away from you. Can I?" Her smile widened at his palpable relief. "You should have seen the look on the Council members' faces."

"I would have given anything to have been there."

"At first, they hesitated. Insisted that all their security had to be maintained internally." When his face darkened, she continued. "Don't worry, Papa, I remembered what you taught me. If I agreed, they would own me eventually or at least try to. So, I stopped them right there and showed them the holes in their security. After presenting what I had discovered on Calcus, they had no choice. The contract I just signed guarantees I'm independent. Congratulate me. I'm going into business for myself."

"What business? I told you to stay away from them."

"I'm expanding from software and going into baking and confections."

"What?" Shaking his head, he stopped. "How does baking have anything to do with Xerxes? I don't understand."

"I need them. Simple as that." Her firm response meant to shake off his concern.

He tilted his head with a raised eyebrow, expecting more of an answer.

Holding proof of their Calcan hijinks, I am in a position to exchange security services for sole importation and distribution rights." Her cheeks flushed. "The Shahrazad Sweets Company. This way, they don't own me. Nobody owns me."

"You named your company after her?"

Jazz nodded with a grin. "I thought Mum would have approved. It appears you do, too."

"I do, but what do you know about baking, much less selling sweets?"

"Forgot who prepared your meals since Mom died? I found a unique product and made it my business to learn the rest."

"What unique—"

Jasmine patted her father's arm and pointed to the bench. "Let's sit here in the sun." She opened her purse and removed a foil-wrapped package. She raised it to her nose and passed it over. "Smell."

He sniffed with hesitation. "What is it"? Smells sweet. I don't eat cake," he said, pushing it away.

"Try it. Something I'm introducing. It comes from the Ail fruit. The public can't get enough of it. It is the culinary sensation everyone is talking about. So much so that I'm having problems meeting demand. Did I mention I control the distribution?"

Valdeez nodded with a grin. "That's my girl."

Jasmine took off her shoe and massaged her foot. "Sorry, Papa."

"Sorry for what? You're going to bring that up again? Look, it's over. I'm good."

"You know, for turning you in."

"I'll admit that I was angry right after I found out. But then, when I thought about it, I came to the same conclusion. If it was going to be anybody, I'm glad it was you. It was the right move. It is what I would have done."

Turned in by your own daughter. She let his words settle to their natural mutual conclusion.

"I hope it was worth it. You made the prosecution's case," he said.

Jazz threw up her hands and shook off the notion of doing anything for nothing. "I negotiated. You should know me by now. Xerxes was going to deny everything. Blame you one way or another. But I had them. So I drove a hard bargain."

"Get what you paid for?"

"You didn't make it any easier, providing amphetamines," she said with a grimace, looking at him for some sign of contrition.

He put out the palms of his hands and shrugged. "It kept them happy and working. So, what did you get out of the deal?"

"I dictated the terms. The school scholarship programs were reinstated… along with Luna's."

"She and that vet caused quite a stink," he said, holding his sides as they broke into belly laughs.

"The Calcans demanded full restitution, the removal of all

Xerxes facilities, and they want their vet back. The corporation has apologized for their part, compensated the Calcans, and sent replacement vets, but the Calcans keep sending them back."

"They got off too easily."

"Not really. When their stock plummeted, I took stock options, which I have since realized. Since then, their price has risen steadily," she said with a grin." I could live comfortably on the profit, but there is too much left to do."

Jasmine put her shoe back on. "Let's keep walking." Her dark business suit contrasted with her father's bright orange prison scrubs. They meandered the walkway, oblivious to the towering surrounding concrete walls. "I negotiated with the prosecution," she said. "In exchange for providing evidence, I got you sent to a Xerxes-run prison. Since the warden loves Ail fruit, I have arranged to be able to see you any time I want." She checked his face for a response and shrugged. "Guess it's only fair. You took away Luna's scholarship so there would be somebody to keep me company. I gave it back so we could be together."

They walked to the waiting room, arm in arm.

"Really, how are you doing, Papa? You have lost weight that you did not need to lose."

"I'm doing okay. Better than fine." When she seemed unsatisfied with the answer, he said, "I've made some friends here."

"Friends? In here? I hope they are not of the buggie kind."

"I tired of playing against the computer and needed live opponents, so I started a chess club." He unwrapped the foil package and took a bite. His eyebrows raised. "You made this?" He wiped the edge of a knuckle and licked the rest clean. "Up for another game?" he asked. "Care for a bite?

No?" Without waiting for her to answer, he said, "Then I'll take white."

"Whatever you say, Papa."

Chapter 20

"What we have once enjoyed, we can never lose. All that we love deeply becomes a part of us."

—Helen Keller

LUNA SLIPPED A boot into the leg of her riding suit.

"Are you sure you won't come with?" her mother asked, shaking her head. "Your dress will get wrinkled in that thing. And those boots certainly do not go with a dress."

"Yes, Mom, I'm sure."

Her mother raised a new pair of dress shoes as an open invitation to take them. "Well, I'm bringing these, anyway. You can change when we get there."

"They were a present from Kai. It's my way of having him along. I wouldn't be here if it wasn't for him."

"I know, dear. I understand how much he means to you."

Luna lifted her other foot into the suit, and the hem of her dress raised. The knee had healed, but scars remained.

"Here, put some of this on," her mom said, pulling makeup from her purse.

"It's okay, Mom. Gotta go," Luna said, grabbing her duffle bag. "There are some things I need to take care of before I meet you there."

"Don't be—" her mother said, but Luna was already out the door.

She hoped to ride the course this hour at the speeder track, reliving the good times. However, underclassmen were already there when she arrived, with open arms and invitations. She declined the offers. "Some other time, guys." After outracing ATVs and trucks, the little bike had nothing to prove.

Her next stop, the stable, was as she liked it. She was alone with familiar horses. Despite the months that had passed, most of the same horses were still there. Daisy was. Bucephalus was not. She couldn't find Trulee anywhere.

Luna stopped at every stall, greeted with whinnies of recognition, and returned their greetings with scratches and rubs. In the stall at the end of the aisle, Daisy stepped up and leaned her head over Luna's shoulder. Luna returned the greeting by hugging the mare's neck and rocking from side to side. Daisy knew. Luna pulled an embroidered handkerchief from her sleeve, wiped her tears, and held Daisy in a goodbye lullaby.

Trilling Rs cut broke the embrace. Trulee had saved herself for last. In the time it takes to pop a pill, the insistent feline had curled up in Luna's arms, just as she had done a year before.

"What are you doing here?" a voice interrupted from the aisle.

"Oh, my gosh. What time is it?" Luna asked, releasing the cradled feline.

"Almost noon. Better hurry if you're going to make it," the crew chief said.

"Close up for me, will you, Sid," Luna said, flying past. She mounted the bike and drove off in a rush. The wind dried her face. It had been raining the last time she left the barn in such a hurry.

Upon entering the Rockwood Academy gates, Luna

slowed to the posted speed limit. She coasted to the admin-istration building, looking for a space in the packed parking lot. The security camera registered the **Sancho 2** license plate. Finding the lot packed, she squeezed between two limos, jumped the curb, and parked beneath Heiman's window.

"Gaudeamus igitur…" The beginning of the school gradu-ation commencement song came through the auditorium doors.

Hear that, Kai. 'Let's rejoice.'

Unzipping her jumpsuit, she grabbed the duffle, and with one leg outside of the suit, she hopscotched up the steps.

"*Venit mors velociter…*"

Death rushes in. Luna translated, kicking off the other pant leg.

Members of the audience, sitting in the back row, turned.

"*Nemini parcetur…*"

"Nobody shall be spared," she said to herself, breathing hard and donning her cap and gown. *I miss you, Kai.* Holding the jumpsuit bunched in her arms, Luna made her way down the aisle to the seats reserved for the graduates. She gave Ziggy a nod and waved to her parents sitting in the audience. Ziggy answered with two thumbs up. Her father stuck out his chest, looking distinguished in his uniform, and her mother, with raised eyebrows, pointed to the time.

Amy was sitting at the end of a row. Luna brushed up and plopped the suit in Amy's lap. Amy gasped. Luna continued down the aisle toward the reserved graduate seats, caught her breath, and, looked back and winked. Amy returned the wink with a smile.

Along the row to her seat, Luna bumped off seated class-mates, all the while excusing herself, blowing the tassel off her nose, and balancing her cap to keep it from falling off her long hair. *Easier than maneuvering through miners' knees on a moving animal transport.*

Arnie removed his cap from her seat and said, "Almost missed your big moment."

Luna answered with a jab.

"Ow. What's that for?" he asked, massaging his shoulder.

Shushes came from behind.

"For dumping me," Luna answered.

"Aw, come on, Luna. You broke it off long before Amy. Remember, it was you who set us up in the first place."

"Just giving you grief," she said and punched him again before placing a hand over his.

"Still friends?" he asked, squeezing her hand.

"*Shhhh.*"

Jeff nudged her other side. "Have you declared a major? Still going to become a vet?"

Principal Heiman stood behind a podium and cleared his throat. "What an honor it… blah, blah, blah… serving as this year's class principal. Blah, blah, blah."

Luna spoke out of the side of her mouth. "Until they come up with a degree in veterinary biochemical engineering, I dunno. At least now, I'll have time to figure it out."

"What about intergalactic culture studies?" a girl's voice asked from behind.

"What's this I hear about fruit?" another asked.

"Are you going to give up racing?" yet another asked.

"Wanna sell the bike?" Jeff asked.

"*Shhhh.*"

The sounds of a tapping cane turned heads to the back of the auditorium. A hunched-over elderly man wearing a bad wig and thick glasses came down the aisle. An elegantly dressed blond woman, who looked young enough to be his granddaughter, escorted him by the arm. Those sitting in the closest row scooched over and made room.

"Before we hand out diplomas, I am proud to announce this year's Xerxes National Scholarship winner is a member of our senior graduating class."

Arnie nudged with his elbow.

"For her innovative study 'Uses of Ail Fruit as a Universal Antidote,' this year's prize goes to…." He paused.

No surprise. The award was announced last week. What's he waiting for?

"Luna Auer."

The auditorium applauded, classmates cheered, and Arnie patted her on the shoulder and whooped.

Not a surprise, but it's nice to feel acknowledged. A whistle blasted from the audience. *Dad? More likely, it was Ziggy.*

"Sorry, he isn't here to see this," Arnie said as he stood to let her by.

"Me too." She sniffled. Bleary-eyed, she blinked multiple times, feeling her way to the aisle. *This is as much for me as it is for you, Kai.*

The applause faded in Luna's ear. The time had come. She was about to face Heiman in front of everyone. *Payback time? Make a scene. Tell everyone what an ass he is. Or let bygones be bygones.* She approached the stage steps, looking into the principal's smug face.

What would Kai do?

To someone sitting in the audience, one would have thought she was stalling, dragging out the acceptance, making the most of her moment.

Of course, ask the right question. She broke into a wide smile. *How to open his mouth?*

I would be in a different place if it hadn't been for

Heiman. She would not have traveled to Calcus nor made friends with miners. Missed riding in a tuk-tuk, not rescued a taurden, and never met Hugo and Gina, nor made friends with Falafel and Reuben. She caught Ziggy's eye and thought of Nastor, Sachi, Anu, her family, and even Rizzo. She had gone so far as to forgive Jazz, accepting her offer to go into business together, importing Ail fruit. Luna's lips pressed into a broad smile. *An omelet made especially for me.* The lessons learned. The taste of Galgani's concoction, joy, regret, and bitterness. The swallow stuck deep inside her throat.

Luna exchanged places at the podium with Heiman. He extended his hand and, with her back to the audience, at the last moment, she withdrew her handshake to adjust her cap. His mouth gaped wide enough to pop in one of Hugo's pills.

As prearranged, Luna accepted the award from Ms. Watkins. The woman had taken the time and gone out of her way to make this happen. Ms. Watkins pointed to her engagement ring and jiggled her eyebrows. Professor Woodson had made it official. Ms. Watkins handed Luna her award, and they reciprocated hugs and congratulations.

Luna took the award to the podium, pulled a prepared speech, and cleared her throat. "Parents, friends, faculty, and students of Rockwood Academy's class of—" Luna felt a poke in her backside. *What the... Was she imagining things? Get on with it. They're waiting.*

In the audience, Arnie's expression nudged her on.

To someone sitting in the audience, one would have thought she was stalling, dragging out the acceptance, making the most of her moment.

"Class of—" It happened again. She was being 'goosed.' She looked behind. Nothing there. What a time for a dress malfunction. Did it have to catch in her butt? Static? *I knew I shouldn't have worn a dress.* Her hand smoothed the backside of her gown. She turned forward and collected herself. Her face strained to remain calm.

Raised and furrowed brows stared back from the audience. She continued. "I am proud to accept this award and feel that none of this would have been possible without the help of—" She turned and nodded to her teachers and winked at Professor Woodson "—My teachers" As she faced forward, she felt the poke. Again. With a free hand, she swatted behind and felt...

A smile erupted in the audience.

She looked over her shoulder. Unseen behind the podium and by the rest of the faculty, a tail wagged. Her eyes widened.

Reuben! She stammered, "And, and, and...."

Family and students looked at each other and shrugged.

Stage fright, they're thinking. Let them think.

Luna bit her lip. Her voice stumbled through the speech as she raised the plaque and scanned the audience's faces.

Seated next to the young lady, the old man took off his glasses. His eyes twinkled.

ACKNOWLEDGMENTS

Thanks to Aesop for providing insight into the personalities of animals, and Hugh Lofting, author of the *Dr. Dolittle* books, for giving them voice. James Alfred Wight, OBE FVERCS, whose *James Herriot's* books have inspired generations to appreciate those who care for animals.

My single mother, who during the 60s, thought nothing of taking me out early from school, to get on a Greyhound bus and go south, for Christmas. After vacation and back in school, the other kids would brag about their family celebrations and presents received. I showed up with a tan. Or, during my last year of grade school, having perceived that we had been living in one place long enough, packed a suitcase, duffle bag, and shopping bags to ride a Trailways bus cross country. Portland, Oregon is a nice place to live, she had read. We arrived in the middle of the night, walked to the closest hotel, and I'd awake the next morning to see her circling apartment newspaper ads. Within days, I was enrolled in school.

A father who inspired a respect and love for animals. An uncle, who told the best stories, and though he did not have to, took the time to show he cared.

OMSI, the Oregon Museum of Science and Industry, where a kid, with limited funds, could win at auction, a dog skeleton. Chicago's Museums for their breathtaking exhibits.

Mr. Woodson, who opened the door to high school biology, and Mrs. Hanley, who thrilled her classes with magical chemical interactions. Drs. Cooper and Libby of Tuskegee Institute, who brought hands-on animal science to a city kid. Dr. Jan Koprowski, lek. wet, mentor. Drs. Prasuhn, Foerner, Kuhn, Hammer, and Gendreau, who helped bring a foreign grad into the fold. Friends and colleagues Drs. Ilarco Lushpinsky and Piotr Warcholek.

Clients and patients, who provided the inspiration. Mark Bradel DDS, who kept me smiling during the writing. Penny Blubaugh for her feedback and other librarians for their invaluable help and those at our local book take-out window, where Savy, Theo, and the author's pic were taken. Erica Damon, for alpha reading and early essential writing direction. Emma Cox, for beta reading and input from a teenager's perspective. Dr. G. Singh, who checked issues pertaining to physics and cultural sensitivity. Nicoleta Dabija for her illustrations.

And finally, you, the reader. For centuries, storytellers have relied on your input to help improve our craft. A grimace or shaken head when the tale took a wrong turn, chuckles that indicated everyone got the joke, raised brows that heightened the scary, and held breaths to culminate the climax. Thanks to you, characters can fly beyond their authors' imaginations.

Some library take-out windows give out more than books.

After graduating from high school with the state's representative scholarship, the author attended the U. of Illinois at Champaign for two and a half years before transferring to the Tuskegee Institute, in Alabama. While there, he represented the school in rodeo and the National Dairy Tasting Competition. During the summers between semesters, he worked for the Federal Animal Disease Testing Laboratory in Salem, Oregon, a ranch in Wyoming, and attended the American Motorcycle Mechanics School. Upon graduation with a bachelor's degree in animal science, he spent a year learning Polish in Krakow before being admitted to the School of Veterinary Medicine in Wroclaw, Poland.

The author jogs with his dogs, rides a Honda Niner along the shores of Lake Michigan, and plays pickleball while reporting on Kai and Luna's next adventure. He lives in Chicagoland with his wife, Dia and dogs, Theo and Savy.

This is his first book.

Made in United States
Orlando, FL
28 July 2023

35521963R00190